The Burned Children
of America ★ ★ ★ ★ ★

ZADIE SMITH INTRODUCES THE BURNED CHILDREN OF AMERICA

HAMISH HAMILTON
an imprint of
PENGUIN BOOKS

HAMISH HAMILTON

Published by the Penguin Group
Penguin Books Ltd, 80 Strand, London WC2R 0RL, England
Penguin Putnam Inc., 375 Hudson Street, New York, New York 10014, USA
Penguin Books Australia Ltd, 250 Camberwell Road, Camberwell, Victoria 3124, Australia
Penguin Books Canada Ltd, 10 Alcorn Avenue, Toronto, Ontario, Canada M4V 3B2
Penguin Books India (P) Ltd, 11 Community Centre, Panchsheel Park, New Delhi – 110 017, India
Penguin Books (NZ) Ltd, Cnr Rosedale and Airborne Roads, Albany, Auckland, New Zealand
Penguin Books (South Africa) (Pty) Ltd, 24 Sturdee Avenue, Rosebank 2196, South Africa

Penguin Books Ltd, Registered Offices: 80 Strand, London WC2R 0RL, England

www.penguin.com

First published 2003
1

Introduction © Zadie Smith, 2003
Editorial selection © Marco Cassini and Martina Testa, 2003
Pages 297–8 constitute an extension of this copyright page.

Set in 11/13 pt Monotype Dante
Typeset by Rowland Phototypesetting Ltd, Bury St Edmunds, Suffolk
Printed in Great Britain by Clays Ltd, St Ives plc

A CIP catalogue record for this book is available from the British Library

ISBN 0–241–14205–9

To the memory of Amanda Davis

Publisher's Note

This book is based on the Italian edition of *The Burned Children of America*, edited by Marco Cassini and Martina Testa, and published by minimum fax (info@minimumfax.com) in 2001.

Please visit *The Burned Children of America* website at www.bcoa.info.

Contents

Introduction

(being the sort of introduction that makes extensive reference to the stories contained within and therefore should be read afterwards)

★ ★ ★ ★ ★ In 1995 an interviewer asked the American writer David Foster Wallace to describe how it felt to live in America. This was his reply:

There's something particularly sad about it, something that doesn't have very much to do with physical circumstances, or the economy, or any of the stuff that gets talked about in the news. It's more like a stomach-level sadness. I see it in myself and my friends in different ways. It manifests itself as a kind of lostness. Whether it's unique to our generation I really don't know.

The occasion of the interview was the publication of his monster-novel, the 1079-pager *Infinite Jest*, college-dorm favourite and the heaviest hardback of its time. It sat like a challenge on the shelves of hipsters everywhere. If you couldn't write a bigger one, you could compete with your room-mate to see how far you could throw it from a standing position. Either way, *Infinite Jest* was the book you were going to have to deal with sooner or later, just as a previous generation had to deal with *Gravity's Rainbow* or *Midnight's Children*, or *The Recognitions*. *Infinite Jest* had other

distinguishing features besides weight, though. It was structurally
and formally experimental in the recently revived fabulist tradition of John Barth and Donald Barthelme; it was societally astute,
'networked', like Pynchon and DeLillo, but it was simultaneously
emotionally engaging, melancholic even. Did I mention it was
funny? What was at stake in Wallace's novel, and has remained
distinct in his work, is an attention to the secret, battered, deflated
spiritual existence of America and Americans. Underneath the
professional smiles there is a sadness in this country that is sunk
so deep in the culture you can taste it in your morning Cheerios.
It is internal and you can't sell anything to it – it's not in the
market for a new pair of sneakers – and so it is also the place the
culture would always rather not go, unless it is *forced* to go there.
You can be unsatisfied in America, or unfulfilled, you can be
unrecognized, unappreciated, you can be unbalanced, unemo-
tional, unnutritionally satisfied and unnumerically rewarded,
you can be unrepresented and unspoken – but you cannot be
unhappy. Unhappiness points gently at the metaphysical, and if
your metaphysical needs are not sufficiently catered for by the
Sci Fi channel, well, then, Houston We Have A Problem. And
yet there remains this sadness. And it exists side-by-side with an
hysterical emphasis on your (yes, your!) happiness which you
will find on the outside of things, with those same Cheerios,
printed all over the packet. Wallace identified it: many, many
people followed him. This collection showcases those writers,
often widely different in style from Wallace and each other, but
one smells a certain sadness coming off them all. Even the
laughter, which is almost consistent throughout, is that laughter
Nabokov loved so: the kind that springs forth in the dark.

*

But here I must digress quickly to explain how and why this collection came about. It was a labour of love, but the contractions were all somebody else's: a man called Marco Cassini. As you might guess, Marco is Italian and heavily bearded. He is very young (for an editor) and he runs his own publishing house in Rome. It is called minimum fax and the centre of operations is a little apartment he shares with his girlfriend, Martina Testa. I met both of them during a literary festival in Mantova two years ago. I was cringing my way through a reading to a big crowd of non-English-understanding Italians, and Marco and Martina were sat in the front row grinning, wearing *McSweeney's* T-shirts. It was incongruous enough a sight in a small medieval town – I grinned back. I think they took this as a sign of affinity; after the reading Marco and Martina dragged me to some kind of taverna, paid for all the red wine and Marco produced a little box out of his jacket in which a still-sweaty bandanna, belonging to David Foster Wallace, sat crumpled up. Marco told me he would never wash it. Tragically, I was impressed. Having established the mutual grounds of our nerddom, we grew more drunk, more friends of Marco arrived. Everybody spoke animatedly about a ragbag of young American writers we were all delighted to find each other had heard of – we got more drunk. I wondered how a drunk like Marco managed to publish anything. And then at about 2 a.m. Marco wrote a contract for my next book on a paper napkin and I lurched forward and signed it. To this day he e-mails me to tell me it is legally binding, despite the wine stains. *I will see you in the court*, he says. Well, we will see.

About a year and a half later, this collection you have in your hands turned up on my own editor's desk. The stories had been compiled by Marco and Martina and published by minimum fax, and included names familiar enough to be a pleasant surprise considering the anthology comes from such a small house. But Marco is resourceful, as we have seen, and had come by many of the stories by making friends with the writers involved, harassing them with e-mail, and then pouncing before the larger Italian publishing houses (who would rather wait and see if these American kids will amount to anything anyway) realized what had been taken from them. The collection amounted to an impressive snapshot of current American talent (although it by no means exhausts the variety of what is out there, particularly the new wave of diverse sub-cultural voices. For this a *Burned Children of America II* will be necessary), and it was the first time I had seen these writers all together in the same place. It was delicious, unexpected, as when a relative utilizes your address book for a surprise party and the result is a room full of lively people who you know, though they may not know each other. There were still more writers in the collection (hanging out in the kitchen, lurking by the fridge, sitting on the stairs) that I had never read and with these I felt the unreasonable pleasure of discovery although the discovery was nothing to do with me. Most of all I felt a thrill that so many people in my literary generation ('literary generations' are to 'a generation' as dog years are to human years; a generation should be properly confined within a five year stretch, but a single literary generation these days stretches from seventeen to thirty-nine) were at this fictional party, writing, and doing so with enthusiasm and verve. It raises the spirits, like seeing someone do a competent moonwalk in the lounge: it makes you want to do better yourself. In short, it was a happy gathering and I was very flattered to be asked to tap my glass three times, raise my voice and deliver these introductory words.

★

Yet the collection itself, the voices it left behind in my mind, presented themselves as a chorus of melancholy. It seemed to me that the writers were offering their readers an America quite different in spirit from the generation that preceded them. Set apart from the exuberant possibilities of Bellow's America, the masculine raging of Roth's, the lyricism of Morrison's. The America of these stories is more muted, the characters less hysterical in their trajectory, at odds with themselves, uncertain. Sad.

But why so sad, people? The community described in these stories (and the people who wrote them) is nothing if not privileged, educated, lucky, rich, most often Wasps, American. Why are these writers burned, what *is* the originating trauma, exactly? Two things seem prominent: fear of death and advertising. The two, of course, are intimately connected. There is no death in advertising, as an industry it is the league of anti-death, and this generation have seen advertising grow to inhabit the very fabric of their lives. Meanwhile death reveals itself as the nasty sting they never imagined at the end of the tale. Fear of disease, accident and attack is everywhere. Some of the fears are new or newish (the frequency of mass-death apocalyptic fantasy in recent American short stories can't be an accident), some are as old as America itself. In 'Comprehension Test' Myla Goldberg questions her fellow Americans about that ultimate plus-sized American fear: being the victim of a crime committed by a black man. It's multiple choice, so the reader will do well to have her pen at the ready. For Judy Budnitz's white middle-class Americans (whose life expectancy probably outranks any other group on the planet), death is still something to be feared in all its forms, we even get a useful list of morbid possibility:

freak accidents, threshing machines gone awry, people caught in giant gears or conveyor belts and torn limb from limb, hands in bread slicers, flimsy walkways over vats of acid. Elevator cases, diving board cases, subway train cases, drowning-in-the-bathtub cases, electrocution-by-blender cases. And then there were the ones that were just called Act of God.

Add this to Sam Lipsyte's story 'The Wrong Arm' – in which the disease has no name but is coming in with the tide anyway – well, one strongly gets the feeling that death is back in American fiction just as it has returned to American life. Not simply happening over there where they are poor and brown and mad about God, but over here where we are rich and have no God to protect us. Death is sort of an affront to American life. It's so anti-aspirational. No matter what you do, how hard you work, how good you are, it seems like you can't avoid it. It's not interested in your rights or freedoms. It just wants to return you to where you came from. Physical death deprives you of body, of consciousness, but there is a second death discussed in these stories with more passion: the death of authenticity. This is an old, old postmodern story, but for so many of the writers in this volume the problem just won't go away. Advertising stalks these stories as a corporeal, evil force in the world, replacing the human voice with advertising copy. *Just one second of unmediated thought, please* – this has become the West's new literary pastoral pose. Where once every writer dreamed of returning to the Virgilian greenwood and the babbling brook, now they just want to write an emotive sentence that has not already been used to sell dehumidifiers, Pepsi or suppositories. In Jonathan Lethem's 'Access Fantasy', we are in a bleak future of ad-patches, applied to the skins of poor people and impelling them to sell whatever, whenever they open their mouths. Ken Kalfus replaces Calvino's invisible cities with invisible malls, palaces to consume in, huge ornate adverts for themselves. A. M. Homes has a boy enamoured with a Barbie doll, 'falling in love in a way that had nothing to do with love', and everything to do with product: 'I ran my tongue back and forth over the slivers, back and forth over the words "copyright 1966 Mattel Inc., Malaysia" tattooed on her back.'

Advertising doubles for life, supplants, creates simulacra – but the stories themselves transcend the artificial worlds that inspired them. There is exquisite melancholy to be drawn out of these new American landscapes so infected with the corporate. Jeffrey Eugenides shows us a crumbling beach community in Florida, a cheap, decrepit hotel block and a whole town conspicuously dedicated to leisure; but wait: the narrator's kindly father owns the block and he works hard to maintain it, he does this for his family, for love of his family. Amidst the artificially transplanted palms out front, the pastel paints, the glimmering pool – the whole crazy, urgent battle to lead a successful American life – we are given a glimpse of the old man trying to pee, thumping himself in the bladder, trying to make it come out. There is an inescapable whiff of mortality about such a scene. It restates a truth that so much of corporate American life is in the business of denying.

The king of corporate comedy, however, is the divine George Saunders, who has single-handedly sunk the rest of his fellow American short-story writers (and this English one) into a maelstrom of bitter envy, formless anger, self-denigration, cycles of depression, spasms of plagiarism, difficulties with peeing etc. In

'I CAN SPEAK!™' the chilling false jollity of corporate language is enacted in the grammar itself (no one else can do so much with exclamation marks, brackets, rhetorical questions). This is a language that is constantly held hostage to some idea of 'appropriate' and 'professional' behaviour. This is the kind of speech that is aware of every possible legal ramification of speech. In place of the 'howdys' and 'how've ya been?' of corner store America (now a sort of fantasy to be found only in old movies on AMC in the afternoons), we are offered stilted, terrified sentences, every word of which we *know* will be checked over by somebody in middle management on the next floor who has the narrator's balls in their hands: 'No, that is not for me to say, Mrs Faniglia, I am only in sales . . .' (American names, if only we had names like these . . . you get so much *mileage* out of them. Ruth Faniglia. Rick Sminks.)

Saunders wrote his first story collection in-between times while working an office job, just as Carver wrote his in between visits to the laundromat. The life Saunders describes may be inauthentic in its spiritual essence, but the authentic description of this inauthentic life feels complete. From an interview:

At an office job, you gain weight, because you're just sitting at a desk for eight hours a day. There's no time for your family except when you're done, and then you're stressed out. And forget your spiritual life; you're just too stressed out. There's a great Terry Eagleton quote about how capitalism plunders the sensuality of the body; I was living that for eight years. Now, I have time to work out, I spend a lot of time with my kids, I have a spiritual life. That difference between seven years ago and now is not trivial. If I'd kept living my life the same way, I'd have died earlier, I'd have died angrier.

And one might expect Saunders's writing to be more angry, but this is not a prose of fury. There is too much sympathy, too many laughs. Certainly A. M. Homes and Matt Klam get closer to anger, with their vicious demarcation of the American gender war; behind Klam we can hear the Updike of *Couples*, behind Homes – well, actually there have been very few women writers like Homes. She is one of many women in this collection, along with Stacey Richter and Aimee Bender, whose writing seems to conform to none of the Maileresque fantasies of what women's writing is – indirect, soft, domestic, emotional. This prose has teeth – in Julia Slavin's case, literally. I feel Homes is one of the best short-story writers to come out of America in thirty years; you cannot shake a Homes story off your mind, you cannot rid yourself of the creeping unease it brings to your bedside table. Not everyone can get as angry as Homes, though, and still keep the prose on an even keel. There is another route, and humour is a large part of it. I am not the first person to note the peculiar tendency of this generation of American writers towards whimsy. Saunders is whimsical in his way but still a realist; he is only trying to show you how absurd the real is. Much of this collection, however, veers towards an abstract whimsy, a gentle scurrying after metaphor, sometimes a dogged pursuit of it, until the metaphor itself becomes the subject. Shelley Jackson takes 'Sleep' and tell us something about half-lived lives and a culture dedicated to escapism – in this America people shape sleep, and throw it around the backyard, and watch it fall from the sky; they fashion substitute wives and husbands out of it. Amanda Davis's schoolgirl 'Faith' is a little schoolgirl stalked by the fat schoolgirl she used to be, Aimee Bender knows a boy who has nine fingers that will open nine different doors, Rick Moody tells you the life and times of a paperclip, Arthur Bradford's characters tell their stories with no linguistic frills, just the thrill of what happens next, and what usually happens next is a really big slug, or some bees or in this case a whole load of frogs. So here is a generation who grew up reading the sort of stories which wanted to do a lot of things: they wanted to impress with intellect, dazzle with literary gossip, vibrate with seedy autobiographical content, scandalize New York – you know, a lot of things. In contrast, this generation genuinely wants to tell you a story – no matter how surreal – and this makes a nice change. The accusation levelled against whimsy, though, is that it is too, too precious – butter wouldn't melt in its mouth. But two of the most enjoyable pieces in the collection could be accused of the most whimsy: Dave Eggers's letters from a dog and Jonathan Safran Foer's truly affecting 'A Primer for the Punctuation of Heart Disease'. What both these pieces seem to be attempting is to make something happen *off* the page, *outside* words, a curious thing for a piece of writing to want to do. Though Eggers has shown himself to be a high-wire stylist before, there is nothing ornate about this piece, his letters from a dog called Steven to the CEOs of major American companies are hardly *Portrait of the Artist as a Young Dog*. Everything is happening off the page – it really shouldn't be any good at all. But there is something priceless about the little sub-narrative in your head you create as you imagine the CEO opening this letter, reading it, frowning, showing it to his secretary, finally shredding it, but never able to quite suppress the little bit of joy a letter from a dog must bring to a man who conducts seven a.m. breakfast meetings. *Esprit de sérieux* of the kind Simone de Beauvoir and her fellow existentialists warned us against – seriousness of the *soul* – is the death of us; everything that prompts the serious man to be serious (nation, corporate allegiance, an opinion on the usefulness of art, a dedication to the ideals of the past) are the ties that bind us, are the objects we put first, leaving the true subjects of existence, other people, to suffer as they will. Basically, what I'm saying is that the CEOs of major companies need to be sent letters written by domestic pets. It's just what needs to happen right now.

Out of the mouths of babes or something . . . Young Mr Safran Foer, a sort of sickening prodigy type, brings us a story offering a system of punctuation for the things siblings never say to each other. And then the things families don't say. And then the things whole religio-cultural groups don't say for fear that the sadness will take them over completely and we'll all have to start walking the streets watching out for people's hearts squished all over the sidewalk. It's a little story that understands that 'Familial communication always has to do with failures to communicate', a story that cares deeply for all the should-haves of our lives. We think we should-have. We think other people should-have. But we don't. The last lines, if you please:

Of course, my sense of the should-have is unlikely to be the same as my brothers', or my mother's or my father's. Sometimes – when I'm in the car, or having sex, or talking to one of them on the phone – I imagine their should-have versions. I sew them together into a new life, leaving out everything that actually happened and was said.

Which is as good a description of a writer's moral obligation as I have ever read. For *should-have* is always a moral question; it is superseded only by *what-if*. The empathic imaginative enacting of *what-if*, after all, is what creates the possibility of *should-have* in the first place. Now, a sad American writer, who feels the sadness all around him, has a responsibility at this present moment to recall the *what-if*, the equal pains of other people, many of them brown-skinned and far away. A sadness that indulges itself is just a sadness, but a sadness that connects this feeling with the sadness other people have felt throughout history and are feeling right now as I write this – this sadness takes on a moral aspect and becomes good writing and good *being* (good writing requires, *demands* good being, I'm absolutely adamant on this point). The *what-if* is the engine of fiction, it is there to produce pleasure, and, more and more these days, to illuminate pain. We will leave off now with George Saunders in an interview quoting Anton Chekhov, a man who existed in the *what-if* every day of his life.

People keep saying to me, 'But you seem so happy.' And I really am. But I love that Chekhov quote: 'There ought to be a man with a hammer behind the door of every happy man, to remind him by his constant knocks that there are unhappy people, and that happy as he himself may be, life will sooner or later show him its claws.' That seems to me to be a very legitimate function for literature: just to tap in the closet. For me it's pretty natural just to say, 'Yes, life's pretty good, but it's not good for everybody. And when it's not good, this is how it might feel.'

Zadie Smith
Cambridge, Massachusetts

I CAN SPEAK!™

★ ★ ★ ★ ★ George Saunders

Mrs Ruth Faniglia
210 Lester Street
Rochester, N.Y. 14623

Dear Mrs Faniglia,

We were very sorry to receive your letter of 23 Feb., which accompanied the I CAN SPEAK!™ you returned, much to our disappointment. We here at KidLuv believe that the I CAN SPEAK!™ is an innovative and essential educational tool that, used with proper parental guidance, offers a rare early development opportunity for babies and toddlers alike. And so I thought I would take some of my personal time (I am on lunch) and try to address the questions you raised in your letter, which is here in front of me on my (cluttered!) desk.

First, may I be so bold as to suggest that your disappointment may stem from your own, perhaps unreasonable, expectations? Because in your letter, what you indicated, when I read it, was that you think and/or thought that somehow the product can read your baby's mind? Our product cannot read your baby's mind, Mrs Faniglia. No one can read a baby's mind, at least not yet. Although believe me, we are probably working on it! All the I CAN SPEAK!™ can do, however, is respond to aural patterns in a way that makes baby seem older. Say baby sees a peach. If you or Mr Faniglia (I hope I do not presume) were to loudly say something like 'What a delicious peach!' the I CAN SPEAK!™, hearing this, through that little slotted hole near the neck, would respond by saying something like 'I LIKE PEACH.' Or 'I WANT PEACH.' Or, if you had chosen the ICS2000 (you chose the ICS1900, which is fine, perfectly good for most babies), the I CAN SPEAK!™ might even respond by saying something like 'FRUIT, ISN'T THAT ONE OF THE MAJOR FOOD GROUPS?' Which would be pretty good, for a six-month-old like Derek, your son, don't you think?

But here I must reiterate: That would not in reality be Derek speaking. Derek would not in reality know that a peach is fruit, or that fruit is a major food group. The I CAN SPEAK!™ knows, however, and, from its position on Derek's face, it will give the illusion that Derek knows, by giving the illusion that Derek is speaking out of the twin moving SimuLips. But that is it. That is all we claim.

Furthermore, in your letter, Mrs Faniglia, you state that the I CAN SPEAK!™ 'mask' (your terminology) takes on a 'stressed-out look when talking that is not what a real baby's talking face appears like but is more like some nervous middle-aged woman.' Well, maybe that is so, but, with all due respect, you try it! You try making a latex face look and talk and move like the real face of an actual live baby! Inside are over 5000 separate circuits and 390 moving parts. And as far as looking like a middle-aged woman, we beg to differ: we do not feel that a middle-aged stressed-out woman has (1) no hair on head and (2) chubby cheeks and (3) fine downy facial hair. The ICS1900 unit is definitely the face of a baby, Mrs Faniglia. We took over twenty-five hundred photos of different babies and using a computer combined them to make this face, this face we call Male Composite 37 or, affectionately, Little Roger. But what you possibly seem to be unhappy about is that

Little Roger's face is not Derek's face? To be frank, Mrs Faniglia, many of you, our customers, have found it disconcerting that their baby looks different with the I CAN SPEAK!™ on. Which we find so surprising. Did you, we often wonder, not look at the cover of the box? On that cover the ICS1900 is very plainly shown, situated on a sort of rack, looking facewise like Little Roger, albeit Little Roger is a bit crumpled and has a forehead furrow of sorts.

But this is why we came up with the ICS2100. With the ICS2100, your baby looks just like your baby. And, because we do not want anyone to be unhappy with us, we would like to give you a complimentary ICS2100 upgrade! We would like to come to your house on Lester Street and make a personalized plaster cast of Derek's real, actual face! And soon, via FedEx, here will come Derek's face in a box, and when you slip that ICS2100 over Derek's head and Velcro the Velcro, he will look so very much like himself! Plus we have another free surprise, which is that, while at your house, we will tape his actual voice and use it to make our phrases, the phrases Derek will subsequently say. So not only will he look like himself, he will sound like himself, as he crawls around your house appearing to speak!

Plus we will throw in several other personalizing options. Say you call Derek 'Lovemeister.' (I am using this example from my own personal home, as my wife, Ann, and I call our son Billy 'Lovemeister,' because he is so sweet.) With the ICS2100, you might choose to have Derek say, upon crawling into a room, 'HERE COMES THE LOVEMEISTER!' or 'STOP TALKING DIRTY, THE LOVEMEISTER HAS ARRIVED!' How we do this is, laser beams coming out of the earlobes, which sense the doorframe. So the I CAN SPEAK!™ knows it has just entered a room, from its position on Derek's head! And also you will have over one hundred Discretionary Phrases to more highly personalize Derek. For instance, you might choose to have him say, on his birthday, 'MOMMY AND DADDY, REMEMBER THAT TIME YOU CONCEIVED ME IN ARUBA?' Although probably you did not in fact conceive Derek in Aruba. That we do not know. (Our research is not that extensive!) Or say your dog comes up and gives Derek a lick? You could make Derek say (if your dog's name is Queenie), 'QUEENIE, GIVE IT A REST!' Which, you know what? It makes you love him more. Because suddenly he is articulate. Suddenly he is not just sitting there going glub glub glub while examining a piece of his own feces on his own thumb, which is something we recently found Billy doing! Sometimes we have felt that our childless friends think badly of us for having a kid who just goes glub glub glub in the corner while looking at his feces on his thumb. But now when childless friends are over, what we have found, my wife, Ann, and I, is that it's great to have your kid say something witty and self-possessed years before he or she would actually in reality be able to say something witty or self-possessed. The bottom line is that it's just *fun* when you and your childless friends are playing cards, and your baby suddenly blurts out (in his *very own probable future voice*), 'IT IS LIKELY THAT WE STILL DON'T FULLY UNDERSTAND THE IMPORT OF ALL OF EINSTEIN'S FINDINGS!'

Here I must admit that we have several times seen a sort of softening in the eyes of our resolutely childless friends, as if they, too, would suddenly like to have a baby.

And as far as Derek flinching whenever that voice issues forth from him? When that speaker near his mouth sort of buzzes his lips? May I say this is not unusual? What I suggest? Try putting the ICS on Derek for a short time at first, maybe ten minutes a day, then gradually building up his Wearing Time. That is what we did.

And it worked super. Now Billy wears his even while sleeping. In fact, if we forget to put it back on after his bath, he pitches a fit. Kind of begs for it! He starts to say, you know, 'Mak! Mak!' Which we think is his word for mask. And when we put the mask on and Velcro the Velcro, he says, or rather it says, 'GUTEN MORGEN, PAPA!' because we are trying to teach him German, and have installed the German Learning module in our ICS2100. Or for example, if his pants are not yet on, he'll say, 'HOW ABOUT SLAPPING ON MY ROMPERS SO I CAN GET ON WITH MY DAY!' (I wrote that one.)

My point is, with the ICS2100 Billy is much, much cleverer than he ever was with the ICS1900. He has recently learned, for example, that if he spills a little milk on his chin, his SimuLips will issue a MOO sound. Which he really seems to get a kick out of! I'll be in the living room doing a little evening paperwork and from the kitchen I'll hear, you know, 'MOO! MOO! MOO!' And I'll rush in, and there'll be this sort of lake of milk on the floor. And there'll be Billy, pouring milk on his chin until I yank the milk away, at which point he bellows, 'DON'T FENCE ME IN.' (Ann's contribution – she was raised in Wyoming!)

I, for one, Mrs Faniglia, do not believe that any baby wants to sit around all day going glub glub glub. My feeling is that a baby, sitting in its diaper, looking around at the world, thinks to itself, albeit in some crude nonverbal way, What the heck is wrong with me, why am I the only one going glub glub glub while all these other folks are talking in whole complete sentences? And hence, possibly, lifelong psychological damage may result. Now, am I saying that your Derek runs the risk of feeling bad about himself as a grownup because as a baby he felt he didn't know how to talk right? No, it is not for me to say that, Mrs Faniglia, I am only in

Sales. But I will say that I am certainly not taking any chances with our Billy. My belief is that when Billy hears a competent, intelligent voice issuing from the area near his mouth, he feels excellent about himself. And I feel excellent about him. Not that I didn't feel excellent about him before. But now we can actually have a sort of conversation! And also – and most importantly – when that voice issues from his SimuLips he learns something invaluable; namely, that when he finally does begin speaking, he will be speaking via using his mouth.

Now, Mrs Faniglia, you may be thinking, Hold on a sec, of course this guy loves his I CAN SPEAK!™ He probably gets his for free! But not so, Mrs Faniglia, I get mine for two grand, just like you. We get no discounts, so much in demand is the I CAN SPEAK!™, and in addition we are strongly encouraged by our management to purchase and use the I CAN SPEAK!™ at home, on our own kids. (Or even, in one case, on an elderly senile mom! Suffice it to say that, though she looks sort of funny with the Little Roger head on her somewhat frail frame, the family takes great comfort in hearing all the witty things she has to say. Just like her old self!) Not that I wouldn't use it otherwise. Believe me, I would. Since we upgraded to the ICS2100, things have been great, Billy looks almost identical to himself, and is not nearly so, you know, boring as before, when we had the ICS1900, which (frankly) says some rather predictable things, which I expect is partly why you were so unhappy with it, Mrs Faniglia, you seem like a very intelligent woman. When people come over now, sometimes we just gather around Billy and wait for his next howler, and last weekend my supervisor, Mr Ted Ames, stopped by (a super guy, he has really given me support, please let him know if you've found this letter at all helpful) and boy did we all crack up laughing when Billy began rubbing his face very rapidly across the carpet in order to make his ICS2100 shout, 'FRICTION IS A COMMON AND USEFUL SOURCE OF HEAT!'

Mrs Faniglia, it is nearing the end of my lunch, and so I must wrap this up, but I hope I have been of service. On a personal note, I did not have the greatest of pasts when I came here, having been in a few scrapes and even rehab situations, but now, wow, the commissions roll in, and I have made a nice life for me and Ann and Billy. Not that the possible loss of my commission is the reason for my concern. Please do not think so. While it is true that, if you decline my upgrade offer and persist in your desire to return your ICS1900, my commission must be refunded, by me, to Mr Ames, it is no big deal, I have certainly refunded commissions to Mr Ames before, especially lately. I don't quite know what I'm doing wrong. But that is not your concern, Mrs Faniglia. Your concern is Derek. My real reason for writing this letter, on my lunch break, is that, hard as we all work at KidLuv to provide innovative and essential development tools for families like yours, Mrs Faniglia, it is always sort of a heartbreak when our products are misapprehended. Please do accept our offer of a free ICS2100 upgrade. We at KidLuv really love what kids are, Mrs Faniglia, which is why we want them to become something better as soon as possible! Baby's early years are so precious, and must not be wasted, as we are finding out, as our Billy grows and grows, learning new skills every day.

Sincerely yours,
Rick Sminks
Product Service Representative
KidLuv, Inc.

There Should Be a Name for It
★ ★ ★ ★ ★ Matthew Klam

★ ★ ★ ★ ★ Lynn's roasting a chicken. She takes out garlic, chili powder, and a lime. 'What's that for?' I say. 'There are pine nuts above your head,' she says. I hand them down to her. Now she butters the pan. She's got the coriander in a bag, cloves, curry, and two oranges. Then other green herbs. Jesus Christ, I'm thinking, all that crap for the chicken.

'All that's for the chicken?'

'What?'

'What? That.' I'm pulling on my eyebrow hair. It's a nervous habit, but I feel like plucking these long curly ones. 'All that goes on the chicken?'

She rinses off her hands and says, 'This is a recipe from my mom.'

It's early summer. It's afternoon, and the kitchen is the brightest room in this house. It's like a greenhouse in here, very sunny. The house itself is small and cheap, though a hundred and fifty years ago somebody planted a sycamore on the front lawn. Protected from the wind and fed by sun and water, the plant grew into a giant. The limbs stretch up – it's like an elephant, white tusks against the sky.

'Up we go,' she says, upending the chicken. She pulls a wax-paper bag from inside it like an envelope and drops it in the sink.

'What the hell is that?' I say. Lynn wipes her forehead with her wrist. She takes the bag out of the sink and tears it open, spilling the contents into her hand. It's meat – it looks like tongues.

'Oh, my God.'

'It's chicken livers. See?'

She flicks them with her finger. It's three glistening pieces of purple meat, but not at all like steak. They look like they were alive five minutes ago. She holds one. She seems to enjoy touching it.

'OK, get rid of it.' Lynn puts the bag and the livers in the garbage. She says, 'You make it with onions. My mother loves it.'

'Yeah.'

This is the whole chicken, an entire animal. Like, I haven't exactly seen this done before by a person my age. We're both kids. We don't know how to cook this stuff. In all the time we've been living together, Lynn's never cooked a whole chicken.

I'm leaning close enough to her that I can smell her shampoo. Her hair is thick and reddish brown, full and shiny, and her skin is the color of creamy tan suede. Mexican mother, Irish father. You know how they airbrush the skin of ladies in *Playboy*? I see Lynn's body every day, I look at her skin up close. I've had my eye an inch above her stomach or her shoulder or her calf, and it's flawless. It's golden skin. Every morning after her shower, Lynn comes and stands in front of me – I'm either getting dressed or making notes for work – then she turns around and I rub cream across her shoulders, underneath the bra straps, bright-white fabric against her tan skin.

She cuts the fat off the chicken, that makes sense, but with scissors, of all things. She holds it like a little playmate, flipping it over, rocking it under the faucet. She washes out the hole in it, pouring some little pieces of red guts into the sink, shaking out the dried blood or cartilage that runs down and sticks in the drain. Sickening. Then she tears off a piece of brown paper bag and folds it, dabbing the outside of the chicken.

'What are you doing?' I ask.

'It gets the old oil out of the skin.'

'Old oil? What, like sweat?'

'No, not like sweat,' she says. 'Like sweat? Chickens don't sweat.'

'I know.'

'I'm cooking you dinner and you're gonna stand here and give me shit?'

'No! No way. This is gonna be sensational.'

I love her. Man! I really do. She's a pistol. It's not placating love, it's really passionate love. Uncharted territory, yes, definitely. But that's what love is – undefined.

'Move aside, termite,' she says to me, grabbing the bottle of olive oil.

'Termite,' I say. 'Good one.'

I love how she says that – 'Are you gonna give me shit?' That's funny. The answer is yes, I am.

Lynn's awesome, though. She knows what she's thinking, and she knows what you're thinking. She's got you. She's a keeper, as they say. I want to keep her.

'Or would you rather I'd left the feathers on?'

I say, 'You're the chef.' I mean, whatever this girl touches turns to gold.

Say something bad happened to her, and we have no control over it. All of a sudden there's a situation. Hang on, let me start this over.

It's hard to explain – poor kid – a month ago Lynn had to get an abortion. What a lead balloon. What a joke. It ain't no joke.

'Give me that,' she says, pointing at the pepper, and I hand it to her. She rubs chili powder on the skin. Now the paprika, now salt, now some other stuff.

In Spanish, the word is *aborto*, a foreign word that even I can master and pretty easy for Celia, Lynn's mother, to yell at her a few times over the phone. '*Aborto! Aborto! Clak-ata-clak-ata-clak-ata.*'

Lynn called home. It was night, we were lying in bed, and I heard everything from my side. I wanted to help, but what could I do? You don't interfere with a family. Lynn nodded into the phone, picked up a pencil and stared at it.

'Mom. We already decided.'

'Goddamn it!' I heard Celia say. 'You slut. You and your jackass boyfriend.'

After two minutes, Lynn hung up. She didn't say anything.

'Jackass boyfriend?' I said.

'She said to tell you she hates you.'

'Thanks.'

In my mind, I saw Celia stomping barefoot through her newly carpeted house with the antenna phone and her 1950s bouffant hairdo and ten pounds of eye shadow, shaking her fist, saying, 'Goddamn jackass,' meaning me, blaming it on me.

Lynn and I have a normal sex life. Whatever that means. Sex is never normal with anyone, it's bizarre, it's wiggly meats, but Lynn was a virgin when we met. And then a couple of months went by, and we were invited to her parents' for Christmas.

We drove from Colorado to Ohio. It's twenty-two hours by

car. You know how it is when you go on a road trip – you're going to a new place together. After five or six hours, the inside of the car smelled like BO; my ass began to hurt; my legs felt like concrete; there were sunflower seeds all over the floor. More miles, and soon we were spitting the shells on each other. Two o'clock in the morning, shit-bag road stop, I'm buying cigarettes in Michigan. Lynn's standing next to me in a pink pajama top and jeans, sunflower-seed shells in her hair, which is all sticking up in knots in the back from her sleeping on it. She gave me two candy fireballs; her hand was warm and clammy. Outside, no cars passed by. It was silent. It wasn't particularly cold for December. There was the gas station and then nothing for miles.

We stood in the unfamiliar light of the store in the middle of nowhere, lost. It was at about that time that I felt anything could happen. Me and my girlfriend, Lynn, on our first road trip together. When you're twenty-three, a road trip is the highlight of your life. I held on to her hand. It's the same person, and she's great, but she seemed different all of a sudden, three-dimensional. Like a person you've just met for the first time and would like to get to know. As we drove off, the car went over a speed bump and out of the corner of my eye I saw Lynn's boobs shake.

They put me in the guest room in the basement. The room had white wicker furniture and green-and-silver jungle wallpaper. Mold in the squishy rug. We'd packed our clothes into the same suitcase, and as I dug through it for my contact-lens holder I came across a bunch of Lynn's underwear. I took a pair out and held them up to the light, weightless flowered cotton panties. They had a lacy edge. They were clean and cute and smelled like powder. Eleven o'clock at night I'm sitting on the bed in the dank basement, white wicker furniture and green jungle wallpaper, the underwear crumpled against my nose and mouth, tracing swirl patterns in the stucco ceiling. I really loved her. Two floors above me my girlfriend lay sleeping, down the hall from her mother and father. I never put pressure on Lynn, for I knew that would be wrong, and yet she must've felt safe. We'd begun to build up trust. This is the part where Lynn loses her virginity. It was the holiday season. The stage was set.

Lunchtime, Celia had made a Mexican specialty, a casserole, a savory thing, cheap cuts of fatty meat, bone chips, dog lips, and I went into the bathroom to get a stain off my pants. Lynn came in to help me, and we both ended up naked from the waist down. She got up on the sink, both of us a little self-conscious, trying to be quiet, except I was so excited my feet itched, the thing so hard it felt like it was pulling off me of its own power. Lynn's like kicking my jeans, she was like Don't come inside me, she was like drooling, her eyes rolled back into her head, kind of grunting, her legs around my waist. And there were her parents – Celia and Phil sitting outside the door sopping up the orange grease on their plates from their Mexican lasagna. Man, it was something. Lynn said, 'I'm supposed to be a virgin, you bastard. My mother is in the next room. Stop it right now. Stop it before I faint,' laughing. 'Somebody, help.' I almost fainted myself, both of us leering and hot as monkeys.

It's terrible the way kids work off their parents.

That week was the best sex I ever had in my life: Celia knocking on the door to Lynn's room during afternoon-nap time, me beneath the blanket, Lynn saying, 'I'll be right out, Mom, I'm getting dressed,' Celia saying, 'Where's Jack, honey?' *and really not knowing where I was!* See? That's why I love the Midwest. Such a dreamy lack of a clue. That's what happens in the Ohio

River valley, even to a transplanted Mexican with citizenship. I'm from New York, where dead people are not that dumb. These folks are idiots. I mean innocent. Other friends of their family would come by, I'd run down to the basement to bring up extra chairs, and I'd feel it dribbling in my pants. Once the first one was out of the way, we did it every time Phil and Celia turned their backs. Every time they went to the food store. They had to go back to the food store so many times because we were eating everything in the refrigerator and losing weight at the same time. Their whole house must still smell from our spooge. I picture that dumpy suburban street – the snow melting in rivers of mud everywhere, her dad walking around in that fisherman hat, the smell of new wall-to-wall carpet everywhere in their house – and I get an exciting feeling inside. It's like the first time we did it all over again.

Lynn holds the chicken's weight in one hand and rubs a stick of butter around it with the other, like a deodorant stick, almost. She sprinkles it with lime, rubbing gently with her other hand around its back and rump. It makes me squeamish sitting there, like it might get up all of a sudden and tap my shoulder, but Lynn's got a pretty sure grip on it. She grabs it by the cavity, sticks it on its back in the pan, and throws in a bunch of herb leaves and pine nuts. Then she cuts up an onion and an orange with the skin still on.

My office mate Amy told me, after she had her baby, how similar an uncooked chicken felt in her hands to the body of her daughter. She said how she held it, rubbing olive oil on it, under the wings, around the thighs, with soft loose pink skin, the small, protective rib cage. It was the same weight and size as her baby.

She said even the elbows had a similar feel in her wet hands. She said it was too funny, so she loaded her camera, naked Elizabeth lying next to the chicken on Amy's leather coat, and all the groceries piled up around them. She stood on a chair and got the two birds on film.

Lynn is standing at the sink now, measuring out rice, and looking at me with those bright-green eyes that say, 'I know what I'm doing here.' She looks like an angel. My knees begin to buckle, and I just want to put her down on the kitchen floor and start the trouble all over again. I want to bare her breast and nod on her nipple. I'm her baby. She's my baby. Everybody's somebody's baby. Let's make a baby.

Lynn says, 'What else besides rice?'

'Do you want salad?' I say.

In April we put a garden in the backyard. The land behind our house is flat. It gets both sun and shade. The grass is long and lush and light green, and right now there are some dandelions. It'll need mowing soon. The garden was our team project, although the day we rented the tiller Lynn was sick and I did everything, and I'd just as soon have Fritos over a vegetable any day of the week. But we both like looking at the garden.

After dinner we go and check out the garden, walking between the rows, careful of where we step. Sometimes she'll pull weeds. When it gets dark we lie on the cold metal basement doors and watch the sky. Above us, the clouds are silently on the move, backlit by the moon. The smell of cut grass is everywhere. The sweet smell and the crickets, and the slick noise of lawn sprinklers hissing in the dark. Grass smells good. There should be a name for it.

'I'll get the salad,' I say. There's a basket we use for the vegetables. I take it off the top of the refrigerator.

'I'll do it,' Lynn says. 'I'm in the mood.' She pulls the basket out of my hands and goes out the back door, the glass doorknob banging against the wall.

The sun is going down. Flat, ginger-colored light is sprayed against every surface inside the kitchen, across the counters and the refrigerator door and the walls that are the color of yellow wine. I hear her say hello to Whiskey, the cat. The people next door own him. Strange name for a cat.

It's Tuesday. It's almost seven. Time to eat.

We said we'd get a cat, but what I really want is a dog – dogs are better – but cats are less permanent. If we had to move, you could give the cat away, or leave it. No one would do that to a dog, and anyway it's against the law. A dog would starve to death.

Our difficulties began one night three months ago. I know the exact night. Lynn came home from class and said, 'I just got my period. It's so early this month.' She said something cute like 'You don't have to worry about rubbers for a while.' I do worry about rubbers. They are my downfall. We did it that night, no rubber. There was an instant – I remember it – when I was deciding whether or not to actually go for it. I followed a certain line of reasoning, and remembered what she said, twinkled over the risks, and then blew my nuts out. It was something to behold. I really enjoyed myself, oink oink, drowning in it. But then her period disappeared the next day. Or I should say it never came.

She was ovulating.

Let me lay this out again. She ovulated that night, thus the dot of blood. Then we did it. Bingo. You morons, you fucking biologists.

She was pregnant. It was April. I'd just turned twenty-four. I'd never been near an abortion clinic. And Colorado's not the laid-back, liberal-Jew neck of the woods I come from. This here's the American West. I work for a software designer, but I've seen guys in spurs all duded up like *Deliverance* on a Friday night.

I felt desperate and called my parents. My mom told me how in Florida a pro-life group stood outside a women's clinic with a bullhorn, yelling, 'If you come out now we'll shoot you, but your unborn child will be spared!' Congress had just blocked the abortion pill for the eighty-second time. She told me that what we were doing was OK. Her voice made me homesick.

The thing about New York City is everything's so jam-packed. It's the crowds, there are so many bums, dead people practically lying on the street. In the winter you die from the cold wind, in the summer you die from the heat. The breeze stinks, the people smell like piss, there's the traffic. It's impossible to park. Everybody's in a rotten mood. No place to hide.

In Colorado, the sun always shines. The sky is usually blue, and when we hang our clean clothes on the line in the backyard they dry in an hour. When you smell them they're crisp and smell like air. The mountains are to the west of town. This is a new town, 120 years old. They shot indigenous peoples to settle this town. You drive up into the Rockies and see powdery snow on the side of the road. Toward the eastern part of Colorado there are cornfields that go clear across the Midwest, I think. That yonder there is Kansas, I reckon. Anyway, it's flat, and kind of stunning from inside a car, cows and fields and vistas slashing out in every direction, and the sky above you is a flawless ceiling.

God, you think, this would be perfect, if only . . . if only I had more money, if only it were a couple of years from now, if only Lynn and I were married, or were ready to get married, if I had more friends here – but old friends – or decent places to hang out at, or more of a feeling of what's next.

They wouldn't let us come in to the clinic yet. She wasn't far enough along. We had to wait almost two weeks to have it done. Seven and a half weeks is the magic number, for all you peckerheads taking notes. Anything less, it's a speck of unremovable dust. Lynn ate saltines before she got out of bed every day, and I brought her a cold glass of club soda. Our friend Tina taught her that.

I'd walk in, hand her the saltines, and sit and look at this girl I've been sleeping next to for months and months – five months by then – and I hated her. She was sick now, and I was sick of her, I hated her little puffy knocked-up ass, she looked like a worried old hag, and out of nowhere I'm just not so sure of anything. Why I all of a sudden don't love her. Because there's something about her that I'm definitely not too sure about. What if she turns into her mother? Celia's a joke.

They say a pregnant woman looks radiant. Lynn went around for two weeks, agitated and angry and with an upset stomach, but she really did look radiant – it was like a cosmetics expert had done something to her face. Her cheeks were flushed all day, and her eyes were as bright as green candy. I can't explain the difference. I kept catching myself staring. For those two weeks she was nauseous and pissed off. Added to that, I was still in training for my job, we were not married or engaged or anything, and Lynn really didn't know, ha-ha, was she maybe ready to be a mother? Maybe she wasn't and maybe she was. Is twenty-two too young? She toyed with the idea while lolling around in the bath, conditioning her hair. Well, I knew. I'm sure. Please ask me.

Out the window now the sun is setting. It's the summer of 1995. I see Lynn is crouched between the vegetables, picking peas and pulling up weeds.

This garden is a pretty thought – it's the nicest thing I've ever done. We have snap peas growing along one row. I read in the paper that they like to climb, so I built a trellis beside the row, crisscross lattice-wood slats, about two feet tall. I painted it white. We have eggplants, squash, tomatoes, and yellow flowers, and next year we'll plant tubers. When I hate Lynn, or when I can't stand to look at her or be near her, when I feel putrid, when I wish God would just erase me, I look at the garden. When she gets angry or yells about something terrible I did and we're fighting, I look out the window at that thing we made, the garden, at the lawn when it's been mowed and raked and looks like a putting green, cool and flat and smells sweet. You want to lie down on it and tear the grass up with your hands. Sometimes I think I'm just about ready to kill her.

How come I never do what I'm supposed to do? How come everything I do is such a fucking disaster? Doesn't anybody get what they want? And that line of hers about how she might want to have it. She came out of the bathtub with a towel on her head, fluffing her hair. 'Honey,' she said. She never called me 'Honey' before in her life. 'Honey, I've been thinking about our child.' I could feel all the blood draining from my head. White flecks on the edges of my vision. There was a narrow window of opportunity there, before I calmed myself, where different pictures whizzed into my mind. Blood, knives, handcuffs, that sort of thing. I told her, You have it alone, honey darling, in your own purple dream world – I'll be in Australia by the time the thing comes out.

There's the immense Colorado sky, there's the grass, there's the clothes on the line, fruit hanging ripe in the trees, the smell of wet cut grass. The land ripping out flat to the Mississippi with the sun leering on top in every direction. And you're standing above it, a million miles from bumper-to-bumper commuter-nightmare New York. You're not there anymore, though, you're here, at the foot of the Rockies, cow-town college town on the American prairie. Great American steer farm. Steroid-fat cows. Transistor radios in barns, cows chewing all night long.

There were five of us in the room during the procedure: the doctor, her assistant, the hand-holder, me, and, of course, Lynn. She was the star. This was her show. Then it would finally be over. The hand-holder was a therapist, trained in female personal crisis. She was never more than a foot from Lynn throughout that long day.

The staff was ready to go. A stainless-steel machine is used by the doctor to vacuum it out, and the doctor needed Lynn's OK to begin. The whole thing was supposed to take five minutes.

Lynn got weepy from nerves, and we all waited while she collected herself. Everyone was anxious to get on with it. I bet Lynn was, too. I held her hand and kissed it; she wasn't even looking at me, she stared up at some poster on the ceiling. The sound, the way she cried, choking some, the way you do when you're sobbing lying on your back, so the spit runs down your throat, swallowing, laughing underneath the crying for how absurd the scene was – even Lynn could see it – lying there with her legs propped up in the air, all these fucking people around her holding her hands and her knees and her privates, watching her like she was – ha-ha! – about to give birth (sorry). Boo-hoo. But in my mind I keep coming back to that sound, not loud, not shrill, that crying, it was almost a noise an animal would make. How much trouble Lynn was having even crying right then, without strangling on her own spit. Is there a way to describe how much I wanted to get the fuck out of there? I wanted to shout, God of New York, turn off that sound, get me out of this room before I'm seared and split open, before I develop breasts myself. The other half of my brain, though, recorded her voice for all time.

'You're OK,' Lynn said to nobody, to herself. 'You're OK.' She'd planned to get through it without tears.

Then it was quiet and she told the doctor to go ahead, and the doctor nodded to her assistant. The assistant turned on the machine, and the machine made a sound like any vacuum.

Lynn is outside, bent over the row of peas. The chicken is sitting over there in the pan. I guess it's ready to bake. She put garlic, butter, lime juice, chili powder, chopped nuts, oranges, cloves, parsley, coriander, half a banana, and paprika on it. What's left? Jean Naté? A cigar up the butt? The rice is cooking away in a pot. The chicken sits there like a drag queen, waiting to get roasted.

When it was over, Lynn went into another room and fell asleep. The therapist came over and said, 'You were so caring today. Guys aren't usually so caring.'

I nodded. The woman looked at me sweetly. I guess I was nice. So what. Maybe it wasn't the norm for her. Or was she just looking for a tip? My voice, though, was so much deeper than everybody else's in the room. Whatever I said that day came out sounding like a frog croak. Like a belch. My voice was unnaturally deep. I nodded as much as possible. Other than an arrest for drunk driving in college, it was the most nodding I'd ever done in one five-hour stretch.

'What are you doing?' I yell to Lynn out the window. She's bent over the rosebush. Her head is down and her shoulders are rounded, as though she's concentrating on something small.

Lynn says, 'There are beetles on the roses.'

I look over at the roasting pan again. 'Do we cook this thing or what? I'm getting hungry. What temperature do you set it at?' No answer. She's busy with the roses.

'Lynn, you didn't turn the oven on. I'm going to come out there and pull you in by your hair.'

Her hair is hanging around her face. She's looking down. 'Relax,' she says. 'The oven is on. What time is it?' I can feel myself getting annoyed, so I take ten deep breaths, counting the numbers slowly, saying the word *relax* as I breathe out.

'Damn it, Lynn, I can't hear you.' She looks up finally.

'It has to cook for an hour,' she says. 'And you have to move the rack.'

The pan is heavier than I thought. She said move the rack. What does that mean, up or down? I grab it and then drop it, hot rack, and then the roasting pan, too, onto the oven door.

'Fuck!'

'What's going on?' she says.

'The rack is on fire.'

'Of course it is, Jack, it's three hundred and fifty degrees in there. Did you burn yourself? Better put cold water on it.'

I stand over the sink and let the water run on my fingers.

There's a welt on my palm. I am a moron. She says, 'Didn't you ever hear of an oven mitt?'

Man. My fucking hand. Did I ever hear of an oven mitt? What is that, sarcasm?

She says, 'Do you want to try something weird?' Out the window I see her looking up toward me, her face flushed from leaning over for so long. 'Should we put dandelions in the salad? Look at this,' she says, clutching a bunch of dandelions from our lawn in a bouquet. 'Mexicans kill for these, the little leaves,' she says. 'And they fry the flowers.' I never ate dandelions before. And who cares.

'Is that too weird?' she says.

'Hey, yeah,' I say, drying my burned hand gingerly on my T-shirt. 'Momma had a baby and the head popped off.' When I was a kid, we used to pick a dandelion and say this when we flicked the head off the stem. The water in the rice pot foams over the sides.

'Excuse me, Momma didn't have a baby and the head popped off,' I say, correcting myself.

I walk over and grab a towel, move the rack down, push the chicken in, and close the oven. The door goes *spring* against the metal. It's 7:02. Nothing comes to mind. Outside she looks up at the window.

'Is that a joke?' she says.

At this angle the sun cuts right through the house. It's orange, purple, rose-colored light, blasting right through the house and spilling against everything.

'Fuck you,' she says.

It's about time somebody said it. I can hear the familiar sound of it ringing in the background.

'You can never keep anything to yourself,' she says.

'What?' I say.

'In your head,' she says, standing at the doorway. 'Forget it.' Over in the rice pot, there isn't any water left. So the bottom is cooking way too fast. It's, like, black. I use a coffee cup and dump some water in. It sizzles, a cloud of steam comes up. One more cup of water. The rice starts cooking again. My eyes are tearing. In a few seconds the whole wet mess is bubbling away. I feel like I scorched my face.

Lynn's basket is overflowing with greenery and edible dandelions.

'Get out of my way,' she says. 'You are an animal.'

'I'm sorry. Why did I say that? Is it too late to take it back?'

'What's wrong with you?' she says.

Lynn goes over to the oven with a dish towel and slides the roasting pan out. She carries it past me, not even hot yet, out the back door, and I hear it go *gong* against the metal basement doors. I step up to the window. The chicken's in the grass, onions, carrots, sliced oranges – the whole thing.

Lynn is standing in front of me now. The dish towel is wound around her hand.

'Cool,' I say. 'How symbolic.'

She says, 'I think we need therapists.'

'What can I say? I'm sorry,' I tell her.

'Why don't you get down on your knees.'

I say, 'I will if you want.' No one moves.

'You're mad at me,' she says. 'How can you be mad at me?'

'I'm sorry. Jesus Christ. It's my fault.'

She shakes her head, staring at me. 'Now what?'

'I'm too hungry,' I say. 'I can't make any big decisions.'

'What the hell happened to your face?' she says.

Outside, I pick up the roasting pan out of a pile of leaves. Lynn comes up beside me and puts the chicken back in it, and we shovel up the vegetables and carry everything over to the garbage and throw it all away, even the cracked enamel pot. Whiskey is already there at the fence, meowing and sniffing around.

'Go on, Whiskey,' I say. 'Not for you.'

'Make sure the lid's on tight,' she says to me. 'I don't want to clean this up a second time from some raccoon.'

Let's say, for the sake of something, that I never loved her, that what we have here is a housing arrangement, with scenes of nude touching, that we joined for this comfort, that it's missing some key element of normal love. It's not normal, it's more like high-school love, or freshman-year-in-college kind of love, the kind you're glad to stick with as long as it doesn't interfere, as long as it doesn't start ruining your life. The very, very flawed kind. That's my idea of love, actually, those endless first two weeks, early on, when all you care about is love.

We get a pizza. We pay the man. We eat the salad she picked and lie on the rug in the living room, eating pizza, watching TV, together on the floor. We have no furniture – we aren't there yet. The vibe between us is two people very tired and in shock, but amiable. I put some cream on my face. The welt on my hand throbs. I'd rather have pizza anyway; chicken sucks. I love her. Who else would accept me in this condition?

I should say I'll make dinner tomorrow night.

'I can make dinner tomorrow night.'

'You gonna make some chicken?' she says.

'White Christmas lasagna,' I say. 'With spinach and salad and bread.'

'Sounds good,' she says. 'Move over,' sliding toward me. She slings her leg over both of mine, sticking her face in my neck. 'This way,' she says, and I move to accommodate her. I can feel Lynn's warm, clean breath on my skin. What a feeling, from one person to another.

'I don't understand anything,' she says. Her eyes close. Her breath slows.

Lynn gets up from beside me and takes the dinner plates with her. I must be insane. She gives me what I need, and I love her. Hollow but true. I have to remember these things, about her and about the chicken in the grass – is that how it works? Perfect. Stupid. Shared. Turn off the TV now. Turn off the lights.

Flush

★ ★ ★ ★ ★ Judy Budnitz

★★★★★ I called my sister and said: What does a miscarriage look like?

What? she said. Oh. It looks like when you're having your period, I guess. You have cramps, and then there's blood.

What do people do with it? I asked.

With what?

The blood and stuff.

I don't know, she said impatiently. I don't know these things, I'm not a doctor. All I can tell you about anything is who you should sue.

Sorry, I said.

Why are you asking me this? she said.

I'm just having an argument with someone, that's all. Just thought you could help settle it.

Well, I hope you win, she said.

I went home because my sister told me to.

She called and said: It's your turn.

No, it can't be, I feel like I was just there, I said.

No, I went the last time. I've been keeping track, I have incontestable proof, she said. She was in law school.

But Mich, I said. Her name was Michelle but everyone called her Mich, as in Mitch, except our mother, who thought it sounded obscene.

Lisa, said Mich, don't whine.

I could hear her chewing on something, a ballpoint pen probably. I pictured her with blue marks on her lips, another pen stuck in her hair.

It's close to Thanksgiving, I said, why don't we wait and both go home then?

You forget – they're going down to Florida to be with Nana.

I don't have time to go right now. I have a job, you know. I do have a life.

I don't have time to argue about it, I'm studying, Mich said. I knew she was sitting on the floor with her papers scattered around her, the stacks of casebooks sprouting yellow Post-its from all sides, like lichen, Mich in the middle with her legs spread, doing ballet stretches.

I heard a background cough.

You're not studying, I said. Neil's there.

Neil isn't doing anything, she said. He's sitting quietly in the corner waiting for me to finish. Aren't you, sweetheart?

Meek noises from Neil.

You call him sweetheart? I said.

Are you going home or not?

Do I have to?

I can't come over there and make you go, Mich said.

The thing was, we had both decided, some time ago, to take turns going home every now and then to check up on them. Our parents did not need checking up, but Mich thought we should get in the habit of doing it anyway. To get in practice for the future.

After a minute Mich said: They'll think we don't care.

Sometimes I think they'd rather we left them alone.

Fine. Fine. Do what you want.

Oh, all right, I'll go.

I flew home on a Thursday night and though I'd told them not to meet me at the airport, there they were, both of them, when I stepped off the ramp. They were the only still figures in the terminal; around them people dashed with garment bags, stewardesses hustled in pairs wheeling tiny suitcases.

My mother wore a brown coat the color of her hair. She looked anxious. My father stood tall, swaying slightly. The lights bounced off the lenses of his glasses; he wore jeans that were probably twenty years old. I would have liked to be the one to see them first, to compose my face and walk up to them unsuspected like a stranger. But that never happened – they always spotted me before I saw them, and had their faces ready and their hands out.

Is that all you brought? Just the one bag?

Here, I'll take it.

Lisa honey, you don't look so good. How are you?

Yes, how are you? You look terrible.

Thanks, Dad.

How are you, they said over and over, as they wrestled the suitcase from my hand.

Back at the house, my mother stirred something on the stove and my father leaned in the doorway to the dining room and looked out the window at the backyard. He's always leaned in that door frame to talk to my mother.

I made that soup for you, my mother said. The one where I have to peel the tomatoes and pick all the seeds out by hand.

Mother. I wish you wouldn't do that.

You mean you don't like it? I thought you liked it.

I like it, I like it. But I wish you wouldn't bother.

It's no bother. I wanted to.

She was up until two in the morning pulling skin off tomatoes, my father said, I could hear them screaming in agony.

How would you know, you were asleep, my mother said.

I get up at five-thirty every morning to do work in the yard before I go in to the office, he said.

I looked out at the brown yard.

I've been pruning the rose bushes. They're going to be beautiful next summer.

Yes, they will.

Lisa, he said, I want you to do something for me tomorrow, since you're here.

Sure. Anything.

I want you to go with your mother to her doctor's appointment. Make sure she goes.

OK.

She doesn't have to come, my mother said. That's silly, she'll just be bored.

She's supposed to get a mammogram every six months, my father said, but she's been putting it off and putting it off.

I've been busy, you know that's all it is.

She's afraid to go. She's been avoiding it for a year now.

Oh stop it, that's not it at all.

She always finds a way to get out of it. Your mother, the escape artist.

She crossed her arms over her chest. There was a history. Both her mother and an aunt had had to have things removed.

It's the same with all her doctors, my father said. Remember the contact lenses?

That was different. I didn't need new contacts.

She stopped going to her eye doctor for fifteen years. For fifteen years she was wearing the same contacts. When she finally went in, the doctor was amazed, he said he'd never seen anything like it, they don't even make contact lenses like that anymore. He thought she was wearing dessert dishes in her eyes.

You're exaggerating, my mother said.

Mich, I mean Lisa, my father said. He's always gotten our names confused; sometimes, to be safe, he just says all three.

She's afraid to go because of the last time, he said.

What happened last time? I said.

I had the mammogram pictures done, she said, and then a few days later they called and said the pictures were inconclusive and they needed to take a second set. So they did that and then they kept me waiting for the results, for weeks, without telling me anything, weeks where I couldn't sleep at night and I kept your father up too, trying to imagine what it looked like, the growth. Like the streaks in blue cheese, I thought. I kept feeling these little pains, and kept checking my pulse all night. And then finally they called and said everything was fine after all, that there was just some kind of blur on the first pictures, like I must have moved right when they took it or something.

You were probably talking the whole time, my father said. Telling them how to do their job.

I was probably *shivering*. They keep that office at about forty degrees and leave you sitting around in the cold in a paper robe. The people there don't talk to you or smile; and when they do the pictures they mash your breast between these two cold glass plates like a pancake.

My father looked away. He had a kind of modesty about some things.

My mother said to me: All those nights I kept thinking about my mother having her surgery; I kept feeling for lumps, waking up your father and asking him to feel for lumps.

Leah, my father said.

He didn't mind that. I think he might have enjoyed it a little.

Please.

Didn't you?

Promise me you'll go, he said.

She's not coming, she said.

The next day we drove to the clinic an hour early. My mother had the seat drawn as close to the steering wheel as she could get it; she gripped the wheel with her hands close together at twelve o'clock. She looked over at me as often as she looked out at the road.

There were squirrels and possums sprawled in the road, their heads red smears.

It's something about the weather, my mother said, makes them come out at night.

Oh.

We're so early, my mother said, and we're right near Randy's salon. Why don't we stop in and see if he can give you a haircut and a blowout?

Not now.

He wouldn't mind, I don't think. I talk about you whenever I go see him to have my hair done. He'd like to meet you.

No.

If you just got it angled on the sides, here, and got a few bangs in the front –

Just like yours, you mean.

You know, I feel so bad for Randy, he looks terrible, circles under his eyes all the time, he says his boyfriend is back in the hospital. Now whenever I go to get my hair cut, I bake something to bring him, banana bread or something. But I think the shampoo girls usually eat it all before he can get it home.

That's nice of you.

I worry about him. He doesn't take care of himself.

Yes.

Why are you still getting pimples? You're twenty-seven years old, why are you still getting pimples like a teenager?

Not everyone has perfect skin like you, I said. Green light. Go.

I do not have perfect skin, she said, bringing her hands to her face.

Both hands on the wheel please. Do you want me to drive?

No, I don't. You must be tired.

I touched my forehead. Small hard bumps like Braille.

She drove. I looked at the side of her face, the smooth taut skin. I wondered when she would start to get wrinkles. I already had wrinkles. On my neck, I could see them.

So, how is it going with this Piotr?

He's all right.

Still playing the – what was it? Guitar?

Bass guitar.

She turned on the radio and started flipping through stations. Maybe we'll hear one of his songs, she said brightly.

I said: I told you he was in a band. I didn't say they were good enough to be on the radio.

Oh. I see. So the band's just for fun. What else does he do?

Nothing. Yet.

So. What kind of name is Piotr? Am I saying it right?

Polish, I said.

I did not feel like telling her that only his grandmother lived in Poland; his parents were both born in Milwaukee, and he had grown up in Chicago and had never been to Poland; Piotr was a name he had given himself; he was not really a Piotr at all, he was a Peter with pretensions and long hair. I did not tell her this.

A black car cut into the lane in front of us. My mother braked suddenly and flung her right arm out across my chest.

Mother! Keep your hands on the wheel!

I'm sorry, she said, it's automatic. Ever since you kids were little . . .

I'm wearing a seatbelt.

I know honey, I can't help it. Did I hurt you?

No, of course not, I said.

When we reached the parking garage my mother rolled down her window but couldn't reach; she had to unfasten her seatbelt and open the car door in order to punch the button and get her parking ticket. I looked at her narrow back as she leaned out of the car, its delicate curve, the shoulder blades like folded wings under her sweater, a strand of dark hair caught in the clasp of her gold necklace. I had the urge to slide across the seat and curl around her. It only lasted for a second.

She turned around and settled back into her seat and the yellow-and-black-striped mechanical bar swung up in front of the car, and I tapped my feet impatiently while she slammed the door shut and rolled up the window. Now she was fiddling with her rearview mirror and straightening her skirt.

Come on, I said, watching the bar, which was still raised but vibrating a little.

Relax honey, that thing isn't going to come crashing down on us the minute we're under it. I promise you.

I know that, I said, and then closed my eyes until we were through the gate and weaving around the dark oil-stained aisles of the parking lot. I would have liked to tell her about some of the legal cases Mich had described to me: freak accidents, threshing machines gone awry, people caught in giant gears or conveyor belts and torn limb from limb, hands in bread slicers, flimsy walkways over vats of acid. Elevator cases, diving board cases, subway train cases, drowning-in-the-bathtub cases, electrocution-by-blender cases. And then there were the ones that were just called Act of God.

I didn't tell her.

Remember where we parked, she said.

OK.

But she did not get out of the car right away. She sat, gripping the wheel.

I don't see why we have to do this, she said. Your father worries . . .

He'll be more worried if you don't go, I said, and anyway there's nothing to worry about because everything's going to be fine. Right? Right.

If there's something wrong I'd just rather not know, she said to her hands.

We got out; the car shook as we slammed the doors.

She was right about the clinic. It was cold, and it was ugly. She signed in with the receptionist and we sat in the waiting room. The room was gray and bare, the chairs were old vinyl that stuck to your thighs. The lights buzzed and seemed to flicker unless you were looking directly at them.

We sat side by side and stared straight ahead as if we were watching something, a movie.

There was one other woman waiting. She had enormous breasts. I could not help noticing.

I took my mother's hand. It was very cold, but then her hands were always cold, even in summer, cool and smooth with the blue veins arching elegantly over their backs. Her hand lay limply in mine. I had made the gesture thinking it was the right thing to do, but now that I had her hand I didn't know what to do with it. I patted it, turned it over.

My mother looked at me strangely. My hand began to sweat.

There was noise, activity, somewhere, we could hear voices and footsteps, the crash and skid of metal, the brisk tones of people telling each other what to do. But we could see nothing but the receptionist in her window and the one woman who looked asleep, sagging in her chair with her breasts cupped in her arms like babies.

I need to use the restroom, my mother said and pulled her hand away.

The receptionist directed us down the hall and around the corner. We went in, our footsteps echoing on the tiles. It was empty, and reeked of ammonia. The tiles glistened damply.

Here, do something with yourself, my mother said and handed me her comb. She walked down to the big handicapped stall on the end and latched the door.

I combed my hair and washed my hands and waited.

I looked at myself in the mirror. The lights were that harsh relentless kind that reveal every detail of your face, so that you can see all sorts of flaws and pores you didn't even know you had. They made you feel you could see your own thoughts floating darkly just under your skin, like bruises.

Mother, I said. I watched her feet tapping around.

Lisa, she said, there's a fish in the toilet.

Oh, please.

No, I mean it. It's swimming around.

You're making it up.

No I'm not. Come see for yourself.

Well, it's probably just some pet goldfish someone tried to flush.

It's too big to be a goldfish. More like a carp. It's bright orange. Almost red.

You're seeing things – maybe it's blood or something, I said; then I wished I hadn't. The clinic was attached to the county hospital; all sorts of things were liable to pop up in the toilets – hypodermic needles, appendixes, tonsils.

No, no, it's a fish, it's beautiful really. It's got these gauzy fins, like veils. I wonder how it got in here. It looks too large to have come through the pipes. It's swimming in circles. Poor thing.

Well then come out and use a different one, I said. I suddenly started to worry that she was going to miss her appointment. You're just stalling, I said.

Come in and see. We have to save it somehow.

I heard her pulling up her pantyhose, fixing her skirt. Then she unlatched the door to the stall and opened it. She was smiling. Look, she said.

I followed her into the stall.

Come see, she said. Together we leaned over the bowl.

I saw only the toilet's bland white hollow, and our two identical silhouettes reflected in the water.

Now where did he go? my mother said. Isn't that the strangest thing?

We looked at the empty water.

How do you think he got out? she said. Look, you can see, the water's still moving from where he was. Look, look – little fish droppings. I swear. Lisa honey, look.

My mother is going crazy, I thought. Let's go back to the waiting room, I said.

But I still have to use the bathroom, she said.

I stood by the sink and waited. You're going to miss your appointment, I said. I watched her feet. Silence.

I was making her nervous. I'll wait for you in the hall, I said.

So I left, leaned against the wall, and waited. And waited. She was taking a long time. I started to wonder if she had been hallucinating. I wondered if something really was wrong with her, if she was bleeding internally or having a weird allergic reaction. I didn't think she was making it all up; she couldn't lie, she was a terrible, obvious liar.

Mother, I called.

Mom, I said.

I went back into the bathroom.

She was gone.

The stall doors swung loose, creaking. I checked each cubicle, thinking she might be standing on the toilet seat, with her head ducked down the way we used to avoid detection in high school. In the handicapped stall the toilet water was quivering, as if it had just been flushed. I even checked in the cabinets under the sink and stuck my hand down in the garbage pail.

I stood there, thinking. She must have somehow left and darted past me without my noticing. Maybe I had closed my eyes for a minute. She could move fast when she wanted to.

Had she climbed out the window? It was a small one, closed, high up on the wall.

She had escaped.

I walked slowly down the halls, listening, scanning the floor tiles.

I thought of her narrow back, the gaping mouth of the toilet, pictured her slipping down, whirling around and vanishing in the pipes.

I tried to formulate a reasonable question: Have you seen my mother? A woman, about my height, brown hair, green eyes? Nervous-looking? Have you seen her?

Or were her eyes hazel?

I came back to the waiting room with the question on my lips, I was mouthing the words she's disappeared, but when I got there the receptionist was leaning through the window calling out in an irritated voice: Ms. Salant? Ms. Salant? They're ready for you, *Ms. Salant.*

The receptionist was opening the door to the examining rooms; the nurses and technicians were holding out paper gowns and paper forms and urine sample cups, Ms. Salant, Ms. Salant, we're waiting, they called; people were everywhere suddenly, gesturing impatiently and calling out my name.

So I went in.

Later I wandered up and down the rows of painted white lines in the lot. I had forgotten where she parked the car. When I finally came upon it I saw her there, leaning against the bumper.

For a moment I thought she was smoking a cigarette. She didn't smoke.

When I drew closer I saw that she was nibbling on a pen.

We got in the car and drove home.

All of a sudden I thought of something I wanted to pick up for dinner, she said at one point.

Some fish? I said.

We drove the rest of the way without speaking.

So how did it go today, ladies? my father said that evening.

My mother didn't say anything.

Did you go with her? he asked me. Yeah, I said.

So, you'll hear results in a few days, right? he said with his hand on my mother's back.

She looked away.

Right, I said.

She looked at me strangely, but said nothing.

I told them not to but they both came to the airport Sunday night when I left.

Call me when you get the news, all right? I said.

All right, she said.

I wanted to ask her about the fish in the toilet, whether it had really been there. Whether she had followed the same route it had. But I couldn't work myself up to it. And the topic never came up by itself.

We said good-bye at the terminal. My hugs were awkward. I patted their backs as if I were burping babies.

I told them to go home but I knew they would wait in the airport until the plane took off safely. They always did. I think my mother liked to be there in case the plane crashed during take-off so she could dash onto the runway through the flames and explosions to drag her children from the rubble.

Or maybe they just liked airports. That airport smell.

I had a window seat; I pushed my suitcase under the seat in front of me. A man in a business suit with a fat red face sat down next to me.

I wondered if my mother even knew what I had done for her. I had helped her escape. Although at the time I hadn't thought of it that way, I hadn't really thought at all; I had gone in when I heard my name, automatic schoolgirl obedience, gone in to the bright lights and paper gowns and people who kneaded your breasts like clay. I began to feel beautiful and noble. I felt like I had gone to the guillotine in her place, like Sydney Carton in *A Tale of Two Cities*.

I called Piotr when I got home. I'm back, I said.

Let me come over, he said, I'll make you breakfast.

It's seven-thirty at night.

I just got up, he said.

My apartment felt too small and smelled musty. I'd been gone three days but it seemed longer. Piotr came and brought eggs and milk and his own spatula – he knew my kitchen was ill-equipped for anything but sandwiches.

He seemed to have grown since I last saw him, and gotten more hairy; I looked at the hair on the backs of his hands, the chest hair tufting out of the collar of his T-shirt.

He took up too much space. As he talked his nose and hands popped out at me huge and distorted, as if I were seeing him through a fish-eye lens. He came close to kiss me and I watched his eyes loom larger and larger and blur out of focus and merge into one big eye over the bridge of his nose.

I was embarrassed. My mouth tasted terrible from the plane.

What kind of pancakes do you want? he asked.

The pancake kind, I said.

He broke two eggs with one hand and the yolks slid out between his fingers.

I can do them shaped like snowmen, he said, or rabbits or flowers.

He was mixing stuff up in a bowl; flour slopped over the edges and sprinkled on the counter and the floor. I'll have to clean that up, I thought.

Round ones please, I said.

There was butter bubbling and crackling in the frying pan. Was that pan mine? No, he must have brought it with him – it was a big heavy skillet, the kind you could kill someone with.

He poured in the batter, it was thick and pale yellow; and the hissing butter shut up for a while. I looked in the pan. There were two large lumpy mounds there, side by side, bubbling inside as if they were alive, turning brown on the edges.

He turned them over and I saw the crispy undersides with patterns on them like the moon; and then he pressed them down with the spatula, pressed them flat and the butter sputtered and hissed.

There was a burning smell.

I'm not feeling very hungry right now, I said.

But I brought maple syrup, he said. It's from Vermont, I think.

The pan was starting to smoke. Pushing him aside, I took it off the flame and put it in the sink. It was heavy; the two round shapes were now charred and crusted to the bottom.

Well, we don't have to eat them, he said. He held out the bottle of syrup. Aunt Jemima smiled at me. She looked different, though. They must have updated her image; new hairstyle, outfit. But that same smile.

There's lots of stuff we can do with syrup, he said, it's a very romantic condiment.

He stepped closer and reached out and turned the knob on the halogen lamp. His face looked even more distorted in the dimness.

What? I said. Where did you get such a stupid idea?

Read it somewhere.

I'm sorry, I'm just not feeling very social tonight, I said. Peter, I said.

Oh come on.

I missed my parents very much suddenly. You're so insensitive, I said. Get out.

Hey, I *am* sensitive. I'm *Mr.* Sensitive. I give change to bums. Pachelbel's Canon makes me cry like a baby.

Like a what? I said.

Why are you screaming at me? he said.

Don't let the door hit you in the ass on the way out, I said. I thought I was being smart and cutting. But he took it literally; he went out and closed the door behind him with great care.

My sister called later that night.

So how were they? she asked.

Fine, I said. Same as always.

Your voice sounds funny; what happened? she said.

Nothing.

Something's wrong. Why don't you ever tell me when something's wrong?

There's nothing, Mich.

You never tell me what's going on; when you think I'll worry about something you keep it to yourself.

I tell you everything.

Well then, tell me what was wrong with you earlier this fall.

Nothing . . . I don't know . . . there's nothing to tell.

That was the truth. All that happened was I got tired of people for a while. I didn't like to go out, didn't shower, and didn't pick up the phone except to call my office with elaborate excuses. The smell of my body became comforting, a ripe presence, nasty but familiar. I lay in bed telling myself that it was just a phase, it would pass. Eventually the bulb on my halogen lamp burned out and after two days of darkness I ventured out to buy a new one. The sunlight out on the street did something to my brain, or maybe it was the kind bald man who sold me the bulb. I went back to work.

So how are you? How's Neil?

Oh we broke up, she said. We had a big fight, and he couldn't see that I was right and he was wrong. It was high drama, in a restaurant with people watching, us screaming and stuff, and this fat waitress pushing between us using her tray as a shield and telling us to leave. So we finished it outside on the street, I made my points, one two three, and did my closing arguments. If we were in court I would have won.

I'm sorry, I said. Why didn't you tell me right away?

Oh, I didn't want you feeling bad for me. I'm glad, really. Smallminded jerk. Did I ever tell you he had all this hair on his back? Gray hair, like a silverback gorilla.

Yes, well. I don't know that I'll be seeing Piotr any more either.

That's too bad.

No, it's not.

That night as I lay in bed I thought of my mother and I felt my body for lumps the way she said she felt hers, and I put two fingers to the side of my throat. And I began to think of her and think of an undetected cancer, spreading through her body unnoticed. It began to dawn on me that I had done a very stupid thing.

I thought of her lying in bed beside my father at that moment, oblivious to the black thing that might be growing and thickening inside her, maybe in tough strands, maybe in little grainy bits, like oatmeal. She would avoid thinking about it for another six months or a year or two years; she'd deny it until her skin turned gray and she had tentacles growing out of her mouth and her breasts slid from her body and plopped on the floor like lumps of wet clay. Only when all that happened would she give in and say, Hmmm, maybe something is wrong, maybe I should see a doctor after all.

I lay awake for most of the night.

At one point I got up to use the bathroom, and as I sat on the toilet in the dark I suddenly became convinced that there was something horrible floating in the water below me. I was sure of it. A live rat. Or a length of my own intestines lying coiled bloody in the bowl. I sat there afraid to turn on the light and look, yet couldn't leave the bathroom without looking.

I sat there for half an hour, wracked with indecision. I think I fell asleep for a bit.

And when I finally forced myself to turn on the light, turn around and look – I was so convinced there would be something floating there that I was horribly shocked, my stomach lurched to see only the empty toilet.

I went back to work on Tuesday.

Did I miss anything? I asked one of the men.

You were gone? he said.

I didn't know his name; all the men who worked there looked

alike. They were all too loud, and had too much spit in their mouths.

I had a cubicle all my own, but I dreamed of an office with a door I could close.

A few days later my father called. Your mother heard the results from the clinic, he said, the mammogram was fine.

That's great, I said.

She doesn't seem happy about it, he said, she's acting very strange.

Oh, I said.

What's going on, Lisa? he said. There's something fishy going on here.

Nothing, I said. Ask your wife, I said. Can I talk to her?

She just dashed out for an appointment, told me to call you. She said you'd be relieved.

Yes.

I'm going to call your sister now, she was waiting to hear. Or do you want to call her?

I'll do it, I said.

It seemed strange to me then that I would need to call Mich; a phone call implied distance, but our family seemed so close and entwined and entangled that we could hardly tell each other apart. Why should you need a phone to talk to someone who seems like she's living inside your skin?

We both went home for Christmas.

Later Mich visited them.

Then I visited.

Then it was Mich's turn again.

When I called home during Mich's visit my father said: Your

mother was due for another mammogram, so I sent Lisa with her to make sure she goes.

You mean you sent Mich, I said. I'm Lisa.

Yes, right, you know who I mean.

A few days later my father called, his voice sounding strained. Your mother talked to the mammography clinic today, he said, but she won't tell me anything. She's been in her room, crying. She's been talking on the phone to your sister for an hour. I guess the doctors found something, but I'll let you know when we know for sure.

O.K.

I hung up and called Mich.

Hello, she said. She sounded like she was choking on one of her pens. Mich, I said, it's yours, isn't it?

She sighed and said: It's ridiculous, but I thought I was doing her a favor, I thought I was sparing her some worry.

You went in for her, didn't you?

You know, Mich said, she's more worried about this than if she was the one with a lump in her breast. She feels like it's her lump, like it was meant for her, like she gave it to me somehow.

That's ridiculous, I said. I felt like I was talking to myself.

Although, you know, if it were possible, I would, Mich said. I mean, if there was somehow a way to magically take a lump out of her breast and put it in mine, I'd do it in a second.

I wish I could do that for you, I said.

Yeah, we could all share it.

One dessert and three forks, I said.

And later as I sat alone on the floor in the apartment I started to lose track of where I stopped and other people began, and I remembered standing in a white room with my breast clamped in the jaws of a humming machine, and I felt for the lump that I thought was mine, and sometimes I thought it was my mother's, and I imagined the mammogram pictures like lunar landscapes. Then I could not remember who had the lump anymore, it seemed we all did, it was my mother's my sister's and mine, and then the phone rang again and I picked it up and heard my father call out as he sometimes did: Leah-Lise-Mich.

Comprehension Test
★ ★ ★ ★ ★ Myla Goldberg

★ ★ ★ ★ ★ After reading each of the following passages, answer the questions to the best of your ability.

We can truly observe America's great melting pot in action in this urban neighborhood which, over the years, has been home to many of America's newest arrivals. As the tides of immigration have shifted, it too has changed. Yet, like a chalkboard upon which yesterday's lesson has been only partially erased, its streets still bear traces of those who came before. Fifty years ago, this neighborhood was home to scores of Eastern European Jews fleeing persecution. Over time, however, Chinese characters have appeared on buildings beside Hebrew ones. What once could have been described as an urban shtetl has become a part of Chinatown.

Shops sell ginger root, dried mushrooms, and preserved duck eggs. Wheeled carts dispense one-dollar cartons of lo mein and rice noodles. An old man sets up his sidewalk stand, resoling Chinese sandals with used tire rubber. Yet around the corner, a row of electronics stores is still staffed by Orthodox Jews with their sidelocks and skull caps. A pickle store still vends its wares in briny barrels.

Though the words RABBI LOEW SCHOOL FOR BOYS are engraved in stone upon this building's facade, it is now an apartment building filled with Chinese families. Dr Lin's ground-floor office neighbors the very playground he visited as a child. By the time Dr Lin's children are grown, this neighborhood will have changed again, but one thing is certain: additions to our great melting pot are what help make America the Beautiful.

1. Dr Lin was shot to death in his office on Friday afternoon. Had he

A) ever felt uneasy in his office?
B) known his assailant?
C) attempted to defend himself?
D) pleaded for his life?
E) cried out for help?

2. Dr Lin's murderer successfully fled. Is it more likely that his shots

A) went unheard?
B) were assumed to be the sound of a car backfiring?
C) were shrugged off as someone else's problem?
D) went unreported for fear of criminal reprisal?
E) went unreported for fear of the law?

3. Were the shots fired

A) in anger?
B) in fear?
C) in desperation?
D) in revenge?
E) in confusion?

4. As a policeman cordoned off the crime scene with POLICE LINE DO NOT CROSS tape, did he feel

A) important?
B) sad?
C) annoyed?
D) angry?
E) nothing?

[Two NEIGHBORHOOD RESIDENTS approach a sign that has been posted on the gate fronting Dr Lin's office. A police sketch appears below the word WANTED. Beside the poster, a scrap of yellow police tape remains tied to the fence. The two men talk while facing the poster.]

RESIDENT 1:   Did you know him?

RESIDENT 2:   No. I passed by yesterday on my way home, but I did not stop.

RESIDENT 1:   I came as soon as I heard the sirens, but I didn't see anything.

RESIDENT 2:   Today I was expecting for police to be everywhere, but there is nothing.

[The two examine the police sketch. It portrays the face of a black man with generic features.]

RESIDENT 1:   I heard a policeman last night say it was a robbery.

RESIDENT 2:   It says that the doctor was shot two times in the back. Do you think he was reaching for his gun?

RESIDENT 1:   I wouldn't have put up a fight. If I got shot, my wife would kill me.

[Both men chuckle.]

RESIDENT 2:   My little boy plays every day at the
              playground. That this happened so close . . .

[RESIDENT 2 *spits and walks away. After he has gone,*
RESIDENT 1 *removes the police tape and puts it in his pocket.*]

5. When Resident 1 visited the crime scene on the night of
the murder, did he feel

A) intrepid?
B) involved?
C) impelled?
D) excited?
E) entitled?

6. On the night of the murder, did Resident 2 continue past
the crime scene without stopping

A) for fear of being branded a 'rubbernecker'?
B) in the belief that bypassing tragedy prevents future
   misfortune?
C) to avoid suspicion, regardless of guilt?
D) indignant that such a thing had occurred in his
   neighborhood?
E) in the hope that what had happened would undo itself if
   ignored?

7. When the two residents spoke, did they avoid eye contact
out of

A) fear?
B) suspicion?

C) respect?
D) shame?
E) habit?

8. If the two crossed paths on the street again, would they most likely

A) wave hospitably?
B) nod curtly?
C) speak genially?
D) pass imperviously?
E) blush self-consciously?

9. If an innocent man walked by the WANTED poster and recognized his eyes or nose, it is *least* likely that he would feel

A) indignant
B) nervous
C) amused
D) unconcerned
E) persecuted

10. If someone who had seen the poster passed by an unknown black man on the street, is it *least* likely that s/he would

A) stare?
B) smile?
C) feel suspicion?
D) return a greeting?
E) avoid eye contact?

11. The WANTED poster disappeared within twenty-four hours of its appearance. Taking questions 9 and 10 into account, is this

A) suspicious?
B) shocking?
C) surprising?
D) understandable?
E) unconscionable?

DOCTOR IS SLAIN

A physician was fatally shot in his office Friday afternoon during an apparent robbery, the police said.

The body of the doctor, Xang Ling, 35, was found on the floor of his office at about 8 P.M. by a building resident who was walking past the first story window and saw him sprawled inside.

The doctor was shot twice in the back and his pockets turned out, said a police spokeswoman.

There was no sign of forced entry, detectives said.

Dr Ling had practiced medicine in the neighborhood for several years, according to a resident of the building.

12. Would a loved one save this article out of

A) obligation?
B) respect?
C) anger?
D) grief?
E) desperation?

13. Would the fact that the victim's name is misspelled affect that decision?

A) Definitely
B) Possibly
C) Maybe
D) Perhaps
E) Not at all

14. Would the victim's story have filled more space if the victim had been

A) young?
B) female?
C) rich?
D) famous?
E) mutilated?

Since the legendary days of the American West, the reward poster has made itself a mainstay of American culture. From the infamous Jesse James to the Most Wanted at any local post office, this very special placard has undergone quite a transformation, on its way making its mark in history as well as art. A lot has changed since WANTED DEAD OR ALIVE made its first appearance in saloons both real and imagined.

Originally, posters were topped with monetary appeals or the word *Reward* itself. While this straightforward method was sure to get the message across, it lacked sophistication. Modern times have seen the refinement of this brand of appeal. Contemporary posters now invoke the reader's desire for justice first, only within the text alluding to a reward for one's efforts.

A fine example of this modern approach can be seen in the poster that appeared a week after Dr Lin was found murdered. Tied with twine to the gate fronting the breezeway, it read HOMICIDE. Though a reward of up to $1,000 was offered for information regarding the murder, this was only revealed within the body of text, in both English and Spanish. The poster was, in fact, a pre-printed form with a blank for the inclusion of a phone number to call and a name to ask for. While its mass production can be seen as evidence that this poster's more subtle approach is effective, society's cynics might point out that its content, in this case, was altered. A week after its appearance at the crime scene, $1,000 was found to have been crossed out in black magic marker on both posters, with $25,000 handwritten above the revision.

15. Is it of greater concern that

A) money was offered for what should be a voluntary act?
B) only $1,000 was offered?
C) it took seven days for the poster to appear?
D) no posters appeared anywhere else?
E) the poster's languages did not include Chinese?

16. Are these posters put up

A) because they work?
B) to appease the neighborhood?
C) to avoid negligence suits?
D) more extensively in better neighborhoods?
E) with higher reward amounts in better neighborhoods?

17. Was the $25,000

A) an offer?
B) a demand?

At first, I found that I could not pass his office without stopping. Day or night, coming or going, I found myself momentarily planted before the metal gate, peering in. I wasn't reassured by the face that the WANTED poster briefly presented before disappearing. Its banality reminded me how impossible it was to determine whether the countless faces I passed each day were vessels for dreams or nightmares.

Each time I stopped, I would gaze intently at the passage leading to the doctor's door, as if staring hard enough would cause the murderer's footprints to appear like a photographic image in a tray of developer. I tried to reason away my newfound fear of the dark; the doctor, after all, had been shot on a sunny afternoon.

Like any bruise, the trauma of Dr Lin's death faded over time. Children returned to the playground. The HOMICIDE poster outside his office yellowed in the rain and eventually blew away.

Days passed without me thinking of the doctor. I realized I wasn't stopping at his gate anymore. In a fit of guilt, I called the local precinct. If the case had been closed, I would be absolved of having gotten on with my life.

'Has Dr Lin's murderer been found?' I asked the officer in charge of the case.

His voice sounded tired in a way that I had never heard before. He told me that the case was still open.

I wanted to feel entitled to an account of everything that this tired man had and had not done to bring Dr Lin's murderer to justice. Instead, I felt grateful to have never experienced his brand of fatigue, a weariness that blanched his every word.

I thanked him and hung up the phone.

18. Does this murder

A) make future murders more likely?
B) make future murders less likely?
C) have no effect on future murders?
D) change the future?
E) confirm the future?

19. Can safety be

A) measured?
B) assumed?
C) proven?
D) granted?
E) taken away?

STOP
You have completed this test.
Move on when you feel it is safe to do so.

Timeshare
★ ★ ★ ★ ★ Jeffrey Eugenides

★ ★ ★ ★ ★ My father is showing me around his new motel. I shouldn't call it a motel after everything he's explained to me but I still do. What it is, what it's going to be, my father says, is a timeshare resort. As we walk down the dim hallway (some of the bulbs have burned out), my father informs me of the recent improvements. 'We put in a new oceanfront patio,' he says. 'I had a landscape architect come in, but he wanted to charge me an arm and a leg. So I designed it myself.'

Most of the units haven't been renovated yet. The place was a wreck when my father borrowed the money to buy it, and from what my mother tells me, it looks a lot better now. They've repainted, for one thing, and put on a new roof. Each room will have a kitchen installed. At present, however, only a few rooms are occupied. Some units don't even have doors. Walking by, I can see painting tarps and broken air conditioners lying on the floors. Water-stained carpeting curls back from the edges of the rooms. Some walls have holes in them the size of a fist, evidence of the college kids who used to stay here during spring break. My father plans to install new carpeting, and to refuse to rent to students. 'Or if I do,' he says, 'I'll charge a big deposit, like three hundred bucks. And I'll hire a security guard for a couple of weeks. But the idea is to make this place a more upscale kind of place. As far as the college kids go, piss on 'em.'

The foreman of this renewal is Buddy. My father found him

out on the highway, where day workers line up in the morning. He's a little guy with a red face and makes, for his labor, five dollars an hour. 'Wages are a lot lower down here in Florida,' my father explains to me. My mother is surprised at how strong Buddy is for his size. Just yesterday, she saw him carrying a stack of cinder blocks to the dumpster. 'He's like a little Hercules,' she says. We come to the end of the hallway and enter the stairwell. When I take hold of the aluminum banister, it nearly rips out of the wall. Every place in Florida has these same walls.

'What's that smell?' I ask.

Above me, hunched over, my father says nothing, climbing.

'Did you check the land before you bought this place?' I ask. 'Maybe it's built over a toxic dump.'

'That's Florida,' says my mother. 'It smells that way down here.'

At the top of the stairs, a thin green runner extends down another darkened hallway. As my father leads the way, my mother nudges me, and I see what she's been talking about: he's walking lopsided, compensating for his bad back. She's been after him to see a doctor but he never does. Every so often, his back goes out and he spends a day soaking in the bathtub (the tub in room 308, where my parents are staying temporarily). We pass a maid's cart, loaded with cleaning fluids, mops and wet rags. In an open doorway, the maid stands, looking out, a big black woman in blue jeans and a smock. My father doesn't say anything to her. My mother says hello brightly and the maid nods.

At its middle, the hallway gives onto a small balcony. As soon as we step out, my father announces, 'There it is!' I think he means the ocean, which I see for the first time, storm-colored and uplifting, but then it hits me that my father never points out scenery. He's referring to the patio. Red-tiled, with a blue swimming pool, white deck chairs and two palm trees, the patio looks as though it belongs to an actual seaside resort. It's empty but, for the moment, I begin to see the place through my father's eyes – peopled and restored, a going concern. Buddy appears down below, holding a paint can. 'Hey, Buddy,' my father calls down, 'that tree still looks brown. Have you had it checked?'

'I had the guy out.'

'We don't want it to die.'

'The guy just came and looked at it.'

We look at the tree. The taller palms were too expensive, my father says. 'This one's a different variety.'

'I like the other kind,' I say.

'The royal palms? You like those? Well, then, after we get going, we'll get some.'

We're quiet for a while, gazing over the patio and the purple sea. 'This place is going to get all fixed up and we're going to make a million dollars!' my mother says.

'Knock on wood,' says my father.

Five years ago, my father actually made a million. He'd just turned sixty and, after working all his life as a mortgage banker, went into business for himself. He bought a condominium complex in Fort Lauderdale, resold it and made a big profit. Then he did the same thing in Miami. At that point, he had enough to retire on but he didn't want to. Instead, he bought a new Cadillac and a fifty-foot power boat. He bought a twin engine airplane and learned to fly it. And then he flew around the country, buying real estate, flew to California, to the Bahamas, over the ocean. He was his own boss and his temper improved. Later, the reversals began. One of his developments in North Carolina, a ski resort, went bankrupt. It turned out his partner had embezzled a hundred thousand dollars. My father had to take him to court, which cost more money. Meanwhile, a savings and loan sued my father for selling it mortgages that defaulted. More legal fees piled up. The million dollars ran out fast and, as it began to disappear, my father tried a variety of schemes to get it back. He bought a company that made 'manufactured homes.' They were like mobile homes, he told me, only more substantial. They were prefabricated, could be plunked down anywhere but, once set up, looked like real houses. In the present economic situation, people needed cheap housing. Manufactured homes were selling like hotcakes.

My father took me to see the first one on its lot. It was Christmas, two years ago, when my parents still had their condominium. We'd just finished opening our presents when my father said that he wanted to take me for a little drive. Soon we were on the highway. We left the part of Florida I knew, the Florida of beaches, high rises and developed communities, and entered a poorer, more rural area. Spanish moss hung from the trees and the unpainted houses were made of wood. The drive took about two hours. Finally, in the distance, we saw the onion bulb of a gas tower with 'Ocala' painted on the side. We entered the town, passing rows of neat houses, and then we came to the end and kept on going. 'I thought you said it was in Ocala,' I said.

'It's a little further out,' said my father.

Countryside began again. We drove into it. After about fifteen miles, we came to a dirt road. The road led into an open, grassless field, without any trees. Toward the back, in a muddy area, stood the manufactured house.

It was true it didn't look like a mobile home. Instead of being long and skinny, the house was rectangular, and fairly wide. It came in three or four different pieces which were screwed together, and then a traditional-looking roof was put in place on top. We got out of the car and walked on bricks to get closer. Because the county was just now installing sewer lines out this far, the ground in front of the house – 'the yard,' my father called it – was dug up. Right in front of the house, three small shrubs had been planted in the mud. My father inspected them, then waved his hand over the field. 'This is all going to be filled in with grass,' he said. The front door was a foot and a half off the ground. There wasn't a porch yet but there would be. My father opened the door and we went inside. When I shut the door behind me, the wall rattled like a theater set. I knocked on the wall, to see what it was made of, and heard a hollow, tinny sound. When I turned around, my father was standing in the middle of the living room, grinning. His right index finger pointed up in the air. 'Get a load of this,' he said. 'This is what they call a "cathedral ceiling". Ten feet high. Lotta headroom, boy.'

Despite the hard times, nobody bought a manufactured home, and my father, writing off the loss, went on to other things. Soon I began getting incorporation forms from him, naming me vice president of Baron Development Corporation, or the Atlantic Glass Company, or Fidelity Mini-Storage Inc. The profits from these companies, he assured, would one day come to me. The only thing that did come, however, was a man with an artificial leg. My doorbell rang one morning and I buzzed him in. In the next moment, I heard him clumping up the stairs. From above, I could see the blond stubble on his bald head and could hear his labored breathing. I took him for a delivery man. When he got to the top of the stairs, he asked if I was vice president of Duke Development. I said I guessed that I was. He handed me a summons.

It had to do with some legal flap. I lost track after a while. Meanwhile, I learned from my brother that my parents were living off savings, my father's IRA and credit from the banks. Finally, he found this place, Palm Bay Resort, a ruin by the sea, and convinced another savings and loan to lend him the money to get it running again. He'd provide the labor and know-how and, when people started coming, he'd pay off the S&L and the place would be his.

After we look at the patio, my father wants to show me the model. 'We've got a nice little model,' he says. 'Everyone who's seen it has been very favorably impressed.' We come down the dark hallway again, down the stairs, and along the first-floor corridor. My father has a master key and lets us in a door marked 103. The hall light doesn't work, so we file through the dark living room to the bedroom. As soon as my father flips on the light, a strange feeling takes hold of me. I feel as though I've been here before, in this room, and then I realize what it is: the room is my parents' old bedroom. They've moved in the furniture from their old condo: the peacock bedspread, the Chinese dressers and matching headboard, the gold lamps. The furniture, which once filled a much bigger space, looks squeezed together in this small room. 'This is all your old stuff,' I say.

'Goes nice in here, don't you think?' my father asks.

'What are you using for a bedspread now?'

'We've got twin beds in our unit,' my mother says. 'This wouldn't have fit anyway. We've just got regular bedspreads now. Like in the other rooms. Hotel supply. They're OK.'

'Come and see the living room,' my father tells me, and I follow him through the door. After some fumbling, he finds a light that works. The furniture in here is all new and doesn't remind me of anything. A painting of driftwood on the beach hangs on the wall. 'How do you like that painting? We got fifty of them from this warehouse. Five bucks a pop. And they're all different. Some have starfish, some seashells. All in a maritime motif. They're signed oil paintings.' He walks to the wall and, taking off his glasses, makes out the signature: 'Cesar Amarollo! Boy, that's better than Picasso.' He turns his back to me, smiling, happy about this place.

I'm down here to stay a couple of weeks, maybe even a month. I won't go into why. My father gave me unit 207, right on the ocean. He calls the rooms 'units' to differentiate them from the motel rooms they used to be. Mine has a little kitchen. And a balcony. From it, I can see cars driving along the beach, a pretty steady stream. This is the only place in Florida, my father tells me, where you can drive on the beach.

The motel gleams in the sun. Somebody is pounding somewhere. A couple of days ago, my father started offering complimentary suntan lotion to anyone who stays the night. He's advertising this on the marquee out front but, so far, no one has stopped. Only a few families are here right now, mostly old couples. There's one woman in a motorized wheelchair. In the morning, she rides out to the pool and sits, and then her husband appears, a washed-out guy in a bathing suit and flannel shirt. 'We don't tan anymore,' she tells me. 'After a certain age, you just don't tan. Look at Kurt. We've been out here all week and that's all the tan he is.' Sometimes, too, Judy, who works in the office, comes out to sunbathe during her lunch hour. My father gives her a free room to stay in, up on the third floor, as part of her salary. She's from Ohio and wears her hair in a long braided ponytail, like a girl in fifth grade.

At night, in her hotel-supply bed, my mother has been having prophetic dreams. She dreamed that the roof sprung a leak two days before it did so. She dreamed that the skinny maid would quit and, next day, the skinny maid did. She dreamed that someone broke his neck diving into the empty swimming pool (instead, the filter broke, and the pool had to be emptied to fix it, which she says counts). She tells me all this by the swimming pool. I'm in it; she's dangling her feet in the water. My mother doesn't know how to swim. The last time I saw her in a bathing suit I was five years old. She's the burning, freckled type, braving the sun in her straw hat only to talk to me, to confess this strange phenomenon. I feel as though she's picking me up after swimming lessons. My throat tastes of chlorine. But then I look down and see the hair on my chest, grotesquely black against my white skin, and I remember that I'm old, too.

Whatever improvements are being made today are being made on the far side of the building. Coming down to the pool, I saw Buddy going into a room, carrying a wrench. Out here, we're alone, and my mother tells me that it's all due to rootlessness. 'I wouldn't be dreaming these things if I had a decent house of my own. I'm not some kind of gypsy. It's just all this traipsing around. First we lived in that motel in Hilton Head. Then that condo in Vero. Then that recording studio your father bought, without any windows, which just about killed me. And now this. All my things are in storage. I dream about them, too. My couches, my good dishes, all our old family photos. I dream of them packed away almost every night.'

'What happens to them?'

'Nothing. Just that nobody ever comes to get them.'

There are a number of medical procedures that my parents are planning to have done when things get better. For some time now, my mother has wanted a face-lift. When my parents were flush, she actually went to a plastic surgeon who took photographs of her face and diagrammed her bone structure. It's not a matter of simply pulling the loose skin up, apparently. Certain facial bones need shoring up as well. My mother's upper palate has slowly receded over the years. Her bite has become disaligned. Dental surgery is needed to resurrect the skull over which the skin will be tightened. She had the first of these procedures scheduled about the time my father caught his partner embezzling. In the trouble afterward, she had to put the idea on hold.

My father, too, has put off two operations. The first is disk surgery to help the pain in his lower back. The second is prostate surgery to lessen the blockage to his urethra and increase the flow of his urine. His delay in the latter case is not motivated purely by financial considerations. 'They go up there with that Roto-Rooter and it hurts like hell,' he told me. 'Plus, you can end up incontinent.' Instead, he has elected to go to the bathroom fifteen to twenty times a day, no trip being completely satisfying. During the breaks in my mother's prophetic dreams, she hears my father getting up again and again. 'Your father's stream isn't exactly magnificent anymore,' she told me. 'You live with someone, you know.'

As for me, I need a new pair of shoes. A sensible pair. A pair suited to the tropics. Stupidly, I wore a pair of old black wingtips down here, the right shoe of which has a hole in the bottom. I need a pair of flip-flops. Every night, when I go out to the bars in my father's Cadillac (the boat is gone, the plane is gone, but we still have the yellow 'Florida Special' with the white vinyl top), I pass souvenir shops, their windows crammed with T-shirts, seashells, sunhats, coconuts with painted faces. Every time, I think about stopping to get flip-flops, but I haven't yet.

One morning, I come down to find the office in chaos. Judy, the secretary, is sitting at her desk, chewing the end of her ponytail. 'Your father had to fire Buddy,' she says. But before she can tell me anything more, one of the guests comes in, complaining about a leak. 'It's right over the bed,' the man says. 'How do you expect me to pay for a room with a leak over the bed? We had to sleep on the floor! I came down to the office last night to get another room but there was no one here.'

Just then my father comes in with the tree surgeon. 'I thought you told me this type of palm tree was hardy.'

'It is.'

'Then what's the matter with it?'

'It's not in the right kind of soil.'

'You never told me to change the soil,' my father says, his voice rising.

'It's not only the soil,' says the tree surgeon. 'Trees are like people. They get sick. I can't tell you why. It might have needed more water.'

'We watered it!' my father says, shouting now. 'I had the guy water it every goddamn day! And now you tell me it's dead?'

The man doesn't reply. My father sees me. 'Hey there, buddy!' he says heartily. 'Be with you in a minute.'

The man with the leak begins explaining his trouble to my father. In the middle, my father stops him. Pointing at the tree surgeon, he says, 'Judy, pay this bastard.' Then he goes back to listening to the man's story. When the man finishes, my father offers him his money back and a free room for the night.

Ten minutes later, in the car, I learn the outlandish story. My father fired Buddy for drinking on the job. 'But wait'll you hear *how* he was drinking,' he says. Early that morning, he saw Buddy lying on the floor of unit 106, under the air conditioner. 'He was *supposed* to be fixing it. All morning, I kept passing by, and every time I'd see Buddy lying under that air conditioner. I thought to myself, Jeez. But then this goddamn crook of a tree surgeon shows up. And *he* tells me that the goddamn tree he's supposed to be curing is dead, and I forgot all about Buddy. We go out to look at the tree and the guy's giving me all this bullshit – the soil this, the soil that – until finally I tell him I'm going to go call the nursery. So I come back to the office. And I pass 106 again. And there's Buddy still lying on the floor.'

When my father got to him, Buddy was resting comfortably on his back, his eyes closed and the air-conditioner coil in his mouth. 'I guess that coolant's got alcohol in it,' my father said. All Buddy had to do was disconnect the coil, bend it with a pair of pliers and take a drink. This last time he'd sipped too long, however, and had passed out. 'I should have known something was up,' my father says. 'For the past week all he's been doing is fixing the air conditioners.'

After calling an ambulance (Buddy remained unconscious as he was carried away), my father called the nursery. They wouldn't refund his money or replace the palm tree. What was more, it had rained during the night and no one had to tell him about leaks. His own roof had leaked in the bathroom. The new roof, which had cost a considerable sum, hadn't been installed properly. At a minimum, someone was going to have to re-tar it. 'I need a guy to go up there and lay down some tar along the edges. It's the edges, see, where the water gets in. That way, maybe I can save a couple of bucks.' While my father tells me all this, we drive out along A-1-A. It's about ten in the morning by this point and the drifters are scattered along the shoulder, looking for day work. You can spot them by their dark tans. My father passes the first few, his reasons for rejecting them unclear to me at first. Then he spots a white man in his early thirties, wearing green pants and a Disneyworld T-shirt. He's standing in the sun, eating a raw cauliflower. My father pulls the Cadillac up alongside him. He touches his electronic console and the passenger window hums open. Outside, the man blinks, trying to adjust his eyes to the car's dark cool interior.

At night, after my parents go to sleep, I drive along the strip into town. Unlike most of the places my parents have wound up, Daytona Beach has a working-class feel. Fewer old people, more bikers. In the bar I've been going to, they have a real live shark. Three feet long, it swims in an aquarium above the stacked bottles. The shark has just enough room in its tank to turn around and swim back the other way. I don't know what effect the lights have on the animal. The dancers wear bikinis, some of which sparkle like fish scales. They circulate through the gloom like mermaids, as the shark butts its head against the glass.

I've been in here three times already, long enough to know

that I look, to the girls, like an art student, that under state law the girls cannot show their breasts and so must glue wing-shaped appliqués over them. I've asked what kind of glue they use ('Elmer's'), how they get it off ('just a little warm water') and what their boyfriends think of it (they don't mind the money). For ten dollars, a girl will take you by the hand, past the other tables where men sit mostly alone, into the back where it's even darker. She'll sit you down on a padded bench and rub against you for the duration of two whole songs. Sometimes, she'll take your hands and will ask, 'Don't you know how to dance?'

'I'm dancing,' you'll say, even though you're sitting down.

At three in the morning, I drive back, listening to a country and western station to remind myself that I'm far from home. I'm usually drunk by this point but the trip isn't long, a mile at most, an easy cruise past the other waterfront real estate, the big hotels and the smaller ones, the motor lodges with their various themes. One's called Viking Lodge. To check in, you drive under a Norse galley which serves as a carport.

Spring break's more than a month away. Most of the hotels are less than half full. Many have gone out of business, especially those further out from town. The motel next to ours is still open. It has a Polynesian theme. There's a bar under a grass hut by the swimming pool. Our place has a fancier feel. Out front, a white gravel walkway leads up to two miniature orange trees flanking the front door. My father thought it was worth it to spend money on the entrance, seeing as that was people's first impression. Right inside, to the left of the plushly carpeted lobby, is the sales office. Bob McHugh, the salesman, has a blueprint of the resort on the wall, showing available units and timeshare weeks. Right now, though, most people coming in are just looking for a place to spend the night. Generally, they drive into the parking lot at the side of the building and talk to Judy in the business office.

It rained again while I was in the bar. When I drive into our parking lot and get out, I can hear water dripping off the roof of the motel. There's a light burning in Judy's room. I consider going up to knock on her door. Hi, it's the boss's son! While I'm standing there, though, listening to the dripping water and plotting my next move, her light goes off. And, with it, it seems, every light around. My father's timeshare resort plunges into darkness. I reach out to put my hand on the hood of the Cadillac, to reassure myself with its warmth, and, for a moment, try to picture in my mind the way to my room, where the stairs begin, how many floors to climb, how many doors to pass before I get to my room.

'Come on,' my father says. 'I want to show you something.'

He's wearing tennis shorts and has a racquetball racquet in his hand. Last week, Jerry, the current handyman (the one who replaced Buddy didn't show up one morning), finally moved the extra beds and draperies out of the racquetball court. My father had the floor painted and challenged me to a game. But, with the bad ventilation, the humidity made the floor slippery, and we had to quit after four points. My father didn't want to break his hip.

He had Jerry drag an old dehumidifier in from the office and this morning they played a few games.

'How's the floor?' I ask.

'Still a little slippy. That dehumidifier isn't worth a toot.'

So it isn't to show me the new, dry racquetball court that my father has come to get me. It's something, his expression tells me, more significant. Leaning to one side (the exercise hasn't helped his back any), he leads me up to the third floor, then up another, smaller stairway which I haven't noticed before. This one leads straight to the roof. When we get to the top, I see that there's another building up here. It's pretty big, like a bunker, but with windows all around.

'You didn't know about this, did you?' my father says. 'This is the penthouse. Your mother and I are going to move in up here soon as it's ready.'

The penthouse has a red front door and a welcome mat. It sits in the middle of the tarred roof, which extends in every direction. From up here, all the neighboring buildings disappear, leaving only sky and ocean. Beside the penthouse, my father has set up a small hibachi. 'We can have a cookout tonight,' he says.

Inside, my mother is cleaning the windows. She wears the same yellow rubber gloves as when she used to clean the windows of our house back in the suburbs. Only two rooms in the penthouse are habitable at present. The third has been used as a storeroom and still contains a puzzle of chairs and tables stacked on top of one another. In the main room, a telephone has been installed beside a green vinyl chair. One of the warehouse paintings has been hung on the wall, a still life with seashells and coral.

The sun sets. We have our cookout, sitting in folding chairs on the roof.

'This is going to be nice up here,' my mother says. 'It's like being right in the middle of the sky.'

'What I like,' my father says, 'is you can't see anybody. Private ocean view, right on the premises. A house this big on the water'd cost you an arm and a leg.'

'Soon as we get this place paid off,' he continues, 'this penthouse will be ours. We can keep it in the family, down through the generations. Whenever you want to come and stay in your very own Florida penthouse, you can.'

'Great,' I say, and mean it. For the first time, the motel exerts an attraction for me. The unexpected liberation of the roof, the salty decay of the oceanfront, the pleasant absurdity of America, all come together so that I can imagine myself bringing friends and women up to this roof in years to come.

When it's finally dark, we go inside. My parents aren't sleeping up here yet but we don't want to leave. My mother turns on the lamps.

I go over to her and put my hands on her shoulders.

'What did you dream last night?' I ask.

She looks at me, into my eyes. While she does this, she's not so much my mother as just a person, with troubles and a sense of humor. 'You don't want to know,' she says.

I go into the bedroom to check it out. The furniture has that motel look but, on the bureau, my mother has set up a photograph of me and my brothers. There's a mirror on the back of the bathroom door, which is open. In the mirror, I see my father. He's urinating. Or trying to. He's standing in front of the toilet, staring down with a blank look. He's concentrating on some problem I've never had to concentrate on, something I know is coming my way, but I can't imagine what it is. He raises his hand in the air and makes a fist. Then, as though he's been doing it for years, he begins to pound on his stomach, over where his bladder is. He doesn't see me watching. He keeps pounding, his hand making a dull thud. Finally, as though he's heard a signal, he stops. There's a moment of silence before his stream hits the water.

My mother is still in the living room when I come out. Over
her head, the seashell painting is crooked, I notice. I think about
fixing it, then think the hell with it. I go out onto the roof. It's
dark now, but I can hear the ocean. I look down the beach, at
the other high rises lit up, the Hilton, the Ramada. When I go to
the roof's edge, I can see the motel next door. Red lights glow
in the tropical grass-hut bar. Beneath me, and to the side, though,
the windows of our own motel are black. I squint down at the
patio but can't see anything. The roof still has puddles from last
night's storm and, when I step, I feel water gush up my shoe.
The hole is getting bigger. I don't stay out long, just long enough
to feel the world. When I turn back, I see that my father has
come out into the living room again. He's on the phone, arguing
with someone, or laughing, and working on my inheritance.

Incarnations of Burned Children

★ ★ ★ ★ ★ David Foster Wallace

★ ★ ★ ★ ★ The Daddy was around the side of the house hanging a door for the tenant when he heard the child's screams and the Mommy's voice gone high between them. He could move fast, and the back porch gave onto the kitchen, and before the screen door had banged shut behind him the Daddy had taken the scene in whole, the overturned pot on the floortile before the stove and the burner's blue jet and the floor's pool of water still steaming as its many arms extended, the toddler in his baggy diaper standing rigid with steam coming off his hair and his chest and shoulders scarlet and his eyes rolled up and mouth open very wide and seeming somehow separate from the sounds that issued, the Mommy down on one knee with the dishrag dabbing point- lessly at him and matching the screams with cries of her own, hysterical so she was almost frozen. Her one knee and the bare little soft feet were still in the steaming pool, and the Daddy's first act was to take the child under the arms and lift him away from it and take him to the sink, where he threw out plates and struck the tap to let cold wellwater run over the boy's feet while with his cupped hand he gathered and poured or flung more cold water over his head and shoulders and chest, wanting first to see the steam stop coming off him, the Mommy over his shoulder invoking God until he sent her for towels and gauze if they had it, the Daddy moving quickly and well and his man's mind empty of everything but purpose, not yet aware of how smoothly he moved or that he'd ceased to hear the high screams because to hear them would freeze him and make impossible what had to be done to help his child, whose screams were regular as breath and went on so long they'd become already a thing in the kitchen, something else to move quickly around. The tenant side's door outside hung half off its top hinge and moved slightly in the wind, and a bird in the oak across the driveway appeared to observe the door with a cocked head as the cries still came from inside. The worst scalds seemed to be the right arm and shoulder, the chest and stomach's red was fading to pink under the cold water and his feet's soft soles weren't blistered that the Daddy could see, but the toddler still made little fists and screamed except now merely on reflex from fear the Daddy would know he thought possible later, small face distended and thready veins standing out at the temples and the Daddy kept saying he was here he was here, adrenaline ebbing and an anger at the Mommy for allowing this thing to happen just starting to gather in wisps at his mind's extreme rear still hours from expression. When the Mommy returned he wasn't sure whether to wrap the child in a towel or not but he wet the towel down and did, swaddled him tight and lifted his baby out of the sink and set him on the kitchen table's edge to soothe him while the Mommy tried to check the feet's soles with one hand waving around in the area of her mouth and uttering objectless words while the Daddy bent in and was face to face with the child on the table's checkered edge repeating the fact that he was here and trying to calm the toddler's cries but still the child breathlessly screamed, a high pure shining sound that could stop his heart and his bitty lips and gums now tinged with the light blue of a low flame the Daddy thought, screaming as if almost still under the tilted pot in pain. A minute, two like this that seemed much longer, with the Mommy at the Daddy's side talking sing-song at the child's face and the lark on the limb with its head to the side and the hinge going white in a line from the weight of the canted door until the first wisp of steam came lazy from under the wrapped towel's hem and the parents' eyes met and widened – the diaper, which when they opened the towel and leaned their little boy back on the checkered cloth and unfastened the softened tabs and tried to remove it resisted slightly with new high cries and was hot, their baby's diaper burned their hand and they saw where the real water'd fallen and pooled and been burning their baby all this time while he screamed for them to help him and they hadn't, hadn't thought and when they got it off and saw the state of what was there the Mommy said their God's first name and grabbed the table to keep her feet while the father turned away and threw a haymaker at the air of the kitchen and cursed both himself and the world for not the last time while his child might now have been sleeping if not for the rate of his breathing and the tiny stricken motions of his hands in the air above where he lay, hands the size of a grown man's thumb that had clutched the Daddy's thumb in the crib while he'd watched the Daddy's mouth move in song, his head cocked and seeming to see way past him into something his eyes made the Daddy lonesome for in a strange vague way. If you've never wept and want to, have a child. Break your heart inside and something will a child is the twangy song the Daddy hears again as if the lady was almost there with him looking down at what they've done, though hours later what the Daddy won't most forgive is how badly he wanted a cigarette right then as they diapered the child as best they could in gauze and two crossed handtowels and the Daddy lifted him like a newborn with his skull in one palm and ran him out to the hot truck and burned custom rubber all the way to town and the clinic's ER with the tenant's door hanging open like that all day until the hinge gave but by then it was too late, when it wouldn't stop and they couldn't make it the child had learned to leave himself and watch the whole rest unfold from a point overhead, and whatever was lost never thenceforth mattered, and the child's body expanded and walked about and drew pay and lived its life untenanted, a thing among things, its self's soul so much vapor aloft, falling as rain and then rising, the sun up and down like a yoyo.

Faith *or* Tips for the Successful Young Lady
★ ★ ★ ★ ★ Amanda Davis

1. You catch more flies with honey than vinegar

★ ★ ★ ★ ★ The fat girl speaks the truth.

There are all kinds of anger, she says. Some kinds are just more useful than others.

We talk a lot, though no one except me sees her. She stands there sucking on a Fudgsicle like the day is blissful and warm, but I'm freezing.

I am not angry, I tell her, though it's not really true.

She smiles. Saying you're not angry is one kind, she says. Not very useful at all, though.

We are outside in the early fall day. School began three weeks ago and I am carefully watching the crowd file by.

The fat girl says, Faith, don't get your hopes up. Sweetie, that is never going to work out. She's talking about Tony Giobambera who has dark curly hair all over his body and smiles with his mouth but not with his eyes; who walks slowly, like a man with a secret.

I say, You never know.

She says, Actually, I do know. Then she sucks off a big piece of chocolate.

2. Carrots make a lovely snack

The fat girl sits behind me in school. All day, in every class. She eats jelly beans and Fritos. Shh, I tell her, you're making too much noise. She just smiles and brushes the crumbs from her mouth to the front of her blue blouse.

You are the only one I bother, Faith, she whispers. No one else cares.

I look around. We are taking an exam in World History and everyone else is focused on their work. The entire class has bowed their heads like they are praying. I have a copy of the exam on my desk but no answers filled in.

The fat girl moves on to Pringles. She reaches in and takes two chips, balances one on the other and wraps her lips around them.

Look, I'm making duck mouth, she mumbles over my shoulder.

I can't hear you, I hiss, and cover my ears with my hands.

The fat girl sits in Andrea Dutton's old seat. Andrea Dutton is a cheerleader and member of Honor Society who's very pretty and can be nice or awful at whim. The fat girl sits in her seat because Andrea Dutton flipped her car three weeks ago and ended up in the hospital in a coma and everybody said what a tragedy it was. I don't know where the fat girl sat before that.

3. A lady pays attention. Every boy likes a good listener

When the bell rings the fat girl and I go outside. Tony Giobambera always smokes a cigarette before fourth period on a bench in between the old building and the new building where, if he was anyone else, he'd be sure to get caught, but he's not.

He doesn't care if you watch, the fat girl tells me, so I find a place on the grass where I can see him but pretend to stare off into space, thinking about more important things than how much I would give up just to have Tony Giobambera run his finger along my cheek and my throat one more time.

Which won't happen, the fat girl says. She is perched beside me eating rhubarb pie.

Where did you even get that? I snarl.

Wouldn't you like to know, she snarls back, and turns away.

But it did happen once.

4. A lady prepares her appearance: Cucumbers make the eyes less puffy. Vaseline can make a smile shine

It was after what I did, the long summer after I'd shed myself completely and was prepared to come back to school like a whole new person, only inside it was still me. And it was at a mostly senior, end-of-the-summer party a week before school started. Everyone was drunk on beer or getting stoned in the basement, and I walked from room to room waiting for someone to notice the new me, but I was invisible.

I wandered out back, down wooden stairs, away from the

bright lights of the house towards the small latticed huddle of a gazebo. Inside there was a bench and I sat, slapping away mosquitoes and feeling a tightness in my chest that made me want to scream.

So far no one had said anything, even though I'd lost fifty-eight pounds and my skin had mostly cleared up. Even though I missed almost a whole semester of school and disappeared for more than six months. Nothing, not a word.

While I was away at Berrybrook, Miranda Turner's parents found a joint in her room, freaked out and shipped her off to an alternative high school in Idaho where no one was allowed to wear makeup; where they had to dig potatoes if they got in trouble. I knew it wasn't just the pot that bothered them, it was me. We'd been best friends since fifth grade, but even though really I was a good friend, Miranda's parents behaved like my unhappiness could infect their daughter. Like somehow she didn't have her own misery.

Miranda managed to smuggle a letter out of the Idaho prison-school. I didn't receive it until after I'd gotten out of Berrybrook . . . *You can't listen to them*, she wrote. *They're afraid that you're going to convince me to try and kill myself too. I'll probably have to give one of the gardeners a blow job to sneak this letter out to you. Can you believe my parents think that's better than leaving me alone so we can be friends like always?*

5. A lady thinks carefully before speaking: ugly thoughts set free can never be recaptured

I sat on a bench in that gazebo, knees to my chest, picking at the vines that climbed a trellis overhead, ripping off leaves and stripping them down to their veins, when Andrea Dutton came stumbling out of the trees. Her clothes were a mess, all twisted and covered in pine needles. A minute later, out stepped Tony Giobambera, zipping up his pants. He caught up to her and threw his arm around her shoulders and I watched them stumble in my direction.

I had nowhere to go, so I stayed. If Miranda had been there, she would have made me believe everything would be okay, but I sat alone and they trudged right up the steps.

Andrea Dutton stopped when she saw me and swayed back and forth. Didn't you used to be that really fat chick? she slobbered.

I seized up but didn't say anything.

I heard about what you did. She pointed her finger in my face, her eyes were bleary and her skin shined. I pressed myself against the grid of the gazebo.

Tony batted her hand away. Jesus, Andrea, you're a lady, huh.

Shut up, you pig. You don't even recognize her.

Tony swung around. Sure I do, he said softly. You're Faith something, right? He reached out with one strong hand and traced the outline of my cheek. You look great, he said. Really.

Andrea punched him in the shoulder. Let's go, okay? He looked at me, smiled, and all my tight dissolved into warm. Then he took Andrea's hand again and they continued up the hill.

6. Everyone appreciates a pretty smile

The fat girl has Oreos.

Don't you ever stop eating, I ask her? You're such a *joke*.

She doesn't say anything, just continues to lick away the frosting and studies me until my face grows warm. I look down at my nails, which are dirty and chewed. We are sitting on a low wall, in the sun near the back of school. I see a football fly in the distance. The sky is cloudless and blue.

Listen, she says quietly, I'm all you have.

7. A lady believes in herself. She's not afraid to follow her instincts

The day I did it was a pretty day. Clear and cold, just before Christmas. I always think about that: how full of promise that day seemed and how that made everything worse somehow. I had planned a little bit, but when it came right down to it I didn't wake up that morning with an idea of what would happen or when I would know. I just knew. I just turned a corner and knew.

I cried when I thought about it, which was all the time. I felt like the light inside me had flickered and gone out. Killing myself would bring erasure. What I wanted was to lift the needle off the record and stop the song abruptly.

I took pills.

I took lots of pills, beautiful pills of all colors. I saved them for months beforehand, scouring medicine cabinets anywhere I went. I didn't even bother reading the labels after a while. What mattered to me was the way they looked together, like colored pebbles, the way they felt when I reached deep in the jar of them and let them run through my fingers: slippery and precious. I saved up. I waited for just the right moment to pour so much possibility down my throat.

8. *No one likes a busybody*

I first met the fat girl the day I heard about Andrea Dutton's car accident – in the bathroom at a movie theater. It was the day before school started, four days after the party where Tony Giobambera touched me. Two girls I didn't recognize were teasing their hair and talking when I walked in. One girl said to the other, Did you hear about Andrea Dutton?

No, the other girl said. What?

Coma, the first girl said. Flipped her car and shit. Can you believe it?

Jeez, said the second girl, then paused to light a cigarette. And she was so popular.

By now I was safely in a far stall but I could smell the smoke.

Hey, who was that? I heard. Maybe she pointed.

I dunno, sighed the first girl. Why? You recognize her?

I swear that's the fat girl from Homecoming, she giggled. Faith whatever.

You are so high, the other girl laughed. As if. And then after a few minutes they both left.

The old weight settled on my chest. My world felt cracked and pressing. I stayed in the safety of my stall and wept.

When I finally pushed open the door to leave, my eyes were

red and puffy. I splashed cold water on my face but it was obvious that I'd been crying.

Don't worry about them, someone said from another stall. One of them'll die in a terrible perming accident and the other will be killed by an abusive boyfriend when she's in her early twenties.

I smiled, I couldn't help it, and hiccupped: That sounds like something my friend Miranda would say.

Miranda Turner? the voice asked. She got sent away to school in Idaho?

Yeah, I answered quietly. I bit my lip. I felt like I wanted to cry again.

The second stall door opened and a girl walked out. She was holding an ice-cream sandwich. Hi, she said. You must be The Fat Girl from Homecoming.

I stared at her. She was enormous, her face almost squeezed shut with excess flesh, her eyes slits, her cheeks gigantic half-melons. Her fingers were huge and thick.

Yeah, I said, but not anymore.

Bullshit, honey, she said. Once a fat girl, always a fat girl.

Then she took my arm and led me out of the bathroom.

9. *Everyone likes a lady*

I do outpatient therapy. I go in twice a week to see Dr Fern Hester who I am supposed to call Fern and tell how much better my life is now that I have lost all the weight and decided to live. Fern sits with her hands clasped lightly and her ankles crossed. Her skirts are always knee length and the same brown as her hair, which is straight and badly cut in a short, off-center pageboy. She has big square glasses that she inches back up her nose by squenching her face together – something it took me a while to get used to.

Whenever I begin, Fern sits quietly. She stares at me with practiced encouragement if I don't come up with something to talk about immediately. Those silent moments are horrible swollen things that make me nauseous and angry, so I try to prepare a few topics before I arrive for something to fall back on.

I never tell her about the fat girl.

I never talk about Homecoming.

Three weeks ago, I told her: This girl at school is in a coma.

Fern nodded, concern peppering her face.

And everyone says she was totally drinking and stuff. I didn't really know her.

I watched Fern. Her glasses were greasy in the light. They reflected me, brown hair hanging limp, pimple near my nose. I touched my face. I had known Andrea Dutton. When we were little kids we played together, when we were five and six, but that didn't give me the right to call her friend now. Yet I felt this urge to associate with her, to own at least part of her tragedy.

Her absence was a huge gaping hole in the fabric of our school, of the town, even. I pictured her lying in a hospital bed, her blond hair cascading along a pillow, her pale skin smooth and pearly, her lips open just enough for a tube to pass through. The room must be lined in flowers, I thought, with her parents holding a vigil by her side. There could be no doubt that people wanted her back.

She goes out with Tony Giobambera, I said softly, then

regretted it, because Fern's eyes lit up like a pinball machine and she leaned towards me expectantly.

Silence. What was there to say about Tony Giobambera? Somehow I think he actually sees me, not just the fat loser I used to be, but me, Faith, a person? I can't breathe properly around him? I want him to save me?

He's kind of popular, I said. She leaned back and scribbled.

10. *Present yourself in a positive manner. A lady is her own best fan!*

In the afternoon I get called into the guidance office to talk about my record. To *explore ways of accenting my candidacy for college.* To *make myself a more attractive applicant.* The fat girl waits in the hall.

You used to be in the choir, before your difficulties . . .

It seems I have no extracurriculars and now that I've *moved over the rocky areas and into such a better place, mentally speaking,* it's time to put the past behind me and think about the future! *A good academic record can be a great academic record with just a few civic activities . . .*

So what am I supposed to do, I ask the guidance counselor, Mrs Twine, who is far too cheerful for the good of anyone. Run for Student Council president, or something?

That sounds like a very good idea, Mrs Twine responds enthusiastically.

No! (I'm angry, I can't help it.) No, it does not sound like a good idea. You have absolutely no idea what a good idea is. I am a joke! Running for Student Council would be so stupid . . .

I trail off leaving us both uncomfortable. Listen, Mrs Twine says, I understand your nervousness. You don't have to run for Student Council. You could join a club. How about that?

Something cold and alert washes over me. Thank you very much for your time, I say, and rise to leave. I extend a hand and Mrs Twine, looking confused but happy as ever, takes it in both of hers.

Faith, she says, it's all going to work out.

And I want to believe her. Despite everything, I want nothing more in the whole world than to believe this stupid, optimistic woman.

11. A lady has a generous heart. She knows forgiveness is the key to friendship

Berrybrook was what you would expect. It was a long white hallway. It was concerned and pointed questions. It was sitting in a circle with other angry teenagers trying to explore our rage.

It was one long pale blur.

I was kept on an extended plan, fed a special diet and made to exercise. My mom probably coughed up a lot of money for that, but Daddy died with good insurance, so weren't we lucky?

I told them what I needed to, but never let on that my head floated like a balloon, far above my body, that from up there I looked down on my exercising self, the nutty group of us talking about our pain, that even my clean white room was seen from somewhere near the ceiling.

But what was hard was when it ended. They told us all along it would be difficult. Still, I wasn't prepared for the sharpness of the outside, the strong smells, the noise, the color. All of it plowed me over. That alone was enough to inspire complacence. As if I wasn't already complacent enough.

12. A lady has a dainty appetite. A moment on the lips, a lifetime on the hips

There's just no way to talk about some things.

I know what you mean, the fat girl says, slurping a milk shake. You're lucky you have me.

We're sitting on the low wall again. The football field is off in the distance. From here it looks like a postcard, a painting. It looks like you could roll it up and cart it away, leaving space for something else to replace it. But that's not the case.

Some things are meant to be buried. Collected and washed into a deep pit, with hot, molten tar poured over them to change their shape and substance forever. I've worked very hard to forget, but I can't. The thing is, I remember.

Homecoming. I wore my favorite blue sweater and sang the national anthem with the choir, my breath cloudy in the cold November air. After the game, I walked around with Miranda, until I got winded and lost her in the crowd. While I rested, a group of junior guys offered me punch, red punch that tasted like Popsicles. We wandered towards the bleachers. They were friendly, they made me feel normal. That's the part I remember clearly.

Yeah, that's a problem, the fat girl agrees, swishing her cup around, trying to find more milk shake. But there are ways to change things.

She turns to me with an intensity that's scary, like everything in her has melted into anger.

I cough.

You are such a crybaby, the fat girl sneers. Her frustration with me is palpable. Okay, back to the real world, she says, and I wipe my eyes and follow her to Chemistry.

13. *Nobody likes a sad sack! Cheerfulness is the road to popularity*

The day stretches on and on until finally it ends. The moon hangs low and bright in the dark sky: it is time to sleep until I have to do it again.

But the fat girl slumps in a chair in the corner of my room, eating popcorn with butter from a large porcelain bowl. Her face is greasy from stuffing handfuls in her mouth. Her flesh ripples and hangs. She is so disgusting.

Things aren't going anywhere, she says, kicking the chair.

This is not the first time I've seen her here, but usually she waits for me to leave the house, or at least my room, before she shows up. I stick my head under the pillow.

You know I'm right, her muffled voice sneers. Don't even try to ignore it.

I sit straight up. I'm pissed. I scream at her: How could I know that?! How the fuck could things go well when you won't leave me alone?!!

She licks her fingers.

You horrible cow! I scream at her, beginning to cry. I'm so angry I can't help the tears. You miserable piece of shit!

In comes Mom, barreling through the door. Faith! she cries, concern in her voice – but I see the truth in the stupid expression she's worn since I came back.

My mother's afraid of me. She's afraid of her daughter the monster and she can't hide it.

Get out, I tell her.

I mean, how am I supposed to explain the fat girl, dripping butter in a puddle on the carpet, when my mother can't even look at me?

You should knock, I sniffle, and swallow my anger. When I look at her it's with a face of stone.

Hello, I'm sixteen and entitled to privacy, I announce. She holds the doorknob like she could swing in or out. Make your choice, Mom, I whisper deep inside my head, but I know she won't choose what I secretly want.

I'm right: she backs out of the room, closing the door quietly, leaving me alone with the fat girl and the ache in my chest.

Things are just never going to be the same, the fat girl whispers. I almost hear sympathy but then she pops M&Ms. Hey Faith, she giggles, what do these remind you of?

Fuck you, I counter, but she's right, of course. The fat girl always speaks the truth. Things are never going to be normal. Things are never going to fly straight or land right or flow from day to day without seeming like a cartoon.

There's no relief. Each day is hot and airless, a festival of shame and humiliation just like it was before, only now I'm invisible.

Time works wonders, the fat girl says through mashed potatoes, and I want to hit her. Sorry, she says, but it does, I'm just saying.

I lie there, crying softly, until I fall asleep.

14. It is important to know your best features. Remember: everyone has inner beauty!

There were no mirrors at Berrybrook. To relieve us of the eyes of the outside world and add to the illusion that inside Berrybrook we were safe, we were not supposed to see ourselves. I was not shown the removal of my outer layers, though I felt my body become firmer and evaporate, felt whole parts of me fall away.

When my mother drove me home that first day out, the world seemed to be made of marshmallows: everything was spongy and bright. She came through a town that was exactly as I'd left it in an ambulance many months before. She relayed little bits of information: *There's a sale on jeans this Thursday. You need new clothes. Your Uncle Harry broke his leg.* I didn't speak.

She pulled into our driveway and our house seemed to quiver. It was a giant stone reproduction of the house I'd imagined for so many months. It didn't seem real.

I waited for her to unlock the door, then bolted to my room. It was extremely clean and I knew it had been pillaged for clues to my unraveling.

While I leaned in the doorway, movement caught my eye. There, in the corner, stood a skinny, stringy-haired girl with huge, terrified eyes. When I moved my hand, she moved hers. I looked to the side, she did the same. I stepped towards her and she grew larger. When my mom came in a few minutes later, she found me weeping with my head to the mirror. I couldn't tell her any of it: I was walking through absence; I felt surrounded by loss; I was missing, even though I was there.

My mother smiled and put her hands on her hips. Dinner? she offered. We were much too careful to talk about anything.

15. Nothing is achieved without determination and sacrifice. Remember: no pain, no gain

The fat girl is full of information. I think about what she says, about what it would mean to strike back, but I can't imagine it would make me feel better.

Oh it would, says the fat girl. It would feel really *good*. She speaks to me like I'm a stupid child. In her lap is a roasting pan with a whole crispy chicken. She severs one wing with a small gold knife. When someone kicks you, she says slowly, you get up and kick them back.

I don't know, I repeat, and the fat girl shakes her head.

What do you want to remember, she asks me, delicately cutting away at the bird, doing what you've been told or changing everything?

Changing everything, I whisper.

Right, she says, and gnaws on a drumstick.

Right, I say, and take the knife she hands me.

16. A lady sits still. A lady doesn't cause a ruckus

After my last class, I go use the bathroom. The fat girl is nowhere to be found. Hey, I call out, but nobody answers. The hallways are deserted, the day is over. I wander through the school looking, but don't see her anywhere. I go outside, to the low wall, but she's not there, either.

Then I see her at the bottom of the hill. She is spinning in loops and arcs in the center of the football field. Her skirt swings over the grass, her body is a giant blue swirl. I get halfway down the hill, then stop.

Homecoming was almost a year ago, I was still huge and lumbering. The bleachers, that night . . . The whole of it sweeps up on me then, sudden and hazy: We stand with our red plastic cups, breath fogging the air. The guys are so friendly and I feel charming. They laugh at everything I say, and punch each other in the arm, clustering around. We talk about something, our voices colliding, our steamy breath forming tiny clouds that spiral up and drift off into the night. A boy with blue eyes whispers, *Where have you been all my life?* I hiccup, giggle. I can't stop grinning. I toss my hair. They buzz around me, all smiles.

She's nice, one boy says to another. Everything is rubbery and unreal. The blue-eyed boy puts his arm around me and leans in close. *You're so pretty, Faith, do you have a boyfriend?* he whispers. I flush, unsteady. *Does someone love you like you deserve to be loved?* No, I think. *More punch,* someone offers, and I take a long drink. The guys nod their heads, closing in around me. A tall boy's voice is loud and clear. *John, you know what they say about fat girls, right?* My head thick and cloudy, I can't really breathe. *What do they say?* answers a boy in a red parka. I don't know what to do. *Fat girls are hungry,* says another boy with a ratty mustache. *Fat girls are hungry,* an echo. I turn to leave but they have my arms. *C'mon, Faith,* Blue Eyes says, *I thought you liked us.* I don't feel well, I whisper. My heart pounds.

Feed the fat girl! Someone pushes me to my knees. Someone

else has my arms, his nails jagged, a striped silver ring on his middle finger. Right in my ear, *You tell anyone and we'll kill you.* I stare at buckles and pockets. He pinches my nose so my mouth falls open. Then the terrible sounds of zippers and one after the other they come at me, chanting. *Feed the fat girl.* Over and over I gag, I can't breathe. *We'll tell what a slut you are.* Then I'm shoved to all fours. I stare at hands, at sneakers and boots, the cuffs of pants and jeans. *The fatter the berry the sweeter the juice.* And laughter. *The fatter the berry the sweeter the juice.*

17. A lady's immaculate reputation is her most prized possession. Remember: there are good girls and there are bad girls

I don't get down the hill. I get halfway, am nauseous and swallow it down. I sit hard on the ground. Far away a lawnmower hums. I smell fresh cut grass, honeysuckle. The field is utterly empty – the fat girl is nowhere, is gone.

I can't breathe right. I close my eyes, cross my fingers and wish desperately for a sign, any sign, that things will be okay. Then I feel a hand on my shoulder.

I shriek.

Tony Giobambera leaps away from me. Sorry, he mumbles, uneasy. I saw you sit. Are you all right?

Yeah, I bellow. I try to say, I'm fine, but instead begin to cry.

Here, he says, helping me to my feet. Here. He puts an arm around my shoulders and leads me to the bleachers. I smell him: cigarettes, sweat, something musky and male. We sit side by side. I don't know what to do.

Huh, he says. He shoves his hands in his pockets. What's wrong?

His voice calms me. I grope around for an answer. Nothing, I say, my voice squeaky and weird. We sit quietly for a minute and I stare. He has clear blue eyes and bumpy skin but his lips are perfect and full. One big black curl falls over his left brow.

I feel like I should say something, anything. I'm real sorry about your girlfriend, I tell him.

Oh, he looks at me. Yeah . . . and trails off.

I don't answer. In my silence are three things: the desire to preserve this perfect, unspoiled moment, and the knowledge that everything in me that hurts wants a say right now, and how afraid I am of what would happen if I let it.

I look out over the field. Far away, by the line of trees I see a large blue shape spin and whirl, then fall down. She stays like that for a minute, then rises, lurches wildly and spins again.

Tony Giobambera lights a cigarette and offers me one. I hesitate, then take it and lean into the flame he cups.

I drag and exhale. My head flutters lightly off my shoulders.

A bug buzzes by. I swat it away. The fat girl spins and falls.

What do you dream? I ask him and he squints at me.

Dumb things, mostly, he says like it's the most normal question in the world. Sometimes dragons or really stupid shit, cars, school . . .

I straighten my skirt and tilt my head towards him.

What about you?

I feel the fat girl's knife in my pocket, its weight solid and warm. I think about my most frequent dream where stars pepper the sky and I stand on a patch of grass, swelling, and rise above everything until I am immense and powerful and throw fear into the hearts of those below. I hang there, swaying back and forth, an enormous hungry moon able to swallow the world, but I always wake falling.

Tony Giobambera's hands are on his knees. His fingers are long and thin. On his right hand is a silver ring. I focus on it, on the pattern of it, but don't answer. I keep it all to myself, as though the power of words could make things come true. In the distance the fat girl spins and falls, spins and falls. She's a violent scratch of blue in the clear green day. She knows everything that matters, everything there is. I inhale and blow smoke up into the sky where it dissolves and disappears.

Nothing dangerous, I tell him. Nothing to be alarmed about.

There's a gentle breeze and the knife is warm against my leg. In the distance the fat girl falls. I wonder, with everything I am, if this is the moment I've been waiting for.

Letters from Steven, a Dog, to Captains of Industry
★ ★ ★ ★ ★ Dave Eggers

★ ★ ★ ★ ★ On August 5, 2000, twenty letters were sent by Daniel O'Mara to the chief executive officers of twenty Fortune 500 companies. These are six of them.

Hugh L. McColl, Jr.
CEO, Bank of America Corp.
100 N. Tryon Street
Charlotte, NC 28255

Dear Mr McColl, Jr.,
I realize that you are a busy man so I will get to the point. I have recently
been writing some passages from the point of view of a dog named Steven,
and I would like you to see an example. Here is one:

I am Steven and I was born in a box of glass, on newsprint cut to ribbons.
I am here now, five years later, and my paws, once white like paper, are now
white like ivory. I have walked streets! And over fields! Have seen things!
The hands of children I've bitten! They look delectable and taste so fine!

I have to move. I have to move. I can jump a mile. I'm that kind of dog –
I can jump a goddamn mile. I'm a great dog. I see colors like you hear
jetplanes.

I'm going to find a hole. I'm going to find a tiny tiny tiny hole and walk
through like goddamn Gandhi.

That is all for now.

Daniel O'Mara
5811 Mesa Drive, #216
Austin, TX 78731

Robert G. Miller
Chief Executive Officer
Rite Aid
30 Hunter Lane
Camp Hill, PA 17011

Dear Mr Miller,
You do not know me and this matter does not directly affect you, but
nevertheless I need your full attention. I have been, for a few weeks now,
writing letters to men like yourself, though from the point of view of a dog
named Steven. Here is one such letter, for you:

I am Steven and I was born just after the children came home from school.
I've spent days barking while not knowing why I was barking. On those
days I would bark and bark, getting hoarse and tired, knowing that I did not
know why I was barking, all the while guessing that I would be able to
figure it out later.

Yesterday I was running under a hundred tall elms, planted in a row. I
was running toward a clearing where the grass in the light was chartreuse
and soft, and while running, eyes glassy from the cold air, I thought of my
sister, who was taken from me all those years ago, before her eyes had
opened. My fur looks like sandpaper but is luxurious to touch.

I still do not know why I bark. Right now, when it's been overcast for a
week or so, I feel good, I feel rested, like I never want to bark again. But soon
enough I will find myself barking, barking until I am hoarse, unable to stop
barking oh God the people stare at me like I'll bark myself to death.

I guess it's back to work for you now, Mr Miller.

D.

Daniel O'Mara
5811 Mesa Drive, #216
Austin, TX 78731

Peter I. Bijur
Chief Executive Officer
Texaco
2000 Westchester Avenue
White Plains, NY 10650

Dear Mr Bijur,
Greetings. I am a resident of Austin, Texas, who is writing to you under the guise of a dog named Steven. Steven is an Irish setter. This here is Steven:

Before we lived in this house a family of four did. They were named the Clutters, and were of course disturbed by the book of Truman's. I asked once if they were related but they ignored me. I have read Mr Capote's book and liked it a great deal.

I sometimes bark. Sometimes I talk to people about my barking; I feel that it's a problem. Or rather, I feel that other people feel it's a problem, which becomes, for me, a problem. When I see headlights in the rear view window I feel menaced. My brother's name is Jonathan and he barks more than I do, but we never bark at the same time because why would we both need to be barking at the same time? I've bitten him so hard I tasted his alkaline blood. Hooo!

I once ate a pizza. I'm not supposed to eat pizza, because I am a dog, but I don't know who makes rules like this, who can eat what. I ate the pizza and was fine. I looked at a solar eclipse and was fine. I jumped from the roof once and was hardly hurt at all. Maybe I'll never die. I'm a fast dog!

I bark all night at least once a month. In cars I'm quiet. I run around trees like a stick in a current around rocks that are smooth. Hoooo! Hooooo! Yeah you got me now, yeah! Man I wish you could have seen all this.

Mr Bijur, you are too kind. Keep up the work.

$\mathcal{D}$.

Daniel O'Mara
5811 Mesa Drive, #216
Austin, TX 78731

Christopher M. Connor
Chief Executive Officer
Sherwin-Williams
101 Prospect Avenue NW
Cleveland, OH 44115

Dear Mr Connor,
You have many important things to do so I will get to the point. I have recently been writing letters to captains of industry, from the point of view of an Irish setter named Steven. Each letter is one-of-a-kind. Here is yours.

There was a night that I ran like I was swimming in deep back water, but quieter. When I ran past other dogs, dogs I knew, silhouettes now or just legged bushes of black, they looked hollow. Samson's eyes, ice-blue in the daylight, were white and reflective. I went by as if carried by a current, not feeling my feet grabbing at the wet wet grass.

I was running why because I wanted to feel the air cool the gaps in my fur. The sky was that gray-blue it is when there are clouds out after dark. The houses bent over me and I curved around trees. Damn I'm a fast dog!

It's so fucking tiring to hear people talk. I hear everything they say, all at once. I mean, every time one of them opens their mouth, I hear them all talking, and hear everything they've all been saying for so long, and it's so much all the same thing, one long angry shrugging complaint. But I say: Hoooo! Hooooooo!

You know how cheetahs run – how you never see their feet touch the ground? That's me, man – only when I run, my brain is circling my body at the same time – a hula hoop hooping around my head as I run like a fucking hovercraft!

I'm just in love with all this.

Mr Connor, I thank you for your time.

D

Daniel O'Mara
5811 Mesa Drive, #216
Austin, TX 78731

David I. Fuentes
Chief Executive Officer
Office Depot
2200 Old Germantown Road
Delray Beach, FL 33445

Dear Mr Fuentes,

Recently, I have been writing letters to other large-company CEOs, all from the point of view of an Irish setter named Steven. For you, though, I will be writing as a small bird, probably a hummingbird, named Buck. Here goes:

When I was young and hungry always, my mother left me and my siblings alone as she hopped around the field, looking for food and sticks with which to line our nest. When she was gone we opened our mouths, waiting for food, our eyes green-blue peas covered with the thinnest pink skin.

When she was gone we sometimes taught each other songs. I don't remember any of the songs, or why we sang them. Months later we all flew away and I never saw any of them again, my siblings or mother. We small birds are unsentimental because we can fly!

But you know what? I'm not actually a small bird. I am a dog named Steven. I could never fool you – I'm a fast goddamn dog and I run around trees like a rocket-seeking rocket. Hoooo! Hoooooo! I don't need any bird, any small bird asking for food! No way, man! I'm running and running on the dry hot grass and it's like I never want to bark again, if I can just keeping running. If I can keeping running, turning like a skier, staying low, I'll never want to just bark and bark and bark – oh sweet Jesus, let me keep running! I'm just so fucking afraid of getting tired, you know, man?

Mr Fuentes, your attention is appreciated.

D.

Daniel O'Mara
5811 Mesa Drive, #216
Austin, TX 78731

Jacques Nasser
CEO, Ford Motor Company
Detroit, MI 33445

Dear Mr Nasser,
Your job is not an easy one and I respect your time. So I will make this relatively brief and it will be, always, to the point.

Nr Nasser, goddamn, you've heard of me and my running! I've seen your buildings and I've seen your sidewalks and all of your carpets, always the same carpets. Ha ha ha ha! It makes me laugh, I am sorry. Someday I will eat some special food and grow 200 feet tall and then – then watch out, Mr Nasser! Watch for my shadow and duck! Watch for my shadow!

I have loved a hundred others, other animals of fur and speed, and now I love you. But not the same way. Maybe the same way. Have you seen me run, motherscratcher? I know what happens when the sun rubs and rubs the trees in the earliest thoughts of morning. I eat the food you give me I eat the food you give me and then I throw it to the world. I am a dog who eats pizza – I eat pizza and am fine! I eat hummus and I retch! Do not underestimate me, Mr Nasser! Mr Nasser I want you to go to your family. I won't step on your house when I am 200 feet tall. Have you seen Clifford? That's what I will look like when I am 200 feet tall. I will be huge and red and tall, but I promise one thing: I will be careful like Clifford.

Mr Nasser, feel my sun. I rub my sun over you and over you and I want you to give it your young ones and then I want you to run with me because while I sit on your bed and eat your food I do not sleep I do not sleep I plan to run I plan to run!

Mr Nasser, your attention is the fuel that spins my hovercraft head.

Daniel O'Mara
5811 Mesa Drive, #216
Austin, TX 78731

Dentaphilia

★ ★ ★ ★ ★ Julia Slavin

★★★★★ I once loved a woman who grew teeth all over her body.

The first one came in as a hard spot in her navel. It grew quickly into a tooth, a real tooth with a jagged edge and a crown, enameled like a pearl. I thought it was sexy, a little jewel in her belly button. Helen would bunch up her shirt, undulate like a harem dancer, and I'd be ready to go.

Then one day I came home from the mill and Helen called for me to come upstairs. She sat at the foot of our bed wrapped in a towel, still wet and shiny from the shower. She lifted her arm. I felt around. With her arm raised I could make out the outline of a row of upper incisors pressing out just under her skin. My God, I thought, the soft underside of her arm would soon resemble a crocodile's jaw. She said it'd been itching and painful there for some time. I told her not to worry. It was nothing. It would go away. I even managed to make her believe me long enough for her to go to sleep and for me to lie awake all night wondering what the hell to do. But in the morning, when she scratched my thigh with a molar that had sprouted in the crease behind her knee, I called Dr Manfred.

'Yes, well . . . yes, well . . .' Dr Manfred murmured as he examined Helen's body with a small magnifying glass that looked like the kind jewelers use to appraise diamonds. With each 'yes, well' my chest expanded, tightening my shirt at the buttons. I thought my ribs would burst out of my shirt and pile up on the floor like sticks.

'Well, what?' I asked.

He drew the glass away from his eye and smiled a phony smile. 'I can see how you thought they were teeth.'

He produced a little scalpel from his white coat and began to scrape away at one of the teeth on the inside of Helen's elbow. It came off in thin translucent strips like the layers of an onion. Helen squeezed her lips together but didn't complain. She was brave when it came to pain. In a metal bowl, he ground the tooth with a marble pestle into a fine white powder like sand.

'You have calcinosis, my dear,' Dr Manfred said. 'It's a calcification condition.' He pushed up on a turquoise soap dispenser and rubbed his hands into a fat lather cloud. 'Sometimes there's a buildup of calcium deposits in the body,' he said, over running tap water. 'We don't normally see the calcification externally, perhaps a plaque in the dermis, a deposit in the nodule. Not a worry, though.' He shook his hands dry in the air. 'We'll run some blood, check the thyroid. These things usually just go away. *Poof!*'

Helen pinched the sand in the metal bowl between her thumb and index finger, rubbed some into her palm, let it run through her fingers back into the bowl. Dr Manfred wrote a prescription for a calcium substitute and told her to lay off salt.

In the morning Helen rolled over and I saw a long series of evenly spaced holes in the sheet, as if boll weevils had been eating the bed. By scraping off the tooth on her elbow, Dr Manfred had just made room for more. Helen had teeth sticking out all the way up her arm. Her shoulder looked like the back of a stegosaurus. A fool could have told me that Dr Manfred was the wrong kind of doctor.

Dr Freedman's waiting room had little chairs and little tables with crayons and coloring books. Some kid had already rifled through and scribbled everything green. Green duck, green cow, green Bo-Peep, green sheep.

'The dentist sees grown-ups too?' I asked the receptionist.

'Yes, grown-ups too,' she assured me, in a little voice.

I gave Helen the last grown-up chair and sat in one of the little ones. My knees came to my head. The kid at my table was really upset about all the coloring books being colored in, and his mother was telling him to try drawing his own pictures from his imagination. He looked at her like she was stupid. Then he noticed Helen. All the kids were looking at her with their mouths open, even when their mothers told them it wasn't polite. Even when Helen smiled at them and said hello, they couldn't stop gaping. The row of lower bicuspids coming in across her cheekbone was too much.

She was in Dr Freedman's office for an hour. I started pacing. Then two hours. The other patients were agitated, and the receptionist was making apologies on the dentist's behalf. 'I'm sure it's an urgent matter,' she said. 'You'll want him to give you the time *you* need when it's your turn.'

'What took so long?' I asked, driving home.

'I have hyperstimulated dentin,' she said, looking out her window at the shadows from the trees. 'He wants me to stop taking the calcium substitute. And he wants to see me in a week.'

'What for?'

'He says I have twelve cavities.' She flipped down the cosmetic mirror on the visor and freshened her lipstick.

'Leave this to me, Hel,' I said. 'You concentrate on getting well, and leave the rest to me.' I reached over and touched her knee.

She turned toward me. 'Can you pull over? I need to walk.'

'Whatever you want,' I said, stopping the truck on the shoulder.

'I'll see you at home.' She climbed down.

'I'll come too,' I said.

'I need to be alone for a while,' she said, and closed the door.

The teeth started coming in pretty regularly. Every morning there'd be something new to report, something pressing against the skin, a toughening between her toes, a hard place on her ear. Then a few days would go by with nothing, and I'd think maybe the whole business was going to go away, as Dr Manfred said. But soon the cramp Helen had been rubbing on her hip would explain itself with a freshly cut tooth or a red spot above her eyebrow would open up to a molar.

'Just how ugly am I, Mike?' she asked one morning, staring out front at some squirrels that were draining the seeds from her bird feeders.

I moved her hair away and looked at her face, which was blotched and speckled with incisors. 'You could never be ugly, Hel,' I said. And I meant it.

I spent a lot of spare time chopping and stacking wood in the back, trying to figure out how to keep Helen from being scared, thinking about how much I loved her and how going through this experience together *confirmed* to me how much I loved her.

One afternoon I heard her singing in the downstairs bathroom: 'Delta Dawn,' to be precise. I leaned my ax against the stump and moved over to where I could see her, in front of the medicine chest mirror, rubbing the teeth on her body with peroxide and a chamois cloth like they were little pieces of carved crystal. She had her hair twisted into a new do with a sunflower barrette and shimmery pink gloss on her lips. She'd bought a new dress, a yellow gabardine that pinched in under her breasts, fit tightly at her waist, and buttoned all the way down. I watched her put on earrings, little zircons that picked up the light, and hook a matching necklace behind her neck. Then she looked over and saw me standing there with my hands against the window, my breath fogging up the glass, and screamed bloody murder.

Helen was at Dr Freedman's office every other day for this or that. 'He says I need another cleaning,' she'd say, or, 'He wants more X-rays.' I'd sit in that kids' waiting room for hours, listening to Helen giggle and squeal in the office. Once, when things got too quiet, I went in. I found her giddy and stupid on nitrous.

'You can't expect her to get treatment with no anesthesia,' Dr Freedman said, snapping off latex gloves. Helen pulled one out of his hand, blew it up into a five-fingered balloon, and let it zip across the room. I pulled her out of the office by her wrist.

In the truck, Helen was furious. She said I was way out of line. I tried arguing with her but she told me not to bother her, she was cutting a tooth on her neck, out of that place just above the spine where, without thinking, I used to reach over and put my fingers on long trips or in traffic.

★

I came home from the mill one night and Helen had left a note saying to go ahead and eat without her. I made a sandwich with a couple of slices of cheese that had hardened around the edges and about half a cup of mayonnaise to mask the taste of some old turkey. Then I watched beach volleyball on ESPN.

Helen was undressing when I woke up. Naked, she was a treasure from King Tut's tomb, a gilded statue covered in jewels. For one sleepy moment I thought she was the most beautiful thing I'd ever seen. Then I realized what I was looking at. 'Are you insane?' I asked, about her rows upon rows of gold fillings. 'We can't afford those. What were you thinking?'

'They were a gift from Dr Freedman.'

That put me over the top. I wasn't going to lose the woman I loved to a dentist. I pulled on my pants, threw on a shirt and shoes, and grabbed Helen by the wrist.

'I thought you'd like them,' she cried, as I yanked her bathrobe off a nail on the door and dragged her from the house. 'I did them for you!'

I forced her into the truck and peeled out of the driveway. With Helen screaming and grabbing onto the strap above the window, I swerved and cut corners, thirty miles over the speed limit.

Dr Freedman lived in a new brick split-level connected to his office. He opened his huge front door when I rapped the gaudy lion-head knocker. He was in pajamas: blue silk. Helen was trying to wiggle out of my grip and kicking me in the shins with her sharp little feet.

'Why don't you come in, Mike. We'll talk it over.' Freedman was trying to sound as if he were the one in control and I was the crackbrain.

'We don't want any of your handouts!' I yelled.

'They were a gift, Mike. Professional courtesy. For all the business Helen's brought.'

'Take 'em out.'

'That's not reasonable, Mike. You're not being reasonable.' Freedman held his skinny little hands up, his only defense, as I moved toward him to bust his mouth in. Helen was screaming. I was hurting her wrist. I let her go and she ran across the lawn. The dentist and I just stood there like a couple of lazy dogs and watched her run, her feet cutting divots into the dentist's grass, her teeth opalescent in the moonlight.

I didn't go to work the next day. I couldn't get out of bed. I called the mill and said I had the flu. I called all of Helen's girlfriends to see if they'd seen her. Around noon I drove around to places Helen liked to go – Hatcher's Boutique, Sweet Nothings, Flower Emporium – knowing full well she wouldn't be seen in any of those places now. I bought some roses at the Emporium, came home, and watched TV. Five o'clock that afternoon Helen came in. She'd had the gold replaced with porcelain. She thanked me for the flowers and went upstairs for a bath. I stood outside the bathroom door and asked her if she wanted a glass of wine, cocoa, warm towels from the dryer, a sandwich, some music, an inflatable pillow for her neck, anything. No, thank you. No, thank you, nothing.

'If you want to do something,' she called, when I ran out of offers and started to move away from the door, 'you can wash my back.'

I pushed open the door. She sat with her arms resting on the sides of the lion-claw tub like a queen. I lowered myself to my knees. She opened her mouth a little and I kissed her. She didn't kiss me back but she didn't push me away either. I dragged my tongue down her neck and around a circle of pointed teeth that surrounded her nipple like a fortress. She raised her chest. Then I scooped the soap out of the dish and rubbed up a lather. She bent forward, causing little murky waves to lap at the sides of the tub. The water was filled with lumps of chalky powder. I looked up at the ceiling to see if the plaster had come loose. Then I looked at her back. The skin was peeling as if she'd had a bad sunburn, rolling up and coming off in shavings.

'I know what it looks like,' Helen said, before I could say anything. 'Wash along the edges. It'll help it along.'

'Help it along to what?' I managed to ask. Underneath the old skin she was tender, wrinkled and pink like a newborn. I was afraid to touch, worried I'd hurt her. She said it didn't hurt, it just itched and stung a bit. Then I saw a couple of teeth bob to the surface of the bathwater like a row of miniature buoys on a dark and rocky bay.

For a little while it seemed like everything was getting back to normal. Every morning we'd find a few more teeth somewhere in the bed or swirling around in the shower drain. Throw them out, get rid of them, I said, but Helen saved them in a little Zulu basket. 'For jewelry,' she said, holding them in her hands like precious stones. 'Maybe a necklace.' I was so happy and giddy during that time, she could have worn the basket on her head and I wouldn't have objected. I bought her things. I took her dancing even though I'm no dancer.

Freedman cautioned otherwise. 'Helen needs special care during this period,' he said. 'She's completely defenseless.' He'd called me into his office to talk about her recent blood test. There was an excess of calcium carbonate in her blood. He was concerned about the shedding.

'You're looking at me like you think I can't take care of my wife,' I said.

Freedman shrugged. I knew he was in love with her. I mean, everybody was in love with Helen. I used to sit on a stool at the Mug, where she bartended, drinking diluted whiskey, waiting for a chance to talk to her. Two other guys did the same. But it was my car she slid into after work one snowy night, my lap she swung her leg over, and my hand that slid the ponytail holder out of her long brown hair. Now she was getting better. She wasn't going to need him anymore. He was losing her and couldn't bear it.

More of the teeth dropped out and the skin on her back healed and in time the calcium in her blood dropped way down.

But then things started to get bad again.

One beautiful spring morning I came out of the mill and Helen was sitting on the hood of our truck, kicking her heels against the tire like a little girl. 'My wisdom teeth are coming in.' She smiled proudly.

I froze. 'Where?'

She lowered her eyes bashfully and raised them. 'Down there.'

'Oh,' I said. What are you supposed to say when your wife tells you something like that? 'Oh.'

She put her arms around my neck and slipped her butt off the hood. She felt like a wisp of grass. Then my brain bucked into action and I realized she was falling. And I was dropping her. I caught her under her arms before she broke on the asphalt.

'I'm fine, Mike. Really fine. Just a little wobbly.' She moved away from me and did little herky-jerky pirouettes around the parking lot, like a glass ballerina on top of a busted music box.

To say the teeth started coming back in would be an understatement. They knocked down doors and *busted* back in. They grew in mounds on top of one another, in notched clumps like fallen stones from a temple ruin, in clusters like tiled mosaics. They grew straight and crooked and upside down and ingrown. You could sit and watch them grow, see them force their way out. Helen said it didn't hurt. She even got excited when she felt one coming. 'Look at that one,' she'd squeal. 'Oh! Here comes another!' And she'd brush and rub them with baking soda and peroxide, spend all day in front of the mirror singing and polishing.

Helen wasn't in Freedman's office fifteen minutes when I lost patience and barged in. He looked at me as if he were really tired of my intrusions. Well, too bad for you, I thought. When I came around the chair I saw he had her legs in stirrups. 'They're impacted,' he said.

The whole business with Dr Freedman had made me crazy. They were always talking on the phone and laughing and having appointments every day. In my mind, I saw them together, passing the rubber tube of the nitrous tank back and forth. I saw her legs hung over the arms of the chair with Freedman crouched down at the yummy end of things. 'Hope you don't mind the drill,' he'd say, and think he was so funny because she'd laugh and wrap her arms around his neck, pulling him up into her.

I started following her, listening in to her phone calls on the other line. But I was a bad spy. I kept getting caught. 'I know you're there, Mike,' she'd say on the phone, talking to one of her girlfriends about a beauty makeover in a magazine. 'I hear you breathing.' And I'd hang up and sit on my hands on the bed. Once she tapped on my car window in the parking lot of the Price Chopper, where I'd fallen asleep watching her shop. 'Relationships have to be based on trust, Mike,' she yelled through the glass, 'or there's *no* relationship.' She was getting nasty. She snapped at me all the time. I couldn't do anything right.

One night she stormed out of the house on the crutches she had to use now that her legs had gone so stiff. She said she and Dr Freedman were going to the symphony.

'The symphony?' I said, from the front stoop.

'Yes,' she hissed back. 'The symphony.'

'What for?' I said.

'For culture,' she growled, right up in my face, three little canines on the end of her pointed chin. 'You and me, Mike, we have no culture.'

That was the night I tried to be with another woman. Robin was a waitress at the Mug who always wanted to get together with me when I only wanted Helen. We went back to her apartment, but I didn't like touching her. She felt too soft and squishy. I missed Helen's rough spots, her premolars and molars, her pointy canines and wisdoms, the soft areas next to the hard areas. I missed being inside Helen and the challenge of going around the sharp places. Robin felt like Silly Putty, like I could stretch and bend her and tie her up with herself.

I apologized to Robin and got up to go. When we were putting our clothes back on, she said there were doctors who could help me with my problem. She said this in a mean way, not in a helpful way.

Helen was in bed when I got home, the sheet pushed down to her waist. In the cool streetlight that shone through the window, I could see the phosphorescent glow of the thick clumps of teeth that stuck all over her back like barnacles. I shucked off my clothes and slid in next to her. We slept on satin sheets, not because they're sexy but because satin was the only material that didn't catch on the teeth that covered most of her body now. She perched herself up on her elbows and waited for me to talk.

'I want things back the way they were,' I said. 'I miss us.'

In the morning we went to Dr Freedman's and Helen told him to pull the teeth. All of them. I expected him to tell me I was a hateful son-of-a-bitch, but he nodded professionally and spread out his tools. He offered gas, Novocain, a sedative. Helen waved him off. He started with the molars on her rib cage. He used tweezers to pluck out the little teeth on her face and pliers for the bigger molars across her collarbone. He yanked, twisted, and pulled and went on to the next. But something bad oozed out of those holes where the teeth had been, not the red blood that inevitably flows after a pulled tooth. This blood was black-red, the kind of blood that comes from deep inside you and doesn't want to be disturbed. Helen let out a low, sorrowful moan.

'Stop,' I said finally. 'No more.'

I took her to the beach. She wanted to smell the salt and feel the air, let the sounds of gulls and waves lull her to sleep. By now her beautiful face was covered in teeth. I wrapped her in a satin quilt and put oven mitts on her hands, which had become rough and bent. I laid her brittle body against a dune, and we stayed there together like that for three days.

She said she was sorry time ran out on us and she wished we'd had kids. She apologized for going to the symphony with Dr Freedman. 'He made me feel pretty,' she said. 'I know it was wrong.'

'I always thought you were beautiful,' I said. 'I still do.'

After the second day she couldn't talk anymore because her tongue had calcified. I told her stories. I made them up out of nowhere. There was the giant turnip that crushed a big city, the eyeballs that took over the world. Her favorite was the talking stadium that fell in love with a cheerleader, got his heart broken, and then realized – too late, because he'd already caved in and killed everybody – that his real love was the hot-dog lady in one of his concession stands who had been there all along inside him.

On the third day I woke up at sunrise and saw her looking up at pelicans flying in formation over the dunes. I'd seen pelicans in the Outer Banks of North Carolina, but never this far north. They flew southeast and faded away. Helen was still looking up.

'Whatcha lookin' at, Hel?' I looked where she was looking. But there was nothing up there. Not even a cloud.

Now and then I stumble on an oasis, palm trees, blue water, and there's Helen leaning on a tree in the yellow dress she was buried in and yellow shoes, holding a banana daiquiri she made for me. I take a drink of the daiquiri, but the cold hits my brain and gives me a headache. She says, 'Poor baby, let me rub it,' and holds out smooth ivory hands. Then she slips through my arms.

Dissolves into sand. I grab at her, but the more I grab, the more sand caves in around me, and it's not until I'm buried to the waist that I realize she's gone.

A Real Doll
★ ★ ★ ★ ★ A. M. Homes

★★★★★ I'm dating Barbie. Three afternoons a week, while my sister is at dance class, I take Barbie away from Ken. I'm practicing for the future.

At first I sat in my sister's room watching Barbie, who lived with Ken, on a doily, on top of the dresser.

I was looking at her but not really looking. I was looking, and all of the sudden realized she was staring at me.

She was sitting next to Ken, his khaki-covered thigh absently rubbing her bare leg. He was rubbing her, but she was staring at me.

'Hi,' she said.

'Hello,' I said.

'I'm Barbie,' she said, and Ken stopped rubbing her leg.

'I know.'

'You're Jenny's brother.'

I nodded. My head was bobbing up and down like a puppet on a weight.

'I really like your sister. She's sweet,' Barbie said. 'Such a good little girl. Especially lately, she makes herself so pretty, and she's started doing her nails.'

I wondered if Barbie noticed that Miss Wonderful bit her nails and that when she smiled her front teeth were covered with little flecks of purple nail polish. I wondered if she knew Jennifer colored in the chipped chewed spots with purple magic marker, and then sometimes sucked on her fingers so that not only did she have purple flecks of polish on her teeth, but her tongue was the strangest shade of violet.

'So listen,' I said. 'Would you like to go out for a while? Grab some fresh air, maybe take a spin around the backyard?'

'Sure,' she said.

I picked her up by her feet. It sounds unusual but I was too petrified to take her by the waist. I grabbed her by the ankles and carried her off like a Popsicle stick.

As soon as we were out back, sitting on the porch of what I used to call my fort, but which my sister and parents referred to as the playhouse, I started freaking. I was suddenly and incredibly aware that I was out with Barbie. I didn't know what to say.

'So, what kind of a Barbie are you?' I asked.

'Excuse me?'

'Well, from listening to Jennifer I know there's Day to Night Barbie, Magic Moves Barbie, Gift-Giving Barbie, Tropical Barbie, My First Barbie, and more.'

'I'm Tropical,' she said. I'm Tropical, she said, the same way a person might say I'm Catholic or I'm Jewish. 'I came with a one-piece bathing suit, a brush, and a ruffle you can wear so many ways,' Barbie squeaked.

She actually squeaked. It turned out that squeaking was Barbie's birth defect. I pretended I didn't hear it.

We were quiet for a minute. A leaf larger than Barbie fell from the maple tree above us and I caught it just before it would have hit her. I half expected her to squeak, 'You saved my life. I'm yours, forever.' Instead she said, in a perfectly normal voice, 'Wow, big leaf.'

I looked at her. Barbie's eyes were sparkling blue like the ocean on a good day. I looked and in a moment noticed she had the whole world, the cosmos, drawn in makeup above and below her eyes. An entire galaxy, clouds, stars, a sun, the sea, painted on to her face. Yellow, blue, pink, and a million silver sparkles.

We sat looking at each other, looking and talking and then not talking and looking again. It was a stop-and-start thing with both of us constantly saying the wrong thing, saying anything, and then immediately regretting having said it.

It was obvious Barbie didn't trust me. I asked her if she wanted something to drink.

'Diet Coke,' she said. And I wondered why I'd asked.

I went into the house, upstairs into my parents' bathroom, opened the medicine cabinet, and got a couple of Valiums. I immediately swallowed one. I figured if I could be calm and collected, she'd realize I wasn't going to hurt her. I broke another Valium into a million small pieces, dropped some slivers into Barbie's Diet Coke, and swished it around so it'd blend. I figured if we could be calm and collected together, she'd be able to trust me even sooner. I was falling in love in a way that had nothing to do with love.

'So, what's the deal with you and Ken?' I asked later after we'd loosened up, after she'd drunk two Diet Cokes, and I'd made another trip to the medicine cabinet.

She giggled. 'Oh, we're just really good friends.'

'What's the deal with him really, you can tell me, I mean, is he or isn't he?'

'Ish she or ishn' she,' Barbie said, in a slow slurred way, like she was so intoxicated that if they made a Breathalizer for Valium, she'd melt it.

I regretted having fixed her a third Coke. I mean if she O.D.'ed and died Jennifer would tell my mom and dad for sure.

'Is he a faggot or what?'

Barbie laughed and I almost slapped her. She looked me straight in the eye.

'He lusts after me,' she said. 'I come home at night and he's standing there, waiting. He doesn't wear underwear, you know. I mean, isn't that strange, Ken doesn't own any underwear. I heard Jennifer tell her friend that they don't even make any for him. Anyway, he's always there waiting, and I'm like, Ken we're friends, okay, that's it. I mean, have you ever noticed, he has molded plastic hair. His head and his hair are all one piece. I can't go out with a guy like that. Besides, I don't think he'd be up for it if you know what I mean. Ken is not what you'd call well endowed . . . All he's got is a little plastic bump, more of a hump, really, and what the hell are you supposed to do with that?'

She was telling me things I didn't think I should hear and all the same, I was leaning into her, like if I moved closer she'd tell me more. I was taking every word and holding it for a minute, holding groups of words in my head like I didn't understand English. She went on and on, but I wasn't listening.

The sun sank behind the playhouse, Barbie shivered, excused herself, and ran around back to throw up. I asked her if she felt okay. She said she was fine, just a little tired, that maybe she was coming down with the flu or something. I gave her a piece of a piece of gum to chew and took her inside.

On the way back to Jennifer's room I did something Barbie almost didn't forgive me for. I did something which not only shattered the moment, but nearly wrecked the possibility of our having a future together.

In the hallway between the stairs and Jennifer's room, I popped Barbie's head into my mouth, like lion and tamer, God and Godzilla.

I popped her whole head into my mouth, and Barbie's hair separated into single strands like Christmas tinsel and caught in my throat nearly choking me. I could taste layer on layer of makeup, Revlon, Max Factor, and Maybelline. I closed my mouth around Barbie and could feel her breath in mine. I could hear her screams in my throat. Her teeth, white, Pearl Drops, Pepsodent, and the whole Osmond family, bit my tongue and the inside of my cheek like I might accidentally bite myself. I closed my mouth around her neck and held her suspended, her feet uselessly kicking the air in front of my face.

Before pulling her out, I pressed my teeth lightly into her neck, leaving marks Barbie described as scars of her assault, but which I imagined as a New Age necklace of love.

'I have never, ever in my life been treated with such utter disregard,' she said as soon as I let her out.

She was lying. I knew Jennifer sometimes did things with Barbie. I didn't mention that once I'd seen Barbie hanging from Jennifer's ceiling fan, spinning around in great wide circles, like some imitation Superman.

'I'm sorry if I scared you.'

'Scared me!' she squeaked.

She went on squeaking, a cross between the squeal when you let the air out of a balloon and a smoke alarm with weak batteries. While she was squeaking, the phrase *a head in the mouth is worth two in the bush* started running through my head. I knew it had come from somewhere, started as something else, but I couldn't get it right. *A head in the mouth is worth two in the bush*, again and again, like the punch line to some dirty joke.

'Scared me. Scared me. Scared me!' Barbie squeaked louder and louder until finally she had my attention again. 'Have you ever been held captive in the dark cavern of someone's body?'

I shook my head. It sounded wonderful.

'Typical,' she said. 'So incredibly, typically male.'

For a moment I was proud.

'Why do you have to do things you know you shouldn't, and worse, you do them with a light in your eye, like you're getting some weird pleasure that only another boy would understand. You're all the same,' she said. 'You're all Jack Nicholson.'

I refused to put her back in Jennifer's room until she forgave me, until she understood that I'd done what I did with only the truest of feeling, no harm intended.

I heard Jennifer's feet clomping up the stairs. I was running out of time.

'You know I'm really interested in you,' I said to Barbie.

'Me too,' she said, and for a minute I wasn't sure if she meant she was interested in herself or me.

'We should do this again,' I said. She nodded.

I leaned down to kiss Barbie. I could have brought her up to my lips, but somehow it felt wrong. I leaned down to kiss her and the first thing I got was her nose in my mouth. I felt like a St Bernard saying hello.

No matter how graceful I tried to be, I was forever licking her face. It wasn't a question of putting my tongue in her ear or down her throat, it was simply literally trying not to suffocate her. I kissed Barbie with my back to Ken and then turned around and put her on the doily right next to him. I was tempted to drop her down on Ken, to mash her into him, but I managed to restrain myself.

'That was fun,' Barbie said. I heard Jennifer in the hall.

'Later,' I said.

Jennifer came into the room and looked at me.

'What?' I said.

'It's my room,' she said.

'There was a bee in it. I was killing it for you.'

'A bee. I'm allergic to bees. Mom, Mom,' she screamed. 'There's a bee.'

'Mom's not home. I killed it.'

'But there might be another one.'

'So call me and I'll kill it.'

'But if it stings me I might die.' I shrugged and walked out. I could feel Barbie watching me leave.

I took a Valium about twenty minutes before I picked her up the next Friday. By the time I went into Jennifer's room, everything was getting easier.

'Hey,' I said when I got up to the dresser.

She was there on the doily with Ken, they were back to back, resting against each other, legs stretched out in front of them.

Ken didn't look at me. I didn't care.

'You ready to go?' I asked. Barbie nodded. 'I thought you might be thirsty.' I handed her the Diet Coke I'd made for her.

I'd figured Barbie could take a little less than an eighth of a Valium without getting totally senile. Basically, I had to give her Valium crumbs since there was no way to cut one that small.

She took the Coke and drank it right in front of Ken. I kept waiting for him to give me one of those I-know-what-you're-up-to-and-I-don't-like-it looks, the kind my father gives me when he walks into my room without knocking and I automatically jump twenty feet in the air.

Ken acted like he didn't even know I was there. I hated him.

'I can't do a lot of walking this afternoon,' Barbie said.

I nodded. I figured no big deal since mostly I seemed to be carrying her around anyway.

'My feet are killing me,' she said.

I was thinking about Ken.

'Don't you have other shoes?'

My family was very into shoes. No matter what seemed to be wrong my father always suggested it could be cured by wearing a different pair of shoes. He believed that shoes, like tires, should be rotated.

'It's not the shoes,' she said. 'It's my toes.'

'Did you drop something on them?' My Valium wasn't working. I was having trouble making small talk. I needed another one.

'Jennifer's been chewing on them.'

'What?'

'She chews on my toes.'

'You let her chew your footies?'

I couldn't make sense out of what she was saying. I was thinking about not being able to talk, needing another or maybe two more Valiums, yellow adult-strength Pez.

'Do you enjoy it?' I asked.

'She literally bites down on them, like I'm flank steak or something,' Barbie said. 'I wish she'd just bite them off and have it over with. This is taking forever. She's chewing and chewing, more like gnawing at me.'

'I'll make her stop. I'll buy her some gum, some tobacco or something, a pencil to chew on.'

'Please don't say anything. I wouldn't have told you except . . .' Barbie said.

'But she's hurting you.'

'It's between Jennifer and me.'

'Where's it going to stop?' I asked.

'At the arch, I hope. There's a bone there, and once she realizes she's bitten the soft part off, she'll stop.'

'How will you walk?'

'I have very long feet.'

I sat on the edge of my sister's bed, my head in my hands. My sister was biting Barbie's feet off and Barbie didn't seem to care. She didn't hold it against her and in a way I liked her for that. I liked the fact she understood how we all have little secret habits that seem normal enough to us, but which we know better than to mention out loud. I started imagining things I might be able to get away with.

'Get me out of here,' Barbie said. I slipped Barbie's shoes off. Sure enough, someone had been gnawing at her. On her left foot the toes were dangling and on the right, half had been completely taken off. There were tooth marks up to her ankles. 'Let's not dwell on this,' Barbie said.

I picked Barbie up. Ken fell over backwards and Barbie made me straighten him up before we left. 'Just because you know he only has a bump doesn't give you permission to treat him badly,' Barbie whispered.

I fixed Ken and carried Barbie down the hall to my room. I held Barbie above me, tilted my head back, and lowered her feet into my mouth. I felt like a young sword swallower practicing for my debut. I lowered Barbie's feet and legs into my mouth and then began sucking on them. They smelled like Jennifer and

153

dirt and plastic. I sucked on her stubs and she told me it felt nice.

'You're better than a hot soak,' Barbie said. I left her resting on my pillow and went downstairs to get us each a drink.

We were lying on my bed, curled into and out of each other. Barbie was on a pillow next to me and I was on my side facing her. She was talking about men, and as she talked I tried to be everything she said. She was saying she didn't like men who were afraid of themselves. I tried to be brave, to look courageous and secure. I held my head a certain way and it seemed to work. She said she didn't like men who were afraid of femininity, and I got confused.

'Guys always have to prove how boy they really are,' Barbie said.

I thought of Jennifer trying to be a girl, wearing dresses, doing her nails, putting makeup on, wearing a bra even though she wouldn't need one for about fifty years.

'You make fun of Ken because he lets himself be everything he is. He doesn't hide anything.'

'He doesn't have anything to hide,' I said. 'He has tan molded plastic hair, and a bump for a dick.'

'I never should have told you about the bump.'

I lay back on the bed. Barbie rolled over, off the pillow, and rested on my chest. Her body stretched from my nipple to my belly button. Her hands pressed against me, tickling me.

'Barbie,' I said.

'Umm Humm.'

'How do you feel about me?'

She didn't say anything for a minute. 'Don't worry about it,' she said, and slipped her hand into my shirt through the space between the buttons.

Her fingers were like the ends of toothpicks performing some subtle ancient torture, a dance of boy death across my chest. Barbie crawled all over me like an insect who'd run into one too many cans of Raid.

Underneath my clothes, under my skin, I was going crazy. First off, I'd been kidnapped by my underwear with no way to manually adjust without attracting unnecessary attention.

With Barbie caught in my shirt I slowly rolled over, like in some space shuttle docking maneuver. I rolled onto my stomach, trapping her under me. As slowly and unobtrusively as possible, I ground myself against the bed, at first hoping it would fix things and then again and again, caught by a pleasure/pain principle.

'Is this a water bed?' Barbie asked.

My hand was on her breasts, only it wasn't really my hand, but more like my index finger. I touched Barbie and she made a little gasp, a squeak in reverse. She squeaked backwards, then stopped, and I was stuck there with my hand on her, thinking about how I was forever crossing a line between the haves and the have-nots, between good guys and bad, between men and animals, and there was absolutely nothing I could do to stop myself.

Barbie was sitting on my crotch, her legs flipped back behind her in a position that wasn't human.

At a certain point I had to free myself. If my dick was blue, it was only because it had suffocated. I did the honors and Richard popped out like an escape from maximum security.

'I've never seen anything so big,' Barbie said. It was the sentence I dreamed of, but given the people Barbie normally hung out with, namely the bump boy himself, it didn't come as a big surprise.

She stood at the base of my dick, her bare feet buried in my pubic hair. I was almost as tall as she was. Okay, not almost as tall, but clearly we could be related. She and Richard even had the same vaguely surprised look on their faces.

She was on me and I couldn't help wanting to get inside her. I turned Barbie over and was on top of her, not caring if I killed her. Her hands pressed so hard into my stomach that it felt like she was performing an appendectomy.

I was on top, trying to get between her legs, almost breaking her in half. But there was nothing there, nothing to fuck except a small thin line that was supposed to be her ass crack.

I rubbed the thin line, the back of her legs and the space between her legs. I turned Barbie's back to me so I could do it without having to look at her face.

Very quickly, I came. I came all over Barbie, all over her and a little bit in her hair. I came on Barbie and it was the most horrifying experience I ever had. It didn't stay on her. It doesn't stick to plastic. I was finished. I was holding a come-covered Barbie in my hand like I didn't know where she came from.

Barbie said, 'Don't stop,' or maybe I just think she said that because I read it somewhere. I don't know anymore. I couldn't listen to her. I couldn't even look at her. I wiped myself off with a sock, pulled my clothes on, and then took Barbie into the bathroom.

At dinner I noticed Jennifer chewing her cuticles between bites of tuna-noodle casserole. I asked her if she was teething. She coughed and then started choking to death on either a little piece of fingernail, a crushed potato chip from the casserole, or maybe even a little bit of Barbie footie that'd stuck in her teeth. My mother asked her if she was okay.

'I swallowed something sharp,' she said between coughs that were clearly influenced by the acting class she'd taken over the summer.

'Do you have a problem?' I asked her.

'Leave your sister alone,' my mother said.

'If there are any questions to ask we'll do the asking,' my father said.

'Is everything all right?' my mother asked Jennifer. She nodded. 'I think you could use some new jeans,' my mother said. 'You don't seem to have many play clothes anymore.'

'Not to change the subject,' I said, trying to think of a way to stop Jennifer from eating Barbie alive.

'I don't wear pants,' Jennifer said. 'Boys wear pants.'

'Your grandma wears pants,' my father said.

'She's not a girl.'

My father chuckled. He actually fucking chuckled. He's the only person I ever met who could actually fucking chuckle.

'Don't tell her that,' he said, chuckling.

'It's not funny,' I said.

'Grandma's are pull-ons anyway,' Jennifer said. 'They don't have a fly. You have to have a penis to have a fly.'

'Jennifer,' my mother said. 'That's enough of that.'

I decided to buy Barbie a present. I was at that strange point where I would have done anything for her. I took two buses and walked more than a mile to get to Toys R Us.

Barbie row was aisle 14C. I was a wreck. I imagined a million Barbies and having to have them all. I pictured fucking one, discarding it, immediately grabbing a fresh one, doing it, and then throwing it onto a growing pile in the corner of my room. An unending chore. I saw myself becoming a slave to Barbie. I wondered how many Tropical Barbies were made each year. I felt faint.

There were rows and rows of Kens, Barbies, and Skippers. Funtime Barbie, Jewel Secrets Ken, Barbie Rocker with 'Hot Rockin' Fun and Real Dancin' Action.' I noticed Magic Moves Barbie, and found myself looking at her carefully, flirtatiously, wondering if her legs were spreadable. 'Push the switch and she moves,' her box said. She winked at me while I was reading.

The only Tropical I saw was a black Tropical Ken. From just looking at him you wouldn't have known he was black. I mean, he wasn't black like anyone would be black. Black Tropical Ken was the color of a raisin, a raisin all spread out and unwrinkled. He had a short afro that looked like a wig had been dropped down and fixed on his head, a protective helmet. I wondered if black Ken was really white Ken sprayed over with a thick coating of ironed raisin plastic.

I spread eight black Kens out in a line across the front of a row. Through the plastic window of his box he told me he was hoping to go to dental school. All eight black Kens talked at once. Luckily, they all said the same thing at the same time. They said he really liked teeth. Black Ken smiled. He had the same white Pearl Drops, Pepsodent, Osmond family teeth that Barbie and white Ken had. I thought the entire Mattel family must take really good care of themselves. I figured they might be the only people left in America who actually brushed after every meal and then again before going to sleep.

I didn't know what to get Barbie. Black Ken said I should go for clothing, maybe a fur coat. I wanted something really special. I imagined a wonderful present that would draw us somehow closer.

There was a tropical pool and patio set, but I decided it might make her homesick. There was a complete winter holiday, with an A-frame house, fireplace, snowmobile, and sled. I imagined her inviting Ken away for a weekend without me. The six o'clock news set was nice, but because of her squeak, Barbie's future as an anchorwoman seemed limited. A workout center, a sofa bed and coffee table, a bubbling spa, a bedroom play set. I settled on the grand piano. It was $13.00. I'd always made it a point to never spend more than ten dollars on anyone. This time I figured, what the hell, you don't buy a grand piano every day.

'Wrap it up, would ya,' I said at the checkout desk.

From my bedroom window I could see Jennifer in the backyard, wearing her tutu and leaping all over the place. It was dangerous as hell to sneak in and get Barbie, but I couldn't keep a grand piano in my closet without telling someone.

'You must really like me,' Barbie said when she finally had the piano unwrapped.

I nodded. She was wearing a ski suit and skis. It was the end of August and eighty degrees out. Immediately, she sat down and played 'Chopsticks.'

I looked out at Jennifer. She was running down the length of the deck, jumping onto the railing and then leaping off, posing like one of those red flying horses you see on old Mobil gas signs. I watched her do it once and then the second time, her foot caught on the railing, and she went over the edge the hard way. A minute later she came around the edge of the house, limping, her tutu dented and dirty, pink tights ripped at both knees. I grabbed Barbie from the piano bench and raced her into Jennifer's room.

'I was just getting warmed up,' she said. 'I can play better than that, really.'

I could hear Jennifer crying as she walked up the stairs.

'Jennifer's coming,' I said. I put her down on the dresser and realized Ken was missing.

'Where's Ken?' I asked quickly.

'Out with Jennifer,' Barbie said.

I met Jennifer at her door. 'Are you okay?' I asked. She cried harder. 'I saw you fall.'

'Why didn't you stop me?' she said.

'From falling?'

She nodded and showed me her knees.

'Once you start to fall no one can stop you.' I noticed Ken was tucked into the waistband of her tutu.

'They catch you,' Jennifer said.

I started to tell her it was dangerous to go leaping around with a Ken stuck in your waistband, but you don't tell someone who's already crying that they did something bad.

I walked her into the bathroom, and took out the hydrogen peroxide. I was a first aid expert. I was the kind of guy who walked around, waiting for someone to have a heart attack just so I could practice my CPR technique.

'Sit down,' I said.

Jennifer sat down on the toilet without putting the lid down. Ken was stabbing her all over the place and instead of pulling him out, she squirmed around trying to get comfortable like she didn't know what else to do. I took him out for her. She watched as though I was performing surgery or something.

'He's mine,' she said.

'Take off your tights,' I said.

'No,' she said.

'They're ruined,' I said. 'Take them off.'

Jennifer took off her ballet slippers and peeled off her tights. She was wearing my old Underoos with superheroes on them, Spiderman and Superman and Batman all poking out from under a dirty dented tutu. I decided not to say anything, but it looked funny as hell to see a flat crotch in boys' underwear. I had the feeling they didn't bother making underwear for Ken because they knew it looked too weird on him.

I poured peroxide onto her bloody knees. Jennifer screamed into my ear. She bent down and examined herself, poking her purple fingers into the torn skin; her tutu bunched up and rubbed against her face, scraping it. I worked on her knees, removing little pebbles and pieces of grass from the area.

She started crying again.

'You're okay,' I said. 'You're not dying.' She didn't care. 'Do you want anything?' I asked, trying to be nice.

'Barbie,' she said.

It was the first time I'd handled Barbie in public. I picked her up like she was a complete stranger and handed her to Jennifer, who grabbed her by the hair. I started to tell her to ease up, but couldn't. Barbie looked at me and I shrugged. I went downstairs and made Jennifer one of my special Diet Cokes.

'Drink this,' I said, handing it to her. She took four giant gulps and immediately I felt guilty about having used a whole Valium.

'Why don't you give a little to your Barbie,' I said. 'I'm sure she's thirsty too.'

Barbie winked at me and I could have killed her, first off for doing it in front of Jennifer, and second because she didn't know what the hell she was winking about.

I went into my room and put the piano away. I figured as long as I kept it in the original box I'd be safe. If anyone found it, I'd say it was a present for Jennifer.

Wednesday Ken and Barbie had their heads switched. I went to get Barbie, and there on top of the dresser were Barbie and Ken, sort of. Barbie's head was on Ken's body and Ken's head was on Barbie. At first I thought it was just me.

'Hi,' Barbie's head said.

I couldn't respond. She was on Ken's body and I was looking at Ken in a whole new way.

I picked up the Barbie head/Ken and immediately Barbie's head rolled off. It rolled across the dresser, across the white doily past Jennifer's collection of miniature ceramic cats, and *boom* it fell to the floor. I saw Barbie's head rolling and about to fall, and then falling, but there was nothing I could do to stop it. I was frozen, paralyzed with Ken's headless body in my left hand.

Barbie's head was on the floor, her hair spread out underneath it like angel wings in the snow, and I expected to see blood, a wide rich pool of blood, or at least a little bit coming out of her ear, her nose, or her mouth. I looked at her head on the floor and saw nothing but Barbie with eyes like the cosmos looking up at me. I thought she was dead.

'Christ, that hurt,' she said. 'And I already had a headache from these earrings.'

There were little red dot/ball earrings jutting out of Barbie's ears.

'They go right through my head, you know. I guess it takes getting used to,' Barbie said.

I noticed my mother's pin cushion on the dresser next to the other Barbie/Ken, the Barbie body, Ken head. The pin cushion was filled with hundreds of pins, pins with flat silver ends and pins with red, yellow, and blue dot/ball ends.

'You have pins in your head,' I said to the Barbie head on the floor.

'Is that supposed to be a compliment?'

I was starting to hate her. I was being perfectly clear and she didn't understand me.

I looked at Ken. He was in my left hand, my fist wrapped around his waist. I looked at him and realized my thumb was on his bump. My thumb was pressed against Ken's crotch and as soon as I noticed I got an automatic hard-on, the kind you don't know you're getting, it's just there. I started rubbing Ken's bump and watching my thumb like it was a large-screen projection of a porno movie.

'What are you doing?' Barbie's head said. 'Get me up. Help me.' I was rubbing Ken's bump/hump with my finger inside his bathing suit. I was standing in the middle of my sister's room, with my pants pulled down.

'Aren't you going to help me?' Barbie kept asking. 'Aren't you going to help me?'

In the second before I came, I held Ken's head hole in front of me. I held Ken upside down above my dick and came inside of Ken like I never could in Barbie.

I came into Ken's body and as soon as I was done I wanted to do it again. I wanted to fill Ken and put his head back on, like a perfume bottle. I wanted Ken to be the vessel for my secret supply. I came in Ken and then I remembered he wasn't mine. He didn't belong to me. I took him into the bathroom and soaked him in warm water and Ivory liquid. I brushed his insides with

Jennifer's toothbrush and left him alone in a cold-water rinse.

'Aren't you going to help me, aren't you?' Barbie kept asking.

I started thinking she'd been brain damaged by the accident. I picked her head up from the floor.

'What took you so long?' she asked.

'I had to take care of Ken.'

'Is he okay?'

'He'll be fine. He's soaking in the bathroom.' I held Barbie's head in my hand.

'What are you going to do?'

'What do you mean?' I said.

Did my little incident, my moment with Ken, mean that right then and there some decision about my future life as queerbait had to be made?

'This afternoon. Where are we going? What are we doing? I miss you when I don't see you,' Barbie said.

'You see me every day,' I said.

'I don't really see you. I sit on top of the dresser and if you pass by, I see you. Take me to your room.'

'I have to bring Ken's body back.'

I went into the bathroom, rinsed out Ken, blew him dry with my mother's blow dryer, then played with him again. It was a boy thing, we were boys together. I thought sometime I might play ball with him, I might take him out instead of Barbie.

'Everything takes you so long,' Barbie said when I got back into the room.

I put Ken back up on the dresser, picked up Barbie's body, knocked Ken's head off, and smashed Barbie's head back down on her own damn neck.

'I don't want to fight with you,' Barbie said as I carried her into my room. 'We don't have enough time together to fight. Fuck me,' she said.

I didn't feel like it. I was thinking about fucking Ken and Ken being a boy. I was thinking about Barbie and Barbie being a girl. I was thinking about Jennifer, switching Barbie and Ken's heads, chewing Barbie's feet off, hanging Barbie from the ceiling fan, and who knows what else.

'Fuck me,' Barbie said again.

I ripped Barbie's clothing off. Between Barbie's legs Jennifer had drawn pubic hair in reverse. She'd drawn it upside down so it looked like a fountain spewing up and out in great wide arcs. I spit directly onto Barbie and with my thumb and first finger rubbed the ink lines, erasing them. Barbie moaned.

'Why do you let her do this to you?'

'Jennifer owns me,' Barbie moaned.

Jennifer owns me, she said, so easily and with pleasure. I was totally jealous. Jennifer owned Barbie and it made me crazy. Obviously it was one of those relationships that could only exist between women. Jennifer could own her because it didn't matter that Jennifer owned her. Jennifer didn't want Barbie, she had her.

'You're perfect,' I said.

'I'm getting fat,' Barbie said.

Barbie was crawling all over me, and I wondered if Jennifer knew she was a nymphomaniac. I wondered if Jennifer knew what a nymphomaniac was.

'You don't belong with little girls,' I said.

Barbie ignored me.

There were scratches on Barbie's chest and stomach. She didn't say anything about them and so at first I pretended not to notice. As I was touching her, I could feel they were deep, like slices.

The edges were rough; my finger caught on them and I couldn't help but wonder.

'Jennifer?' I said, massaging the cuts with my tongue, as though my tongue, like sandpaper, would erase them. Barbie nodded.

In fact, I thought of using sandpaper, but didn't know how I would explain it to Barbie: *you have to lie still and let me rub it really hard with this stuff that's like terry-cloth dipped in cement.* I thought she might even like it if I made it into an S&M kind of thing and handcuffed her first.

I ran my tongue back and forth over the slivers, back and forth over the words 'copyright 1966 Mattel Inc., Malaysia' tattooed on her back. Tonguing the tattoo drove Barbie crazy. She said it had something to do with scar tissue being extremely sensitive.

Barbie pushed herself hard against me, I could feel her slices rubbing my skin. I was thinking that Jennifer might kill Barbie. Without meaning to she might just go over the line and I wondered if Barbie would know what was happening or if she'd try to stop her.

We fucked, that's what I called it, fucking. In the beginning Barbie said she hated the word, which made me like it even more. She hated it because it was so strong and hard, and she said we weren't fucking, we were making love. I told her she had to be kidding.

'Fuck me,' she said that afternoon and I knew the end was coming soon. 'Fuck me,' she said. I didn't like the sound of the word.

Friday when I went into Jennifer's room, there was something in the air. The place smelled like a science lab, a fire, a failed experiment.

Barbie was wearing a strapless yellow evening dress. Her hair was wrapped into a high bun, more like a wedding cake than something Betty Crocker would whip up. There seemed to be layers and layers of angel's hair spinning in a circle above her head. She had yellow pins through her ears and gold fuck-me shoes that matched the belt around her waist. For a second I thought of the belt and imagined tying her up, but more than restraining her arms or legs, I thought of wrapping the belt around her face, tying it across her mouth.

I looked at Barbie and saw something dark and thick like a scar rising up and over the edge of her dress. I grabbed her and pulled the front of the dress down.

'Hey big boy,' Barbie said. 'Don't I even get a hello?'

Barbie's breasts had been sawed at with a knife. There were a hundred marks from a blade that might have had five rows of teeth like shark jaws. And as if that wasn't enough, she'd been dissolved by fire, blue and yellow flames had been pressed against her and held there until she melted and eventually became the fire that burned herself. All of it had been somehow stirred with the lead of a pencil, the point of a pen, and left to cool. Molten Barbie flesh had been left to harden, black and pink plastic swirled together, in the crater Jennifer had dug out of her breasts.

I examined her in detail like a scientist, a pathologist, a fucking medical examiner. I studied the burns, the gouged-out area, as if by looking closely I'd find something, an explanation, a way out.

A disgusting taste came up into my mouth, like I'd been sucking on batteries. It came up, then sank back down into my stomach, leaving my mouth puckered with the bitter metallic flavor of sour saliva. I coughed and spit onto my shirt sleeve, then rolled the sleeve over to cover the wet spot.

With my index finger I touched the edge of the burn as lightly as I could. The round rim of her scar broke off under my finger. I almost dropped her.

'It's just a reduction,' Barbie said. 'Jennifer and I are even now.'

Barbie was smiling. She had the same expression on her face as when I first saw her and fell in love. She had the same expression she always had and I couldn't stand it. She was smiling, and she was burned. She was smiling, and she was ruined. I pulled her dress back up, above the scarline. I put her down carefully on the doily on top of the dresser and started to walk away.

'Hey,' Barbie said, 'aren't we going to play?'

Sleep

★ ★ ★ ★ ★ Shelley Jackson

★ ★ ★ ★ ★ Sleep is falling. The crumbs run in drifts down the street, collect in the gutters.

Sleep falls every day at noon here, with soothing regularity. Sometimes it melts on the way down, and falls as golden rain, or in cold weather, golden sleet, but mostly our siesta is warm and dry. The occasional sleepstorm is cozy and harmless: a war waged with croutons and dinner rolls. Once, years ago, when the children were young, we woke to find we were slept in: I opened the front door and the living room filled with gold. We had a sleepball fight around the sofa, which my wife won – she was always fierce in defense of her own. The drifts blew away by evening, but our house was gilded until the next rain, and the shrubs were like torches!

Where we live, the skies are heavy with sleep. Sometimes high-flying jets come down encrusted with it, like bees dusted with pollen. Fielded by Midas and thrown home, how beautiful these shining apparitions are. They roll unsteadily to a stop, transformed into fairy-tale coaches. A crack opens, a patch of golden coral swings aside, stairs descend, and then the baffled pilot emerges like a new Aphrodite from a peculiar Edenic shell.

Permanent banks and shoals of sleep drowse above us. They can be thick enough, it is whispered, to slow a plane to a standstill and hold it fast above the earth. Some planes disappear and are never found. Some fall to earth, but no human remains are discovered in the wreckage. Many years ago, a pilot landed a plane alone, and insisted forever after that everyone else got out *above*, forced open the emergency exits in mid-flight and stepped out into a landscape of gilt towers and archways.

Sleep sometimes coagulates in the shapes of animals: bruin and bunny are the most common, though I have seen sheep and cows as well. These form naturally, like snowflakes. Under favorable conditions these sleep-sheep 'stalk the earth,' the colloquial term for wafting or 'mere wafting,' as O'Sullivan pointedly calls it, eschewing what he calls the 'credulous jargon of simpletons and charlatans.' He is practically alone in his refusal to see familiar forms in sleep, of course. Animalcules take shape in every substance known to us; it is a tendency written into the very structure of matter, a statistically significant swerve towards animaloid structures, especially cute ones. The universe, we now know, is far from that chill mechanical model so unaccountably adored by physicists past. The world that gave rise to feathers, pill-bugs, cookies and whales is silly, showy, comfy. Above all, it is kind.

O'Sullivan and his humorless cronies are just the latest incarnation of our abstemious church fathers, who held it a sin to sink into the friendly pillowing of sleep, in which every living thing delights. Sleep, they taught, is the dross of souls rejected by God, who chews us up en masse, strains the juices through his baleen, and spits out the crud. 'The damned will stay in hell as broth and yeast,' says Luther. Sleep is that broth, that yeast.

Of course, sleep is literally both broth (add water) and yeast: a few grains of it scattered over warm, honey fattened water will bewitch bread into a fantasia of dough turrets, minarets, grottos, candelabras and credenzas, now sadly out of culinary fashion, but still traditional at Sleepmastide. Its flavor is unremarkable, though children love it, but I find it has a mild intoxicating effect, albeit short-lived. The taste is reminiscent of cardamom, with an incongruous hint of spearmint. A few grains on the tongue will calm a fretful baby; cooked up and injected, its effects are stronger but still mellow, hence its reputation as a drug for hippies and beginners, though it is probably more frequently taken by users of all descriptions than this reputation would suggest.

Exotic varieties of sleep, named for the region in which they're gathered, are popularly believed to have special qualities, though scientists say there is no significant difference between these and our domestic sleep. My private investigations (the wayward probings of a curious mind) have brought me to the same conclusion. These rare strains of sleep are some countries' biggest cash crop, so their governments turn a blind eye to the traffic, and are not very hospitable to foreign scientists who want to test on-site the exaggerated claims that circulate about the properties of the sleep when fresh.

There are gnostic teachings of another sleep, the opposite in every respect of our sunny everyday sleep. One reads of a dark, greasy, subterranean sleep, which seeps out of solid rock and hardens into strange fungal forms, and plugs underground rivers with a glassy but flexible mass that can be reliquified by one blow of a pickaxe. Miners have staggered out of shafts and told tales of slow-motion tsunamis of sour treacle. Do not sample this sleep, they say; it will spoil your appetite for every other thing. Nevertheless, I cannot help wishing that someday I will be given a chance to taste it. I love sleep, I confess, and as I watch the grains fall slowly outside the window, I think how lucky we are. Into our difficult lives this surplus falls. This gift.

I have not mentioned the greatest consolation sleep grants us. At the proper time and with the proper ceremonies, you may make yourself a substitute out of sleep. How to do it must be writ in our genes. I watched my children miming it in sandboxes; like birds building nests, they needed no tutors. You may fail at every other endeavor, but you will not fail at this one. Even the clumsiest become deft and knowing as they pat and roll the golden column, persuading it into human form.

This substitute or scapegoat is legally empowered to act as a person in your stead. Your substitute can vote for you, take a test or a beating, deliver a public speech, perform the marital duties, or commit suicide for you. Politicians are all substitutes, as are firemen, astronauts, and most people forced to make public apologies, but substitutes are often made for sadder, more personal reasons. I have watched friends grow ever more restless and unhappy, until one day the complaining stops, and I know they have gone to start a new life and left this diplomat behind. We say they are 'dreaming.' I am happy for them in their bright new world.

My children are already dreaming. So young! At their age I kept telling myself, *A better time will come. I can endure this moment.* And when the next moment came, I found I could endure that one too, and so on, to this day. But I don't think less of them for making their escape. We are all waiting for our chance. Out of care and duty leaps the shocking blossom of the new: vibrant, imperious, reeking of pollen. It is a subpoena, a lure, a gauntlet. If we are honest and brave we have little choice: we kick over our happy home and go. We step out of the airplane onto a golden cloud.

It is a terrible thing when it is the substitute that is sent to find a new life, a sign that a person yearns for change but cannot imagine creating it herself. The irony is that her failure of imagination marks her proxy too. When you see someone creeping through life, as if everything in the world were new, yes, but in its newness an assault, she is sure to be one of these.

An action is in the works to protect the rights of substitutes. It is bound to fail, because the substitutes themselves show no interest in it; the meetings of the Substitute's Union are all attended by solicitous originals who – in an odd reversal – are empowered to vote for their substitutes! These good-hearted citizens betray a basic confusion about the existential condition of the substitutes. If scapegoats feel pain, it is only the delegated pain of their originals.

Use your substitute well: you will not get another. If you use it too early – to feign a teen suicide, maybe, or escape the school bully – you must live out your own life from then on, and that is a hard, lonely prospect. People who use their substitutes frivolously find that they have given all their frivolity away, and are compelled to be serious characters from then on, while their substitute dutifully practises dissolution.

Eventually, of course, the substitute has suffered enough knocks that it no longer looks quite human. Dents alter the form little by little; scratches expose the waxy interior.

It is the originals' responsibility to lay their substitutes to rest when this time comes, but not surprisingly, they often fail to take this in hand. (Those battered pawns we've all seen staggering around are a civic disgrace.) When the original is ill or badly hurt, on the other hand, the substitute's pupils turn white, while if the original should die, the substitute falls in its tracks and turns to sleep again, sifting out of the sleeves and collar. This can be a brutal shock to family members who did not know their loved one was a substitute.

If an enterprising person is standing by, this sleep can be patted together again; it is the only time a person can make a second substitute. These secondary substitutes, lit as it were on the embers of the one before, have certain specific defects that do not vary: they cannot enunciate the consonants *d* or *t*, they cannot create nested sentence structures, they are color-blind, and they have recurring nightmares of spiral forms and infinitely mounting abstract quantities.

No substitutes can have children, of course, although they make kind, responsible parents. A substitute wife can become 'pregnant' and in due course deliver a waxy figurine, but this baby will not move or cry, since it has no original and is not a true substitute.

There is a mystical tradition that if two substitutes fall in love (true love must be specified, for many marriages are made up of a pair of substitutes, in fact nothing is more common), their child has a fifty-fifty chance of being an original. If such a child is born, and reality thus springs from the loins of artifice, then all people will fall to their knees before it. It will be the living god, and this can be proved by conjuring it to make a substitute for itself. The sleep will fall apart in the child's hands: the real Original can have no substitutes.

Last night I lay awake, and in one of the thousand insomniac hours before dawn I switched on a lamp. A fine scar on my wife's eyelid caught the light and gleamed like a gold thread. I turned back the sheets, I examined her entire body, and I found incontrovertible proof. My wife is a substitute. As I got out of bed, she mumbled something and reached for me. I touched her hand and saw her smile into the pillow.

I am not shocked. Is that dreadful? She could not endure the demands of our love and she left. I understand this as I have understood other surprises she has given me in the past. I feel lonely, and yet in a curious sense there is something right about this. I have spent my life in adoration of sleep. I may have loved it better – more carefully, more knowledgeably – than I've loved the people in my life. Its beauty, its mystery. The evidence it bears of a universe capable of mercy. Now when I say, I love sleep, I can also say, I love nothing else. Everything I love is made of it.

The sleep is falling steadily. I could go out and gather it. I could pat it together. My hands would know what to do. I used to be a pilot, did I mention that? I would like to make one more flight. This time I would not let my chance go by.

I could leave my life. I could change completely. Is it time?

The First Men

★ ★ ★ ★ ★ Stacey Richter

★ ★ ★ ★ ★ I'm riding up an escalator with Roxy explaining how she's the worst mother in the world. Some of my students, I say, have really bad mothers, but she takes the cake. Roxy, who's a real cunt, says something along the lines of 'you ungrateful whore' and storms off to Ship 'n' Shore, which is retailese for Fat and Ugly.

I go to the Ladies' Lounge and vomit then proceed to Lingerie to buy a couple of push-up bras on credit. Look, it isn't my fault that Teddy drinks too much, okay? I just want to say that. EVERYBODY ACTS LIKE EVERYTHING IS MY FAULT AND IT ISN'T MY FAULT. I hate it, hate it, hate it. And I wanted that perfume, that's why I lifted it. What do you want me to say? That it's a disease? I have news for you, baby. Greed is not a disease.

A little later, an ugly clerk at the Sunglass Hut is explaining why these three-hundred-dollar glasses are ultimately *me* when Roxy swoops past with her nose in the air, jingling her car keys so I'll notice she's leaving without me. She wants me to run after her, but I'm not going to give her the satisfaction – I mean, is this any way to treat your own daughter? I'm stranded with no nutritional options but corn dogs, frozen yogurt, and the giant cinnamon buns that stink up all the stores west of The Gap. I've maxed out most of my cards. I am not drunk, I haven't scored in several days, nor have I been laid. I'm considering trying to go easy on drugs because of the children. Think of the children! That's what Roxy says, but give me one good reason why I should listen to her.

Besides, I do think of the children. Right now I'm thinking of Roger Wells, everyone calls him Pig Pen – cute. He's in my third period Health Ed class, and he sells me downers at a reduced rate in exchange for a guaranteed B+. This was a good deal for everyone until Pig Pen started skipping class entirely. How am I going to buy drugs when he won't fucking come to class? 'It's no big deal, Miss Roberts. Whatever you say, Miss Roberts.' That kid is a liar and a degenerate – B+ or not, I'm filling in the negative comment bubbles with a number two pencil on that one. I am TRYING to teach a unit on reproduction, very touchy vis-à-vis the school board, the PTA, the textbook company, and there are only so many things I'm authorized to say according to state law. I keep repeating *abstinence, abstinence* when Pig Pen slinks in late and tosses a note on my desk that says I owe him big money. Through the window, I get a peek at his drones circling. This kid is a really bad kid.

You want to know how they get that bad? Some are born bad. Some of them have bad parents. Some of them watch too much MTV and it spoils them. You can spot the ones that have been corrupted by heavy metal music from the slogans on their T-shirts and their constant, vulture-like slouch. Some of them have been in accidents and received blows to the head. When they wake up, they're bad. Pig Pen may have been bad due to any of these influences, or he may have gone bad during a gym class trauma – getting picked last for a year, pantsing, taunts concerning penis size. It's been known to happen. One day they're little boys and girls, and the next they're criminals and drug addicts.

After the bell rings I tell Pig Pen I need a few days to get the money together, and would he please get me some more of those good downers? For a while he had a pharmaceutical source and could obtain the best, best shit, and when I looked at him I swear I almost started to drool. Pig Pen said Okay, Miss Roberts.

God's honest truth, I was going to pay the kid. Good, bad, I didn't care, he had what I needed. Unfortunately I had to go and drop in on Roxy and have my entire head screwed up, a task that took her about twenty minutes. She's sitting in her kitchen, in a warm-up suit patterned after the British flag, trying to make me eat a pound cake. She's accusing me of having an eating disorder and keeps saying, 'Let me look in your mouth, let me look in your mouth,' as though I'm a farm animal she's thinking of buying. Then she puts a slice of cake with whipped cream and strawberries in syrup in front of me – a sort of witch test. If I don't eat it, I'm mentally sick. If I do, I'll turn into a fat slug like her.

I pick up the fork. Roxy informs me that I am a heathen, and that I have picked up the wrong fork. I pick up another fork. She sighs and wedges her lumpy hips more firmly in her chair, but after thirty-two years of this I'm certain that this fork is the one. I cut the cake into bite-sized pieces. I consume it daintily. I wait until she's running the insinkerator before I duck into the bathroom to vomit.

After that, she starts whining that we never go anywhere together so we make a date to go to the mall on Saturday. My friend Wanda won't talk to me anymore, but when she did, she used to say WHY DO YOU SPEND SO MUCH TIME WITH THAT WOMAN IF SHE DRIVES YOU CRAZY? But what she doesn't understand is that Roxy has accused me of taking her boyfriend Teddy out drinking when the truth is Teddy is an alcoholic and doesn't need anyone to 'help' him drink. We went to the Golden Nugget once or twice, but HE called ME and asked for a ride. Shit. Do you want to know why I'm bad? My mother made me this way.

The upshot is that after the cake incident I was so stressed out I went to Rossingham's and bought four gold chains and a cubic zirconia tennis bracelet with instant credit and a small down payment. I have Roxy to thank for this little spree. The next thing I know it's already Saturday and I'm broke, stranded at the mall, pausing in the food court to watch captive sparrows pecking crumbs off the floor. I think the smell lures them through the automatic doors and the poor things are too stupid to figure out how to get out. Or maybe it's the greatest deal; maybe for a sparrow the mall is the lap of luxury, like living in the Hyatt for a human.

So I'm bird watching and calmly sipping my Diet Coke when I look up and who should be approaching? Not Pig Pen, thank God, but one of his worker drones, Seymour Jackson, to whom I'd given a D the year before in biology. Seymour Jackson is a big white kid with a military crew-cut and arms that reach almost to his knees. He has the deadened, blank face of a jock but Seymour is not a jock because he's a bad boy and a drug dealer who smokes cigarettes incessantly. In class, he'd chew tobacco and spit into a Big Gulp cup that he liked to balance on the edge of my desk on his way out. Those of Seymour's peers not too frightened to refer to Seymour at all refer to Seymour as 'Action.'

The way it goes for high school teachers these days is you generally don't want to chitchat with kids you've given a D, particularly strapping lads who work for an organization to whom you owe money for narcotics. Nevertheless, Action Jackson comes right up to me and looks at me – just looks. Very mean. Very tall.

'Miss Roberts?' He seems confused.

'What can I do for you, Seymour?'

'You're at the mall?'

Let me tell you a little bit about these kids. They're not bright. They sniff nail polish remover and drive around with handguns tucked under their registration slips. They wear sunglasses in the rain and get gum stuck in their braces. In my class they think it's really funny to act like retarded mental idiots when I call on them. There are no class clowns anymore – the youth of today are too dimwitted for wisecracking. When I see the instructions 'shake and pour' on a carton of orange juice I think Thank God, because these kids are in desperate need of instruction. So I say to Action, enunciating clearly: 'Yes, Seymour. I *am* at the mall.'

He's drumming his hands on his stomach, rolling his head around in a weak imitation of Stevie Wonder. Teenage boys, Jesus Christ. They can't hold still for a second and they can't look you in the eye. You can practically smell the hormones steaming from them – it's repellent, but at the same time it's a struggle not to take them home and fuck their brains out. I AM NOT referring to Brandon Murray here. Brandon Murray is a pathological liar who is 'at risk' and any charges he's made against me should be regarded as impeachable fantasy.

Then Action wants to sit down. 'Miss Roberts, Miss Roberts, can I sit here a minute?' What am I supposed to say? I am thinking this kid might have a gun in his jeans. I owe seven bills and some change to Pig Pen, which isn't all that much, considering these guys drive Camrys and carry cell phones in their backpacks, but they watch a lot of TV, a lot of movies, and they've picked up all manner of bullshit about loyalty, manhood, honor, prompt payment.

'Miss Roberts.' He tosses a pack of cigarettes on the table, then his backpack, then a clump of keys with a little pot leaf on the ring. 'That book you made me read, the one about the cavemen . . .'

'They're called Homo erectus, Seymour.'

'Homo whatever. Look, I know I didn't pay attention in class, but I keep thinking about it. The whole thing about him hunting giant tree sloths and adapting and working in groups . . .' Action's foot is going up and down as if it were electrified. It's possible he's on speed, but he's so hyper to begin with it's hard to tell. He's puffing a cigarette too, pinching the filter really hard, like he wants to prevent it from escaping. 'I keep thinking,' he says, 'about the acquisition of language.'

'Hey, Action. Do you have anything for me?'

'Like what?'

'Something powdered. Or in capsule form.'

Action drums on the tabletop. He's moving so much of his body in such a fitful manner that looking at him is like watching something under a strobe light. 'I can't do it, Miss Roberts,' he finally says. 'Pig Pen says you gotta pay up first.'

'What are you on right now? Can you get some for me?'

'Right now?'

'Yeah, right now.'

'Okay,' he says. 'Wait here.'

Action walks around to the other side of the carousel, by the booth where they sell personalized Barbie books imprinted with your child's name. It looks like he's talking on his cell phone, but I'm not sure. I'm thinking that if I manage to escape with my life, I might go to Dillard's and buy some Lancôme eye shadow in smoky gold. Also, if I manage to escape with my life as well as score some drugs, I'll buy a pound of chocolates and eat them without vomiting.

After a few minutes Seymour comes back with a Styrofoam cup in each hand. As he walks across the food court, I detect a bulge under his left arm, through his warm-up jacket. This is bad news. Seymour occasionally seems nice and vulnerable, like a kid, but the truth is he's too young to understand how dangerous he is. It's too bad Roxy ditched me, because I should have already made an exit myself.

'Here you go, Miss Roberts.' Seymour places a Styrofoam cup in front of me and tucks his long arms under the table. The cup is half full of black liquid.

'What is this?'

'Espresso. Rocket fuel of the gods.'

'That's all you've got for me?'

'Hey. It's stronger than you think.'

'Seymour, I have to go now.' I gather my bags. Action scoots his chair over to my side of the table and touches my arm – very gentle. Very soothing.

'You can't go just yet, Miss Roberts. You gotta wait awhile.'

'Why?'

'You gotta answer me about Homo erectus, okay? I read that First Man book and it was freaking me out.' He's leaning toward me, suddenly calm, patient. There's something almost paternal about him. 'I mean, it says that in monkeys, feelings go straight into the brain, right? Like an injection.'

'There's something called the limbic system, Seymour. Fear, pleasure, pain.'

'The reptile brain!'

'Sorta, right. Seymour, I have to go.'

'Wait.' His hand is on my knee, not in a sexy way, but in an anchoring one. 'Homo erectus – he added another step. Like, a filter, right?'

'More or less. Speech centers. Symbolic thinking. Like, if I say the word "cup" you can think of a generic cup, this cup on the table, whatever, and your brain sorts through the possibilities and figures out what I'm talking about. Ta-da, you've got language. You and I communicating. Understand?'

'And this is like, an amazing leap, right? That book said it took a million years.'

'Fuck, Seymour. I don't know how long it took. I wasn't there.'

Seymour's big face goes slack. He's disappointed, but what did he want me to say? I'm not even trained in science but the district is so strapped that half of us cross-teach. My field is Spanish and I'm a licensed family counselor. For some reason the district has declared I'll teach health, biology, and remedial math. I am, however, familiar with the book Seymour is referring to, *The First Men*, a title in the Time-Life series I assign as extra credit when a student is failing because it has a lot of pictures. It also happens to have been written by Edmund White, father of the gay literary renaissance and author of a great biography of Jean Genet, a bad boy if ever there was one. If he could ever learn French, I'm sure Seymour would have gotten along great with Jean Genet.

His cell phone is ringing. 'Will you please excuse me?' The

more polite Action is, the more I figure I'm in trouble. He turns
away but keeps his foot on top of my shoe – I have to pretend to
ignore this. The more I act like everything is cool, the more likely
it is that everything WILL be cool. I'm beginning to think, however, that I'm not going to score any drugs off Seymour on this
particular day.

He's on the phone saying *uh-huh, uh-huh.* The way he looks at
me with one eye, his body tense but motionless – it's giving me
a chill. It's as though every trace of the little boy has been
precipitated out of him and what remains is cool and gray. He
reminds me of a pair of stiletto heels I tried on in Dillard's. When
was that? Less than an hour ago.

'Okay,' he says, hanging up the phone. 'You're going to have
to come with me, Miss Roberts.'

'I have a lot of people waiting for me upstairs. My ex-husband.
He's a cop.'

'You're going to have to hook up with them later, Miss Roberts.
I'm really, really sorry about this.'

There's a car and then another car parked by a Dumpster. Action
nods at a pair of kids I haven't had in my class and urges me into
the back of an Econoline van, license plate PMD 525. The two
guys in front look like brothers – weak chins, slicked hair, sunken
cheeks smothered in clumps of cystic acne. Both are so thin that
their bones show through their clothes, but it's not like I could
take them. They would have weapons.

'You boys,' I ask, 'do you go to Salpointe?'

They are not saying anything to me. They are not even turning
around and acknowledging that I've spoken.

Action climbs in the back beside me and encourages me to

buckle up. I feel he wants this not for safety, but to hold me immobile.

'Hey,' I say, 'I can get some stuff for your face that'll give you the complexion of a baby – my esthetician makes it. You can't buy it in stores.'

The boy in the passenger seat twists around and fixes me with dull, sleepy eyes. His face looks like it got pinched by the forceps on the way out, and right where the tongs would have gone, there's a particularly nasty jumble of welts and pus.

'Miss Roberts,' says Action, 'would you mind keeping quiet?'

'This stuff is a miracle. If you boys hurt me, you'll throw away any chance of ever clearing up your skin.'

'Hey, Miss Roberts . . .' Action sounds pissed.

'And I know how devastating acne can be for kids your age. Okay. I'm through.'

The boys start up the van and it feels like we're driving in circles. I can't see outside because the windows are covered with aluminum foil, though I could see through the windshield if Action would scoot over. Action is on the phone again. He's calm, gliding in his movements, and I know this isn't good. He whispers something to the driver, then turns to me.

'We've gotta go see Pig Pen, okay, Miss Roberts? You've gotta give him the money now, today.'

'Give me the phone, Seymour.'

'I'm not allowed.'

'Give it to me or else you're expelled.'

'I got expelled already.'

'I can get you back in. Seymour. Are you listening to me?'

'It's not my choice, Miss Roberts. We got certain agreements between us. We use language to make agreements in order to do business. We're working together like Homo erectus did to hunt the woolly mammoths. I'm right about that, aren't I?'

'Yes, Seymour.'

'You didn't know I was smart, did you?'

'You're a very bright boy.'

'Then why'd you give me the D?'

'Because you didn't do the reading, you didn't take the tests, you didn't come to class. You left tobacco spit on my desk. Seymour, look at me.' Seymour has started to vibrate again, subtly, in the fingers and feet. 'I don't have the money.'

The van is no longer traveling in circles. We could easily be out in the desert. People die in the desert all the time – hikers, thieves, Mexicans dodging Immigration. They find them days, weeks, or years later, beneath paloverde trees, huddled in pathetic disks of shade.

'Do you want to go to the prom? I could get you back into school. Take whoever you want.'

Action scratches his ear and stares at the foil over the window. After a minute he lights up another cigarette. 'Miss Roberts,' he says, 'I gotta ask you this thing about evolution. Millions of years of things building up – fire, language, hunting, society. I mean, all those stone tools, people trying to form words and their mouths aren't big enough or something. It all builds up to what? To me, like, riding in this van, talking to you?'

'Listen, Seymour. I don't have the money.'

He looks away and pats at his hair cautiously, as though it were a toupee. 'I know that, Miss Roberts.'

'Call my mother – Roxy Ingram. She'll pay Pig Pen.'

'Pig Pen already spoke to Roxy, Miss Roberts. She said she wasn't going to pay your debts no more. She said to tell you.'

The van makes a right. After a while the ride turns bumpy and I'm almost certain we're on a dirt road. The sun pouring in the windshield is very bright. We all rock from side to side in our seats, the four of us looking very crisp, all the stains on our clothes visible, all of our wrinkles and pimples standing out in the light as though we were under a microscope, being examined for the defect that keeps our mothers from loving us.

'The thing that bothers me, though' – Action's eyes list sideways to some pensive arena – 'is what it means. You know? Man evolving from guys with big jaws and shit – is that, what, science? $x = y$ or whatever? Or is it some kind of a miracle?'

Action is a handsome kid. His skin is dewy and he works out at the gym I guess because his arms are big and he doesn't have that inchoate, half-formed look a lot of juniors have. There's something oddly beautiful about the way he can't sit still and can't complete a thought and can't finish exhaling before he inhales, and even though it's likely he'll spend most of his life in jail, and fucking deserves it, at this point in his development it seems entirely obvious that he's a wonder of creation anyway – graceful and predatory, like a shark.

'Yeah, Seymour, I think it's a miracle. I think it's a miracle and a marvel that you've evolved to the point where we can sit here discussing evolution, even as you're driving me out to the middle of nowhere to stab me or shoot me or suffocate me with a couch cushion.'

'Ha!' He sucks on his cigarette with deep satisfaction. 'I thought so. I thought I was a miracle.'

Action leans against the door so I can finally see outside. We're in the desert, clipping past saguaro and cholla, weird plants that look like freaks of evolution themselves. At least I can see the sky, rushing toward us, so blue I feel like if I took a swipe at it, pigment would come off on my hand.

'It's not just you, Seymour,' I say. 'It's me. I'm a miracle too.'

He isn't listening. He's making funny noises with his mouth that are probably meant to mimic an electric guitar. I think the song is 'Back in Black.' Also, he's playing a set of air drums and vibrating his knees, both of them, up and down with astonishing speed. I rip the foil off the window. We're moving through a valley carpeted with beautiful, thorny plants, about half of them dead. There's a different time scale in the desert; things move slowly. Saguaro don't sprout their first arms for a hundred years, and even then they're just adolescents.

The van rolls to a stop. The two boys in front twist around and look at me eagerly, like I'm suddenly going to put on a big show or something. Action opens the door and ushers me out to a place that's saved from being described as the middle of nowhere by very little – just the foundation to a house that was either never built or burned to the ground. There's a border of concrete with four steps leading up to a dirt lot – a rectangle filled with weeds and some bleached beer cans. It's an island of nothing in the middle of the desert, which is, as always, surprisingly green and filled with motion. Out here, without any people, everything seems strangely removed, like I'm looking through a veil. The wind reminds me of other times I've felt the wind. The sun could be on film. And all the different plants growing in the dirt. They all have names.

'Is he going to?' The driver says this as though I'm not there.

'Could you do me a favor, Miss Roberts?' Action, again, is smooth and steady, taking my hand as the wind blows his shirt tight against his torso. In other times he would have been the model for a Greek statue, a Roman foot soldier, a quarterback, the one who invented the spear. Even now I can see that he's in his element, gliding. Nothing, for him, is veiled. 'Could you go up there?' he says to me. 'Would you mind please climbing up those steps now?'

The wind is blowing around scrub and trash on the little platform. Up above drift thick, white clouds.

I start climbing. These boys aren't going to hurt me. These boys are good boys. These boys will let me go.

The Leading Man
★ ★ ★ ★ ★ Aimee Bender

★ ★ ★ ★ ★ The boy was born with fingers shaped like keys. All except one, the pinkie on the right hand, had sharp ridges running along the inner length, and a flat circle at the tip. They were made of flesh, with nerves and pores, but of a tougher texture, more hardened and specific. As a child, the boy had a difficult time learning to hold a pen and use scissors, but he was resilient and figured out his own method fast enough. His true task was to find the nine doors.

Door one he found as a kid; it was his front door key. He did not expect this because it seemed so obvious but one day he came home from school and was locked out; his mother, usually home, had just begun taking some kind of sculpture class and was off molding clay and forgot to leave a key under the welcome mat. So he was unwelcome, in his own home. He cried for a bit and tromped on some pansies as revenge and got so frustrated staring at the lock, such a simple piece of metal separating him from his palace of food and bed and TV and telephone, that he stuck the index finger of his right hand inside. It shoved deep into the lock, bumping around, ridges trying to find a perfect spatial match. Nothing clicked. But he'd enjoyed the sensation so he tried the middle finger next. Too big. The pinkie on the left hand: too small; it wiggled inside like a wire. It was the ring finger on his right hand that slipped inside, easy as a glove, ridges filling the humps and the boy settled it deep, rotated his entire hand, heard a click, and the door opened cleanly. He was inside. He ripped his finger from the door and let out some kind of vicious delighted laugh.

When his mother came home, two hours later, hands red with clay, he pulled her straight to the door and showed her the trick. Shove in, turn, click, open. His mother kept laughing. And I didn't even want to buy this house! she said, holding him close. And to imagine, what if we hadn't? The boy shrugged. He had no idea how to answer that question.

The second key fit the lock of the bank deposit box that held all the securities of the family. The two had gone on a trip to the bank and the boy was bored in the room of security boxes while his mother spoke worriedly with an accountant. He stuck the pinkie on his left hand into their security box and ta da: it opened. He was very surprised. So was his mother. I didn't especially like this bank either, she said. I considered the one closer to home but this one was bigger, she said. Can I have some of this money? the boy asked, looking with interest at the large piece of gold sitting in the box like a glowing turd. No, she said, but I'll buy you a burger. They went out to his favorite burger joint where the lettuce was shredded and sat together and she told him about how she was making a clay version of him. It's you, she said, but you are surrounded by doors. You are standing on doors and wearing doors and your hand of keys is held up like a deck of cards. The boy splayed his fingers out on the table. Gin, he said.

The third, fourth and fifth keys opened his camp trunk, the neighbour's car, and the storage room of the school cafeteria, respectively. He opened the cafeteria door one day at school when he was wandering around, not wanting to go home yet because there was nothing to do and no one to be with. All the other kids were off playing sports. The boy opened the back of the cafeteria with his right pointer, to his own almost dulled surprise that day, and sat with the frozen chicken nuggets for awhile. It got boring quickly so he went home, opened the door with his other finger and watched TV. His father was away at war. No one knew what war it was because it was an unannounced war, which made it worse because he could tell no one because that would cause great governmental problems. So he just held on to that information and when his friends asked where his dad was on Open House Night at school, he said: He's away on business. He wanted to yell out: The business of saving everyone's lives! but he knew that would cause further questions so he kept his mouth shut.

His mother brought home the clay sculpture. It was about two feet tall and looked very little like him, and the doors resembled flying walls. One day when he was home alone and she wasn't back yet, having enrolled in another course, this one called How to Make Glass, he threw some baseballs at the sculpture but the clay held strong. The boy was twelve now. His hands were growing, but his fingers still fit the same locks. Somehow they stayed the size they needed to be, while the rest of the hand – palm, knuckles, wrist – grew with him.

The sixth and seventh keys fit doors in France. His mother and he went to Paris to visit his father who was on leave from the mysterious war and together the three of them had lunch at a café with iron lamp poles nearby and ate crusty bread and red ripe tomatoes. His father looked older and stronger than ever, with big arms and a ruddy tan, and the boy stood next to him and wanted to push all his keys at once into the man's palm, to click and turn his father open, to make him tell what was happening. Secrets. His father and mother shared a room in the hotel and the boy had the room next door, with its strange smelling comforter and a weird phone that had numbers in different configurations. He learned how to say *Où est la porte?*, which means Where is the door?, and the porter at the hotel, after ignoring the question for the first five times, finally showed him a door, standing alone, on the lobby level, hoping to shut the boy up. Using the middle finger on his left hand, boom, the boy opened the door to reveal just a closet, empty, with a few clothes hanging up and several swinging hangers. The porter babbled in amazement, *Mais qu'est-ce que c'est que ça?!* and took one of the hanging shirts straight away to the maître d' at the restaurant who had been bemoaning the loss of it for over a year and the boy said, to no one: I suppose I'm just going to sit here, and he went inside the closet and sat down. The porter, when he returned, was worried about the boy, so solemn!, and brought him a glass of wine and a piece of apple. The boy ate the apple and drank the wine and fell asleep. When his mother found him, she hugged him for a long time and he showed her how his hand was international.

At the Louvre, the boy felt the pointer finger on his left hand itch after greeting Mona Lisa under glass. He found the docent room the way a hound finds blood, and played gin rummy with a pooped guide whose earrings were little diamond stars. His father was off doing business that day. When they returned to the hotel, the mother angry at the boy because he'd vanished, they found the father weary on the bed, looking worried, his ruddy tan fading like a bright couch left in the sun for fifty years.

On the airplane home, the mother cried and the boy went to the bathroom and thought of his father as he peed, and then when he flushed he sent his pee like a message to his father because he imagined it flying out of the plane, free of him, into the world.

Go win the war, the boy thought, and come home. Or, he thought, don't win the war and come home. Or, he thought, don't come home but make mother stop missing you. Or, he thought, make me stop missing you.

He rubbed his keys against his palm. He was almost thirteen. He washed his hands with the lavender airplane soap and returned to his seat.

He didn't fit his eighth key until he was twenty years old.

His father did come back from the war after another sixteen months, but he was not the same man. He was scared of noises and he had a strange white blindness that he experienced when the day got too hot. The family considered moving, over and over, to cooler quarters; considered it, then unconsidered it. The boy took drama classes but always played the funny weird guy and never the leading man. He watched his mother take How to Make Glass II, the second in the series of five, and one afternoon she came home with a tote bag full of huge clear squares. She said this was her final exam for the class, and she'd gotten an A. Look, she said, pointing, no bubbles, she said. The boy asked her what they should do with it now that she'd made it. She said break it. So they took it outside and broke it in two and then his mother looked sad and sat down and the boy broke it in four, then eight, then sixteen, and his mother was still sad, she started to weep, softly, and the boy shattered the glass into a hundred pieces.

His first girlfriend bought a chastity belt as a joke. He couldn't open it. They scrambled around, used the tin key that it came packaged with, opened her up, had sex anyway. Her underwear was thin and full of holes and the boy kept it that night in his bed, after they had parted, and thought about the way she butted her head into his shoulder like a goat. When they broke up, he walked to the bank and put the underwear in the safe deposit box right on top of that one piece of gold. His mother never said a word about it. The bank had changed ownership by now and had a new color scheme – navy and dark green – but the lock was exactly the same.

His father went to the hospital for the blindness. He told the doctor that he saw whiteness everywhere, as if he'd been driving in the snow for days and days, and that he couldn't find his balance or his peace. The hospital gave him painkillers and sunglasses. The boy's father sat in the kitchen with a cup of milk in a mug, his palm covering the opening so he wouldn't have to look at its white flat top and he said: It's not like I saw anything that horrible. The son said really? and the father said: Son, the truth is I can't even quite remember what I saw. Is it bright in here? he asked. The son looked outside at the setting sun and the lucid calm of dusk.

The eighth key fit the cabinet at the weapon store. He went there for his college war class to learn the difference between muskets and spears. The man who owned the weapon store had a big belly and cheeks stretched over his face like poorly upholstered furniture. He would be hard to make in clay. The man was reading a book called *How to Meet Girls*, and when the boy asked to see some stuff, the man said he'd lost the key to the back cabinet where the small revolvers lived. The boy felt his finger itching, walked over, and opened it himself. The man's cheeks raised a full inch on his face, furniture renewal. The boy shot some targets and wrote up a brilliant report. He read *How to Meet Girls* cover to cover.

His mother came to his college graduation. His father could not because the light of the sun blinded him and seeing people all dressed in one kind of uniform reminded him of the army and made his head feel like it would explode. I can't stand it, he told his son. All those bodies on the lawn in black graduation gowns. It's like one huge goddamn foxhole. His mother wore a dress she'd made in her sewing class, with contrasting patches of velvet, burlap, silk.

He went to France for a graduation present. He returned to the Louvre, deciding he wanted to play more gin rummy. He located the door, but when he stuck his finger in the lock, it didn't fit anymore. He tried all the other fingers – no go. They had apparently changed locks since his last visit. This made him feel unsettled, as if kicked out of his own home. He wondered if that finger would find a new lock now. He thought: yes. And no. And I don't know.

He met a French girl named Sophie, sitting in a yellow-and-brown wicker chair at a café, eating a butter-and-sugar crêpe. He fell in love with her within a couple of days. She puffed her lips when she spoke, like the French do. In bed, he put his finger inside of her, the ring finger on his left hand, the finger that means marriage, as if to turn her inside, and unlock her body. She came fast; she was loose and loving, and loud, and luscious, but she hadn't been locked, either. I love you, she told him, after a week, with a thick French accent, lips puffing. He decided to stay for the rest of August. They made love all the time and he told her his uncle couldn't see because he'd watched bad things in the war and Sophie said What war? and the boy shook his head. I don't know, he said. Some war somewhere kind of near here. She had him to dinner at her parents' house and they served so much wine he threw up halfway through dinner, in the bathroom, privately, washing his hands repeatedly with the soap so that no one would ever know, spraying the toilet seat with the cleanser he found under the sink.

When he left France, Sophie said she'd write but she only sent one letter total. He returned to his hometown and found an apartment near his mother and father. He went to the man, still sitting around the kitchen.

Who were you fighting? he asked.

Some other guy, said his father.

What did you see? asked his son.

Not much, said his father. Some blood, he said. I think something got taken away from me, his father said. I think they took something from me but I never even felt it happen when they did.

The boy stood there. He put his right hand of keys into his father's open palm: the security box, the neighbor's car, the closet in France, the docent room at the Louvre that had been changed.

You say you've opened eight so far? said his father. Which is the ninth?

The son waggled his ring finger on his left hand. Well, go open some doors, his father said. The one you open with the ninth key will be connected to the woman you will marry. Maybe.

The boy agreed that would be very sweet, if it worked out like that. He was feeling bothered by the mundane nature of the other eight keys. There was a report on the news that NASA had lost the key to the space shuttle, and so the boy called up right away and offered his assistance. The whole flight over he had the national anthem singing in his head. NASA took him straight away to a sealed white room with serious people who shook his hand and had ridiculously fierce eye contact, and members of the FBI lined the walls like blue columns in case he was a terrorist in disguise. The boy tried all his fingers twice but none worked. The NASA people shook their heads, and he heard someone say I told you so. He had a fleeting feeling of terror that the FBI might arrest him for something his father had done and an even bigger wish that an FBI man would arrest him, take him aside, and tell him what had happened. He flew home, shaken, with the only song in his head being the one from a burger commercial. He shoved his finger into every door he could see for a few weeks, but decided to stop, as it was starting to make him unhappy, and signed up for a sculpture class.

In the second class in the series on figure sculpture, the boy met a woman he wanted to marry. After a year, they married. They spent the gold piece in the safe deposit box on the wedding and did it up, and also did it dark so that his father could stand it. It was a night wedding. His father stood at the microphone and made a toast with his eyes closed. The son danced with his bride, luminous in her white dress; his father never once looked at the bride for fear his head would explode. That night, in the hotel room, the bride looked at the ring on his key finger and asked him what that one opened and he said he didn't know. They made love in the big hotel bed with the strange-smelling comforter and fell asleep face to face, feet tangled together.

They went to Paris on their honeymoon and found the closet in the hotel that the boy, now a man, could open, and when the porter wasn't looking, they snuck inside and made love. Due to the intrusion of the walls, sex was uncomfortable in the closet, so they ended up going to the front desk and getting a room anyway. There on the bed in the hotel, the man told his new wife about his father and the war. He told her everything he knew which was very little but still, other than the quick 'uncle' confession to Sophie, he'd never told anyone. He had to continually smother down a fear of the FBI busting into the wire-tapped room and taking him to FBI jail as he spoke. The new wife was understanding but equally confused. We were at war then? she said. The man said: You are the first person I have ever really told. Her face was dim in the light of Parisian dusk, filtering through the windows and turning the room golden. He felt glad he'd married her. They went downstairs and had a huge feast of duck in apricot sauce in the hotel dining room and the porter, who was now significantly older, recognized him and gave him a free crème brûlée. After dinner, the porter insisted he open the closet again, which he did, although embarrassed, because to him, it still smelled exactly like his wife's desire and not like an abandoned closet in the least.

They found a good apartment in town, near his parents. They got a dog at the pound who had been abused but was responsive. His mother came over with teas from around the world and sat at the kitchen table in her patchwork outfits, and she and the dog got along. The son tried to ask his father the right question that would reveal everything but all he ever got in reply was a sad shaking of the head.

On his thirtieth birthday, he was walking to work, to the factory where he broke glass for a living, when he heard screaming in the streets. He passed a TV in a bar, and the local news was explaining how a little boy was locked in a metal shed by accident and the door was too thick and couldn't be banged down. The young man took a detour on his route and went towards the noise and the banging. Apparently the boy had been in the shed for hours and air would run out soon. This was a special boy too – the one known about town whose elbows were pointed in such a way that made it easy to open tin cans.

The young man had that one key finger left.

As he approached, the crowd, who knew him well, parted willingly as the Red Sea when they saw him walk forward. Inside he could hear the boy in the metal room, sobbing up the air. The young man with the hands of keys paused a moment in front of the metal door. He could feel his finger itching. He wanted to wait for a second, and hold this moment, the moment before he became a finite person. He could feel the air ringing with it – his lifespan a lifespan, the world a round ball. The crowd screamed and the boy sobbed and the young man put the ring finger on his left hand in the lock.

Click.

Hero.

The trapped boy ran out crying, gasping, elbows in wings, and the town lifted the key finger man on their shoulders and he had headlines and got a medal and the mayor shook his now-complete hand.

After the award ceremony, he went to his parents' house. His father was sleeping in a quiet dim room, and the young man slipped the metal medal over his father's head. He'd passed many doors that day and thought: so I can't open that one or that one or that one. From now on, all the doors in the world were as closed to him as to everyone else. The older man kept sleeping and the young man hummed a song to himself inside the cool dark room.

Invisible Malls
★ ★ ★ ★ ★ Ken Kalfus

★ ★ ★ ★ *Kublai Khan does not necessarily believe everything Marco Polo says when he describes the indoor shopping malls visited in his travels around the empire, but he listens to the young Venetian with greater attention than he has shown any other messenger or explorer. He has already heard Marco's tales of invisible cities, of Diomira and Despina, of Zirma and Isaura, calvinoed metropolises built from memory and desire, and he waits for further intelligence. The aged emperor has reached the melancholy moment in his life in which he needs to comprehend his conquests, when the illuminated maps hand-drawn in rare inks and paints by Tartary's greatest cartographers only frustrate him. As beautiful as these maps are, they are unable to show the borders of his vast territory, and they are also very difficult to fold. The Khan has no use for the blunt, irrelevant reports of functionaries, emissaries, generals, and spies. Only in Marco Polo's account is the Khan able to understand what his will has accomplished.*

Indoor Shopping Malls and Memory 1

Leaving there and proceeding for three days toward the east, you reach Monica, an indoor shopping mall entirely occupied by the past. Crowding one boutique after another are Mickey Mouse watches and souvenir ashtrays from the 1939 New York World's Fair, stretched Coke bottles, incense candles and Day Glo posters, smile decals and fake gas lamps, pet rocks and electronic pet birds. Monica's merchants have already placed orders for merchandise nearly obsolete but not yet in fashion. The mall has structural defects and a short lease on the land, but the merchants know they will stay in business forever. They envy their customers, who believe they were happy when they owned what the merchants own now.

Indoor Shopping Malls and Desire 1

In the shops of Alice, you can buy philosopher's stones, golden fleeces, holy grails, concubines of absolute beauty and passion, books that answer the questions posed by wise men and children, and elixirs that deliver eternal life. Each of these items, however, is priced at slightly more than you think it's worth, plus sales tax. After you've left without making a purchase, you feel the difference between what you want to pay and what the goods cost as a little hole burning into the lining of your stomach. You realize that the item is worth more than you thought. You return to the store but find the price has been raised to a new figure that is really unreasonable. Annoyed, you again leave empty-handed, reconsider and return, find the price has been raised again, leave once more, and so on, forever.

Indoor Shopping Malls and Sleep 1

The items in Larissa's shops relate to the many aspects of sleep. These include sheets and bedspreads, of course, and pillows as soft as clouds, comforters of perfect comfort, gossamer negligees woven by genetically engineered Peruvian spiders, as well as bedside tables, bedside lamps and bedside books that, in the disjointedness of their narratives and the vagueness of their metaphors, are written to ease the transition from wakefulness. Across the way, a small shop sells a single line of alarm clocks that are individually calibrated in order to rouse each customer with the most urgency that can be obtained with the least amount of discomfort. The other shops that line Larissa's softly lit corridors supply the foreshortened hours between night and dawn: for example, notebooks whose pages have been chemically treated to better capture the evaporating details of your dreams. These shops also sell the committed sleeper devices to intensify the vividness of his dreams, others to minimize the same dreams, computer software that program dreams, and mass-produced dream rentals. Here are scales that measure the weight of your nightmares and calipers to measure their width.

Indoor Shopping Malls and Desire 2

There is no parking lot at Carolyn. Would-be shoppers drive around it for hours, looking for a place to leave their cars. Bewitched by the illusion of a parking space glimpsed in a rearview mirror, or through the windows of intervening vehicles, or in some parallel universe visible only from the corner of the eye, some drivers abruptly back up, turn, accelerate without warning, or attempt to squeeze between other cars. There are numerous collisions. Most of the drivers, however, allow themselves to be entertained by their car radios, snack on whatever provisions they have brought with them, and then return home. If they voice any complaint, it is only with the amount of traffic they have encountered.

Indoor Shopping Malls and the Sky 1

Like other indoor shopping malls, Rachel is roofed, its internal climate regulated by hidden machinery. Daylight is allowed into the building only through its doors. Yet before the shopper can focus his eyes on the racks and display windows ahead of him, they are directed upwards to a fantastic apparition. Where in other malls are nondescript ceilings, Rachel's master engineers have installed an intricate mechanism of lamps, gears, pulleys, cams, flywheels, springs, and weights that approximate the silent churnings of the universe. Clockwork drives a mammoth lamp, the mall's sun, across a painted sky, and then raises a lesser lamp, a manic face etched in its glass, the mall's moon. The mechanism's motion is accelerated to encompass a full day, from sunrise to sunrise, during the mall's business hours. Planets move forward and then in retrograde, and hundreds of thousands of lights suspended by wires wheel above our heads. As a service to their customers, Rachel's merchants have also arranged to make visible to the unaided eye what God cannot: galaxies, nebulae, clusters, quasars, pulsars, novae, planetary discs, meteor swarms, and interstellar dust clouds. The shopper need not emulate the astronomer's patient attendance to the heavens. Rare and spectacular celestial events, such as eclipses, occultations, conjunctions, and transits are scheduled to appear at least once every day.

Indoor Shopping Malls and Desire 3

From the moment you step into Sophie, you are overcome by aromas sweet, pungent, sour, and meaty. Sophie is exclusively a food court, offering not only ice cream, pizza, popcorn, and tacos, but also manna, loquats, and ambrosia, all of it deep-fried. Strolling down the concourse with a sixteen ounce cup of immortality-conferring amrita in one hand and a hot dog in the other, you pass strangers who are drinking kvass or goat's milk, or nibbling Uzbek plov or shark nuggets, and, enveloped by the grease-laden steam wafting over the formica counters, you wonder what you will eat next. But food is the least of your desires. Where are the public restrooms?

Indoor Shopping Malls and Time 1

Not a single watch or clock is sold in Lucy. Indeed, visitors are asked to leave their timepieces at the coat check, lest the relentless ticking of their mechanisms fracture the delicate goods within, as it does outside the mall. Lucy is devoted to time in its deepest, sourish essence and diverse manifestations: lost time, time made, time that stands still, daylight savings time. Aware that their product is a sensory illusion caused by physical motion, the merchants run the entire mall on a railroad track around the parking lot. The shopper is invited to stand still and allow the eons to wash over him like an ocean on its way to becoming a desert. For clients who are habitually late for their appointments and trysts, Lucy's retailers sell packets of time purchased wholesale from those who are always punctual or even early. The former conventionally swindle the latter; Lucy imposes an orderly and just economy upon them.

Indoor Shopping Malls and Memory 2

Emma is so up-market that its boutiques are named for designers that you have never heard of; nor are you allowed to hear of them. If you do learn the names of these designers, Emma's security commandos abduct you to a secret location within a remote discount store and chemically induce memory loss. If the commando team fails (induced memory loss is still a developing field), the shop goes out of business and is replaced by a store dedicated to an even more exclusive designer, selling clothes at prices too high to be pronounced by the human voice.

Indoor Shopping Malls and the Dead 1

In malls from Paramus to Zanzibar, adolescents wash down every promenade, crowd every aisle, besiege every register, and monopolize every video game. A population in pained transition, its records, jeans, toys, and bedroom decor are also in transition, coveted one day and discarded the next. The exception to this state of affairs is Gloria, an indoor shopping mall located in a subterranean fissure. It is patronized exclusively by the dead, who shop without hurrying, who can wait for closeout sales, and who buy goods to last forever.

Marco Polo does not know if the Great Khan is sleeping or awake: his eyes are closed and his breathing is slowed, but the long lines of his face are drawn into a contemplative frown. The emperor is, in fact, awake, considering indoor shopping malls so far unmentioned, in Manhasset and Shaker Heights, in Boca Raton and Bel Air. He is thinking of the Galleried legions, and of big old GUM staring down at the tsars. 'So this is my empire,' Kublai Khan murmurs. 'These are the subjects who send me their tributes and raise my armies, who follow my laws and who whisper my name to either threaten or calm their children. These are the people whose poets address their songs to me.' 'No, sire,' Marco Polo replies. 'The malls are only home to goods. The promenades are emptied, the shutters are drawn, the fountains are stilled, and the coin purses are fastened shut with the fall of dusk, except on Wednesdays, when they are open to nine. The shoppers return to their residences, where they are alone as if in death, subject to nothing, part of nothing. Your empire is quiet halls and shelves, locked display cases and bare cash drawers.' As night rushes into his palace's luxuriant gardens, the emperor cannot tell if the traveler smiles or weeps. But he knows now, at least, why Marco Polo has so many charge cards.

The Snow Frog

★ ★ ★ ★ ★ Arthur Bradford

PART ONE / *The Egg*

★★★★★ Elizabeth was in the kitchen with the rest of us, trying once again to do that trick with the egg. I'd been watching her out of the corner of my eye while someone else was talking. She picked up a fairly small egg, a white one from the farm, and she was sort of caressing it with her fingers. She probably knew somebody was watching her. Before she did it she said quietly, 'Okay, here goes . . .'

Then she popped the egg, shell and all, into her mouth. She tilted her head back and made a loud gulping sound. I stood up from my chair. So did Tom. He was the oldest person there. He was probably seventy-five years old. He'd been watching her too, I guess.

'Don't do that,' he said.

But it was too late. Elizabeth's neck was bulging out now, swollen with the presence of that egg. She hadn't even chewed. It just went straight down and lodged itself in her throat. Her eyes popped out wide and I thought about lunging forward and socking her in the stomach so that the egg might shoot back up. But then she gulped again and swallowed it right down into her belly.

'Oh great,' said Grace. She was the one who owned the farm. 'What are we going to do now?'

'This happened before,' said Tom. 'She's done this trick before.'

'She was okay before,' I said.

221

'Are you okay, Elizabeth?' asked Grace. 'Can you breathe now?'

'Yes,' said Elizabeth. 'I can.'

And then she smiled. Elizabeth had thin lips, with hardly any color in them. She was very skinny. Perhaps the egg would break apart in her stomach, I thought. It would nourish her and do her good. I took comfort in this notion as I sipped at my hot chocolate.

Grace's farm was a place for people who couldn't fit in anywhere else. She let us all stay there as long as we did work and kept out of trouble. Some people, like Tom, had been there for a long time, ten or twenty years. I'd been there for about a year. Elizabeth was the most recent arrival.

A few days after that egg incident Elizabeth and I were out behind the house, by the woodpile. Grace had sent us there to clean things up and get the stacks in order for the coming winter. We were just standing there though, not doing any work.

I put my hand on Elizabeth's bony fingers and leaned a little closer to her. I thought I might try to kiss her. But then she put her hand over her mouth and coughed a little.

'I don't feel so well,' she said.

'Oh, okay,' I said.

'I think I need to sit down.'

'All right.'

But before she could sit down she coughed again. She held onto her belly and I thought she was going to throw up. Her throat made this raspy noise and now it seemed like she might be choking on something.

'Are you choking?' I asked her.

Elizabeth doubled over and retched. Her thin body heaved

and a small object popped out of her mouth and into her hands. Her hair was covering her face and I couldn't see what it was.

Then she stood up and held her hands out to me. There, cupped within them, was a little baby chick. It was wet from her saliva, but it was moving, alive.

'You gave birth, Elizabeth,' I said.

'I know,' she said. 'Look at that.'

The tiny chick squeaked and flapped its wings a little.

'Let's take it to the chicken coop,' said Elizabeth. 'One of them will take care of it. That's a good idea, don't you think?'

'Sure,' I said. 'I think so.'

We walked over to the chicken coop with Elizabeth cradling the chick carefully in her two hands.

'Don't tell anyone about this,' she said to me. 'I want for this to be a secret.'

'Okay Elizabeth,' I said, 'I won't tell anybody at all . . .'

PART TWO / *What Tom Found*

Tom and I were down in the barn finishing up the chores from the list Grace had given us. Tom was talking to the animals, like he always did, saying things like 'How now brown cow?' or 'What's shakin' bacon?' He'd say that to the pigs. He was a fairly funny guy for an old man.

I was raking hay from one of the stalls and Tom went out to the pigs' trough to empty it and hose it down. I heard him say, 'Hey, are those worms or snakes?'

'What?' I said.

'Come here.'

I went outside and saw him bent over the trough, staring down at something in the muck. I joined him there, looking down. That's when I saw what he was talking about. There were little bodies in there, long and rounded, like puffy sausages. They were pale, translucent, and slightly green. About a dozen of them were wobbling in a small pile among the food scraps and sour milk. A clear jellylike goo surrounded them, holding their bodies together.

'I don't think those are snakes,' I said.

'Neither do I,' said Tom.

'Maybe they're larvae,' I said.

'You don't even know what larvae is,' said Tom.

'Well, they don't look like worms.'

'Big worms maybe.'

'Do you think the pigs ate them?' I asked.

'I hope not,' said Tom.

We decided not to tell Grace about these creatures. 'She worries too much,' said Tom. 'She'll make us spray the whole place down with poison.'

Tom took his shovel and scooped the big worms into a plastic bucket. Then we carried them across the fields and out into the woods where we dumped them in a hole. I was going to cover them up with dirt but Tom said not to do that.

'Don't bury things alive,' he said to me. 'It's not right.'

Elizabeth and I were in the barn after dinner. It was dark out and we had lit a candle. Once again, I wanted to try to kiss her, but she didn't seem interested. She was sitting on a bale of hay, bouncing up and down, and looking around the barn.

'Hey,' I said, 'would you like to see what Tom and I found this afternoon?'

'Yes, I would,' said Elizabeth.

I knew that Tom wouldn't be happy with me for telling Elizabeth, but I was at a loss for interesting things to say. I wanted to show her something impressive. I picked up the candle and told Elizabeth to follow me. Together we walked out towards the spot in the woods where Tom and I had left the worms. I carried the candle with me and tried to hold my hand in front of the flame so that the wind wouldn't blow it out. This was difficult to do because I was excited and walking quickly. Eventually the wind sneaked around my hand and the flame went out.

In the darkness up ahead I spotted the hole we had dug. It was easy to see because there was a dim green light coming from inside it, like someone had lit a small campfire at the bottom of the hole.

'This is it,' I said to Elizabeth.

We walked over to the hole and gazed down at the worms. They were quivering together in a little mass, still covered in that jelly. Their inner organs glowed green through their pale skin. That's where the green light came from, their insides.

'Oh wow,' said Elizabeth. She got down on her knees and scooped one up. She had to use two hands because it was so slippery. Tom and I hadn't touched them that afternoon. We were too afraid.

'Careful,' I said. 'Did it sting you?'

'No,' said Elizabeth. 'It feels warm.'

She held it up and her skinny face was illuminated by the worm's green light. Her teeth appeared green when she smiled. Elizabeth handed the worm to me. It seemed bigger now, about the size of a hot dog. It felt soft and warm, like it was filled with heated pudding.

'What is it?' I asked her.

'A glow-worm,' said Elizabeth, 'a giant one.'

The worm slipped out of my hands and fell on the ground. A little bit of glowing liquid dropped onto my boot.

'I hope they aren't poisonous,' I said.

'Me too,' said Elizabeth.

With the tip of her shoe she pushed the stray worm back into the hole with the others. 'It needs the others to stay warm,' she said.

We watched the worms crawl upon each other and twist their glowing bodies around in a jellied pile. A cold wind picked up and Elizabeth moved closer to me.

'We'd better head back,' she said.

She was right. Grace would be expecting us at the house. The temperature was dropping. I could feel it. It was nearly winter. I took Elizabeth's hand and we walked back through the woods and across the fields.

PART THREE / *Winter Comes*

'It's snowing.'

Early in the morning Elizabeth stood next to my bed shaking my arm with her cold fingers.

'Look outside,' she said.

I sat up and saw that the ground was covered in deep white. It was the first snow of the year. The ground had been bare when we went to bed, and I wondered how so much snow had fallen in just one night.

Grace was downstairs preparing a warm breakfast. Some of the others were already awake. Elizabeth looked at me with worried eyes.

'The worms,' she said. 'They'll freeze.'

'We'll check them after breakfast,' I said.

It was my job to start the wood furnace. I went down to the basement and got it going. By the time I was done everyone upstairs had eaten most of the eggs. I looked around the kitchen for Elizabeth.

'She's not here,' said Grace.

Tom looked up at me and shook his head. I think he knew I'd told Elizabeth about the worms. I grabbed a piece of toast and went outside.

It was still snowing, big blankets of it rushed across the fields. I could see Elizabeth's footprints leading towards the woods. The wind had almost smoothed them over and erased her tracks. I pushed forward, following the faded path into the trees. The big snowflakes melted on my face and dripped down my shirt.

Elizabeth was knelt down digging in the snow when I found her. I got down beside her and dug too. I'd forgotten to wear gloves so my hands got cold quickly.

'Where are they?' she asked me.

'Maybe they crawled away,' I said, 'maybe they found some-place warm.'

'I don't think so,' she said.

My hand hit upon something hard, like a small stone. I dug more and uncovered the pile of them, all frozen together, no longer glowing. Now they were a dull, sickly yellow, like rotten fruit.

Elizabeth began to cry. Then I did too. I wasn't that sad about them dying, I just didn't like the way it looked, the pile of them there, helpless in the snow. And my hands were numb with the cold.

Elizabeth gathered up the hardened bodies and held them in the front of her sweater, like the way you carry apples.

'I'm bringing them home,' she said.

Down in the basement, Elizabeth laid the worms out in neat rows next to the wood furnace. She thought they might thaw out in the heat and resurrect themselves. The worms had grown larger before they died; some of them had developed little pointed tails and rounded heads. It seemed possible that they weren't really worms at all, but there was no point in dwelling on that now.

'Don't let Grace see this,' I said to her.

'Don't worry,' said Elizabeth.

Tom poked his head downstairs and looked over the limp bodies.

'They grew,' he said.

'But now they're dead,' I pointed out.

'Well,' said Tom, 'that's what happens.'

The worms didn't revive themselves like Elizabeth had hoped. They just got wet and droopy and began to smell a little. Tom, Elizabeth, and I went out behind the barn and buried them the next day. We found a patch of mud where the snow had melted and we dug the grave there. Elizabeth said a quiet prayer and I shoveled the mud over their bodies.

'It's okay to bury them now,' said Tom. 'Now it's proper.'

PART FOUR / *Incubator*

I was brushing my teeth in the bathroom and Elizabeth knocked
on the wooden door. I let her in and she shut it behind her. She was
barefoot and wearing a thin white nightgown, the kind you could
almost see straight through. Her eyes were wide and excited.

'What's going on?' I asked her.

Elizabeth said 'Shhhh' and turned out the light.

'Look,' she said to me.

Elizabeth stood before me like a ghost, all white in her flimsy
gown. Except for her stomach. It was glowing green, just a little.
I could make out the faint shape of one of those worms, nestled
snugly underneath her skin just below her belly button. The
worm was illuminated, alive, growing inside of her.

'You ate one,' I said.

'That's right,' she said. 'I swallowed it down when it was
frozen and hard.'

'It's still alive.'

'Just like the egg,' she said, 'that turned into a chick.'

Elizabeth took my hand and guided it into her belly. It was
very very warm.

PART FIVE / *Christmas*

Tom's job was to kill a turkey for the Christmas dinner. Elizabeth
and I went with him to the pen where the birds were kept and
helped him pick one out. We hadn't told anyone about her

worm, not even Tom. The cold winter weather had allowed her to wear bulky sweaters that concealed the radiant bulge underneath.

Together we looked over the flock of birds and chose a big one, not the biggest, but a good-sized one, for our dinner.

Before he took it down to the slaughterhouse Tom said to both of us, 'You know, if there's anything you don't want to discuss with Grace, you always can bring it up with me first.'

He gave a quick nod towards Elizabeth's belly and then went off to wrestle the bird into its cage. I guess that worm wasn't so well hidden after all.

The next night, after the big turkey dinner, Elizabeth and I were supposed to do the dishes, but she could barely stand up. She held onto the edge of the sink and wiped the sweat from her forehead with a rag.

'I think I'm sick,' she said.

Grace felt her forehead and pulled her hand away quickly. 'You're hot,' she said. 'You'd better go lie down.'

'Okay,' said Elizabeth. She stumbled up the stairs and into her bed.

'She probably ate too much,' I said.

Grace pursed her lips and nodded. Then she set to work with me on the dishes.

Tom woke me up near midnight. He was standing over my bed, fully dressed.

'Wake up,' he said.

We went down to the kitchen where Elizabeth was rolled up into a ball on the floor, clutching her stomach.

'I'm too hot,' she moaned, 'I'm burning up.'

I was afraid she'd wake everybody in the house. I picked up her heated body and carried her outside. Tom followed me. It was a clear winter night. The snow was deep and the stars gave everything a pale hue.

'Let's go to the barn,' said Tom.

We laid her down upon some hay and Tom placed a cool wet towel on her forehead. The animals shifted about in their stalls, neighing and grunting at our presence.

Elizabeth rolled over onto her back and it was then that her bathrobe dropped open and Tom saw the glowing shape within her belly. He stared at it quietly for a moment. Then he looked at me.

'She ate one,' I said.

'So I see,' he said.

The bulge was pretty large now, about the size of a melon, and it was glowing bright. We could feel the heat coming off it as we knelt down next to her.

The animals began to make a lot of noise, kicking at the ground and pushing at each other in their pens. Tom went over to calm them. 'Oh hey,' he said to them. He let a few of the sheep out so that they would quit banging on the walls. Some pigs wandered around as well.

Elizabeth started to cough and grabbed her stomach. She rolled onto her hands and knees and began that same retching sound I'd heard before, from the time when we were out behind the woodpile.

'It's coming up,' I said to Tom. I patted Elizabeth softly on the back. I said to her, 'You'll be okay,' although I wasn't really so sure.

Her retching grew louder and then it stopped. Her muscles tightened and a few short squeaks escaped from her mouth.

'She's choking,' said Tom.

'Can you breathe?' I asked Elizabeth.

She pounded her hands on the ground and put her head down, like she was giving some kind of prayer. The pigs squealed and ran away from her. Her whole body convulsed in strange spasms. Still nothing came out of her.

'She's going to pass out,' I said.

Tom stepped forward and placed his arms around her waist. He lifted her up and locked his hands together under her stomach. Elizabeth's face turned blue and her eyes rolled back in her head.

'Help her, Tom,' I said.

Tom jerked his arms together. It was the Heimlich maneuver, just like we'd all been taught. Some green goo spurted out from Elizabeth's mouth.

'Do it again,' I said.

Tom yanked again and more goo flew out of her mouth. Then she coughed and a deep monstrous belch rose up within her. Tom let her go and she fell to her hands and knees again. Her body heaved and out of her mouth poured forth buckets of the green goo, more than I would ever have thought could be inside her. Then, slowly, the glowing shape emerged. Its bulbous tip poked forth from Elizabeth's mouth and her jaw seemed almost to unhinge in order to allow its passage. The green blob plopped out onto the barn floor and began to squirm. Elizabeth gasped, sucking in an enormous breath of air. Then she fell on her side.

The glowing form that had spouted from Elizabeth's mouth wriggled about before us. It was covered in a filmy membrane sac, its limbs poking away at it from the inside, struggling to break free.

'Help it,' said Elizabeth. 'Do something.'

I crept forward on my knees and touched my finger lightly upon the slimy skin. The whole blob was about the size of a large grapefruit. Whatever was inside really wanted to get out. I stuck two fingers into the membrane and hooked them around it. Then I pulled back, tearing a little hole in the surface.

A long, thin leg emerged, and then another. Elizabeth sat up and moved closer to me. Tom stood quietly behind us. The membrane sac slipped away and there before us, among the goo and slime on the barn floor, stood a very large glowing frog.

It stared at us with two enormous glassine eyes, its long legs tucked neatly under its slimy body. It was glowing very brightly now, giving off a green hue so strong that it lit up the entire barn. It was warm too, as if we were sitting in front of a small fire.

'That's the most beautiful frog I've ever seen,' said Elizabeth.

'He's very handsome,' said Tom.

The frog turned and hopped away from us, heading towards the door.

'Open it up,' said Elizabeth. 'He wants to go outside.'

I stood up and opened the big barn door for him. The cool air rushed in and a little snow blew into the barn. I was worried that this would bother the frog, but he didn't mind at all. He paused at the snow-covered field in front of him, and then he hopped forward, taking big leaps into the air and landing softly on his strong legs. When he stood still, the snow around him began to melt, such was the heat he gave off from his skin.

Tom, Elizabeth, and I went out to the field to join him and

we spent much of the night following him around and marveling at the amazing sight of his glowing body hopping through the fields of snow. We decided then that he would be called the Snow Frog.

Over the next few days the frog grew larger, fed steadily on a diet of slop and beans which he shared with the pigs in their trough. He preferred to sleep after his morning meal, and he wouldn't wake until nightfall, when he liked to venture out into the fields and hop about, glowing green under the winter moon. When he reached the size of the smaller piglets, about twenty to thirty pounds, he stopped growing. This was his full size.

Of course, now you see snow frogs that are much bigger in size than this original member of the species. Some of them are as large as full-sized hounds. And the sight of them bounding through the snow, glowing brightly on a cold winter night, is almost commonplace in the North Country and high alpine regions. The children in these rural towns and villages are often heard to beg their parents for permission to stay up late into the evening so that they may run out in the fields and play happily with the good-natured beasts. There is no vision more wonderful to me than the sight of children around Christmas time frolicking in the snow with those warm, fat, glowing frogs.

Over the years Elizabeth birthed many wondrous creatures from her unique womb, including more snow frogs, and it was those she was most proud of. They were her favorites. And I imagine that among the frogs she has now achieved her rightful place in their own lore, passed down from one generation of frogs to the next: Mother Elizabeth, the devoted creator of them all.

Access Fantasy

★ ★ ★ ★ ★ Jonathan Lethem

★ ★ ★ ★ ★ There was a start-up about a half-mile ahead the day before, a fever of distant engines and horns honking as others signalled their excitement – a chance to move! – and so he'd spent the day jammed behind the wheel, living in his Apartment On Tape, waiting for that chance, listening under the drone of distant helicopters to hear the start-up make its way downtown. But the wave of revving engines stalled before reaching his street. He never even saw a car move, just heard them. In fact he couldn't remember seeing a car move recently. Perhaps the start-up was only a panic begun by someone warming their motor, reviving their battery. That night he'd dreamed another start-up, or perhaps it was real, a far-off flare that died before he'd even ground the sleep out of his eyes, though in the rustle of his waking thoughts it was a perfect thing, coordinated, a dance of cars shifting through the free-flowing streets. Dream or not, either way, didn't matter. He fell back asleep. What woke him in the morning was the family in the Pacer up ahead cooking breakfast. They had a stove on the roof of their car and the dad was grilling something they'd bought from the flatbed shepherd two blocks away, a sheepsteak or something. It smelled good. Everything about the family in the Pacer made him too conscious of his wants. The family's daughter – she was beautiful – had been working as Advertising, pushing up against and through the One-Way Permeable Barrier on behalf of some vast faceless

corporation. That being the only way through the One-Way
Permeable Barrier, of course. So the family, her Ma and Pa, were
flush, had dough, and vendors knew to seek them out, hawking
groceries. Whereas checking his pockets he didn't have more
than a couple of dollars. There was a coffee-and-donuts man
threading his way through the traffic even now but coffee was
beyond his means. He needed money. Rumors had it Welfare
Helicopters had been sighted south of East One Thousand, One
Hundred and Ninety-Fourth Street, and a lot of people had left
their cars, drifted down that way, looking for easy cash. Which
was one reason the start-up died, it occurred to him – too many
empty cars. Along with the cars that wouldn't start anymore,
like the old lady in the Impala beside him, the dodderer. She'd
given up, spent most days dozing in the back seat. Her nephew
from a few blocks away came over and tinkered with her engine
now and again but it wasn't helping. It just meant the nephew
wasn't at his wheel for the start-up, another dead spot, another
reason not to bother waiting to move. Probably he thought now
he should have walked downtown himself in search of welfare
money drifting down from the sky. The state helicopters weren't
coming around this neighborhood much lately. Alas. The air
was crowded with commercial hovercraft instead, recruiters,
Advertising robots rounding up the girl from the Pacer and others
like her, off to the world on the other side of the One-Way
Permeable Barrier, however briefly. The world of Apartments,
real ones. Though it was morning he went back to his latest
Apartment On Tape, which was a four bedroom two bath co-op
on East One Thousand, Two Hundred and Fifteenth Street, just
a few blocks away but another world of course, remote from his
life on the street, sealed off from it by the One-Way Permeable

Barrier. He preferred the early part of the tape, before any of the furnishings arrived, so he rewound to that part and put the tape on slow and lived in the rooms as hard as he could, ignoring the glare of sun through his windshield that dulled his view of the dashboard television, ignoring the activities of the family in the Pacer up ahead as they clambered in and out of the hatchback, ignoring the clamor of his own pangs. The realtor's voice was annoying, it was a squawking, parroty voice so he kept the volume down as always and lived in the rooms silently, letting his mind sweep in and haunt the empty spaces, the rooms unfolding in slow motion for the realtor's camera. While the camera lingered in the bathroom he felt under his seat for his bottle and unzipped and peed, timed so it matched to the close-up of the automatic flushing of the toilet on his television. Then the camera and his attention wandered out into the hall. That's when he noticed it, the shadow. Just for a moment. He rewound to see it again. On the far wall of the hallway, framed perfectly for an instant in the lens the silhouette of a struggle, a man with his hands on the neck of another, smaller. A woman. Shaking her by the neck for that instant, before the image vanished. Like a pantomime of murder, a Punch-and-Judy show hidden in the Apartment On Tape. But real, it had to be real. Why hadn't he noticed before? He'd watched this tape dozens of times. He rewound again. Just barely, but still. Unmistakable, however brief. The savagery of it was awful. If only he could watch it frame by frame – slow motion was disastrously fast now. Who was the killer? The landlord? The realtor? Why? Was the victim the previous tenant? Questions, he had questions. He felt himself begin to buzz with them, come alive. Slow motion didn't seem particularly slow precisely because his attention had quickened.

Yes, a job of detection was just what he needed to roust himself out of the current slump, burn off the torpor of too many days locked in the jam at the same damn intersection – why hadn't he gone Downtown at that last turnoff, months ago? Well, anyway. He watched it again, memorized the shadow, the silhouette, imagined blurred features in the slurry of video fuzz, memorized the features, what the hell. Like a police sketch, work from his own prescient hallucinations. Again. It grew sharper every time. He'd scrape a hole in this patch of tape, he knew, if he rewound too many times. Better to have the tape, the evidence, all there was at this point. He popped the video, threw it in a satchel with notebook, eyeglasses. Extra socks. Outside, locked the car, tipped an imaginary hat at the old lady, headed east by foot on West One Thousand, Two Hundred and Eighth Street. He had to duck uptown two blocks to avoid a flotilla of Sanitation hovertrucks spraying foamy water to wash cars sealed up tight against this artificial rain but also soaking poor jerks asleep, drenching interiors, the rotted upholstery and split spongy dashboards, extinguishing rooftop bonfires, destroying box gardens, soap bubbles poisoning the feeble sprouts. Children screamed and giggled, the streets ran with water, sluicing shit here and there into drains, more often along under the tires to the unfortunate neighboring blocks, everyone moaning and lifting their feet clear. Just moving it around, that's all. Around the next corner he ran into a crowd gathered staring at a couple of young teenage girls from inside, from the apartments, the other side of the Barrier. They'd come out of the apartment building on rollerblades to sightsee, to slum on the streets. Sealed in a murky bubble of One-Way Permeable Barrier they were like apparitions, dim ghosts, though you could hear them giggle as they skated through the hushed, reverent crowd. Like a sighting of gods, these teenage girls from inside. No one bothered to spare-change them or bother them in any way because of the Barrier. The girls of course were oblivious behind their twilight veil, like night things come into the day, though for them probably it was the people in cars and around the cars that appeared dim, unreachable. He shouldered his way through the dumbstruck crowd and once past this obstacle he found his man, locked into traffic like all the rest, right where he'd last seen him. The Apartments On Tape dealer, his connection, sunbathing in a deck chair on the roof of his Sentra, eating a sandwich. The backseat was stacked with realtor's tapes, apartment porn, and on the passenger seat two video decks for dubbing. His car in a sliver of morning sun that shone across the middle of the block, benefit of a chink in the canyon of towers that surrounded them. The dealer's neighbors were on their car roofs as well, stretching in the sun, drying clothes. 'Hello there, remember me? That looks good what you're eating, anyway, I want to talk to you about this tape.' 'No refunds,' said the dealer, not even looking down. 'No, that's not it, I saw something, can we watch it together?' 'No need since there's no refunds and I'm hardly interested –' 'Listen, this is a police matter, I think –' 'You're police then, is that what you're saying?' still not looking down. 'No no, I fancy myself a private detective, though not to say I work outside the law, more adjacent, then turn it over to them if it serves justice, there's so often corruption –' 'So turn it over,' the dealer said. 'Well if you could just have a look I'd value your opinion. Sort of pick your brain,' thinking flattery or threats, should have chosen one approach with this guy, stuck with it. The dealer said, 'Sorry, day off,' still not turning his head, chewing off another corner of sandwich. Something from inside the sandwich fell, a chunk of something, fish maybe, onto the roof of the car. 'The thing is I think I saw a murder, on the tape, in the apartment.' 'That's highly unlikely.' 'I know, but that's what I saw.' 'Murder, huh?' The dealer didn't sound at all impressed. 'Bloody body parts, that sort of thing?' 'No, don't be absurd, just a shadow, just a trace.' 'Hmmm.' 'You never would have noticed in passing. Hey, come to think of it, you don't have an extra sandwich do you?' 'No, I don't. So would you describe this shadow as sort of a flicker then, like a malfunction?' 'No, absolutely not. It's part of the tape.' 'Not your monitor on the fritz?' 'No,' he was getting angry now, 'a person, a shadow strangling another shadow.' The chunk of sandwich filling on the car roof was sizzling slightly, changing color already in the sun. The dealer said, 'Shadows, hmmm. Probably a gimmick, subliminal special effects or something.' 'What? What reason would a realtor have for adding special effects for God's sake to an apartment tape?' 'Maybe they think it adds some kind of allure, some thrill of menace that makes their apartments stand out from the crowd.' 'I doubt very much –' 'Maybe they've become aware of the black market in tapes lately, that's the word on the street in fact, and so they're trying to send a little message. They don't like us ogling their apartments, even vicariously.' 'You can't ogle vicariously, I think. Sounds wrong. Anyway, that's the most ridiculous thing I've ever –' 'Or maybe I'm in on it, maybe I'm the killer, have you considered that?' 'Now you're making fun of me.' 'Why? If you can solve crimes on the other side of the Barrier why can't I commit them?' The dealer laughed, hyenalike. 'Now seriously,' he continued, 'if you want to exchange for one without a murder I'll give you a credit towards the next, half what you paid –' 'No thanks. I'll hold onto it.' Discouraged, hungry, but he couldn't really bother being angry. What help did he expect from the dealer anyway? This was a larger matter, above the head of a mere middleman. 'Good luck, Sherlock,' the dealer was saying. 'Spread the word freely, by the way, don't hold back. Can't hurt my sales any. People like murder, only it might be good if there was skin instead of only shadow, a tit say.' 'Yes, very good then, appreciate your help. Carry on.' The dealer saluted. He saluted back, started off through the traffic, stomach growling, ignoring it, intent. A killer was at large. Weaving past kids terrorizing an entire block of cars with an elaborate tag game, cornering around the newly washed neighborhood now wringing itself out, muddy streams between the cars and crying babies ignoring vendors with items he couldn't afford and a flatbed farmer offering live kittens for pets or food and a pathetic miniature start-up, three cars idiotically nosing rocking jerking back and forth trying to rearrange themselves pointlessly, one of them now sideways wheels on the curb and nobody else even taking the bait he made his way back to his car and key in the lock noticed the girl from the Pacer standing in her red dress on the hood of the car gazing skyward, waiting for the Advertising people to take her away. Looking just incidentally like a million bucks. Her kid brother was away, maybe part of the gang playing tag, and her parents were inside the car doing housework dad scraping the grill out the window mom airing clothes repacking bundles so he went over, suddenly inspired. 'Margaret, isn't it?' She nodded, smiled. 'Yes, good, well you remember me from next door, I'm looking for a day or two's work and do you think they'll take me along?' She said, 'You never know, they just take you or they don't.' Smiling graciously even if a little confused, so long neighbors and they'd never spoken. 'But you always – ' he began pointing out. She said, 'Oh once they've started taking you then – ' Awkwardly, they were both awkward for a moment not saying what they both knew or at least he did, that she was an attractive young girl and likely that made a huge difference in whether they wanted you. 'Well you wouldn't mind if I tried?' he said and she said 'No, no,' relieved almost, then added 'I can point you out, I can suggest to them – ' Now he was embarrassed and said hurriedly, 'That's so good of you, thanks, and where should I wait, not here with you at your folks' car, I guess – ' 'Why not, climb up.' Dad looked out the door up at them and she waved him off, 'It's okay, you know him from next door he's going to work, we're going to try to get him a job Advertising.' 'Okay, sweetheart, just checking on you.' Then she grabbed his arm, said, 'Look.' The Advertising hovercraft she'd been watching for landed on the curb a half-block ahead, near the giant hideous sculpture at an office building main entrance, lately sealed. Dad said, 'Get going you guys, and good luck,' and she said, 'C'mon.' Such neighborliness was a surprise since he'd always felt shut out by the family in the Pacer but obviously it was in his head. And Margaret, a cloud of good feeling seemed to cover her. No wonder they wanted her for Advertising. 'Hurry,' she said and took his hand and they hopped down and pushed their way around the cars and through the chaos of children and barking dogs and vendors trying to work the crowd of wannabees these landings always provoked, to join the confused throng at the entrance. He held onto his satchel with the video and his socks making sure it didn't get picked in this crowd. She bounced there trying to make herself visible until one of the two robots at the door noticed her and pointed. They stepped up. 'Inside,' said the robot. They were ugly little robots with their braincases undisguised and terrible attitudes. He disliked them instantly. 'I brought someone new,' she said, pulling him by the hand, thrusting him into view. 'Yes, sir, I'd like to enlist –' he started, grinning madly, wanting to make a good impression. The robot looked him over and made its rapid-fire assessment, nodded. 'Get inside,' it said. 'Lucky,' she whispered, and they stepped into the hovercraft. Four others were there, two men, two women, all young. And another woman stumbled in behind them, and the door sealed, and they were off. Nasty little robots scurrying into the cockpit, making things ready. 'Now what?' he said and she put her finger to her lips and shushed him, but sweetly, leaning into him as if to say they were in this together. He wanted to tell her what he was after but the robots might hear. Would they care? Yes, no, he couldn't know. Such ugly, fascistic little robots. Nazi robots, that's what they were. He hated placing himself in their hands. But once he was Advertising he would be through the barrier, he'd be able to investigate. Probably he should keep his assignment to himself, though. He didn't want to get her into trouble. The hovercraft shuddered, groaned, then lifted and through the window he could see the cars growing smaller, his neighborhood, his life, the way the traffic was so bad for hundreds of miles of street and why did he think a start-up would change anything? Was there a place where cars really drove anymore? Well, anyway. The robots were coming around with the Advertising Patches and everyone leaned their heads forward obediently, no first-timers like himself apparently. He did the same. A robot fastened a patch behind his right ear, a moment of stinging skin, nothing more. Hard to believe the patch was enough to interfere with the function of the One-Way Permeable Barrier, that he would now be vivid and tangible and effective to those on the other side. 'I don't feel any different,' he whispered. 'You won't,' she said. 'Not until there's people. Then you'll be compelled to Advertise. You won't be able to help it.' 'For what, though?' 'You never know, coffee, diamonds, condoms, vacations, you just never know.' 'Where –' 'They'll drop us off at the Undermall, then we're on our own.' 'Will we be able to stick together?' The question was out before he could wonder if it was presuming too much, but she said, 'Sure, as long as our products aren't too incompatible, but we'll know soon. Anyway, just follow me.' She really had a warmth, a glow. Incompatible products? Well, he'd find out what that meant. The hovercraft bumped down on the roof of a building, and with grim efficiency the ugly Nazi robots had the door open and were marching the conscripts out to a rooftop elevator. He wanted to reach out and smack their little exposed-braincase heads together. But he had to keep his cool, stay undercover. He trotted across the roof towards the elevator after her, between the rows of officious gesticulating robots, like they were going to a concentration camp. The last robot at the door of the elevator handed them each an envelope before they stepped in. He took his and moved into the corner with Margaret, they were really packing them in but he couldn't complain actually being jostled with her and she didn't seem to be trying to avoid it. He poked into the envelope. It was full of bills, singles mostly. The money was tattered and filthy, bills that had been taken out of circulation on the other side of the Barrier. Garbage money, that's what it was. The others had already pocketed theirs, business as usual apparently. 'Why do they pay us now?' he whispered. She said 'We just find our way out at the end, when the patch runs out, so this way they don't have to deal with us again,' and he said 'What if we just took off with the money?' 'You could I guess, but I've never seen anyone do it since you'd never get to come back and anyway the patch makes you really want to Advertise, you'll see.' Her voice was reassuring, like she really wanted him not to worry and he felt rotten not telling her about his investigation, his agenda. He put the envelope into his satchel with tape and socks. The elevator sealed and whooshed them down through the building, into the Undermall, then the doors opened and they unpacked from the elevator, spewed out into a gigantic lobby, all glass and polished steel with music playing softly and escalators going down and up in every direction, escalators with steps of burnished wood that looked good enough to eat, looked like roast chicken. He was still so hungry. Margaret took his hand again. 'Let's go,' she said. As the others dispersed she led him towards one of the escalators and they descended. The corridor below branched to shops with recessed entrances, windows dark and smoky, quiet pulsing music fading from each door, also food smells here and there causing his saliva to flow, and holographic signs angling into view as they passed: FERN SLAW, ROETHKE AND SONS, HOLLOW APPEAL, BROKEN SMUDGED ALPHABET, BURGER KING, PLASTIC DEVILS, OSTRICH LAKE, SMARTINGALE'S, RED HARVEST, CATCH OF THE DAY, MUTUAL OF FOMALHAUT, THNEEDS, et cetera. She led him on, confidently, obviously at home. Why not, this was what she did with her days. Then without warning, a couple appeared from around a corner, and he felt himself begin to Advertise. 'How do you do today?' he said, sidling up to the gentleman of the couple, even as he saw Margaret begin to do the same thing to the lady. The gentleman nodded at him, walked on. But met his eye. He was tangible, he could be heard.

It was a shock. 'Thirsty?' he heard himself say. 'How long's it been since you had a nice refreshing beer?' 'Don't like beer,' said the gentleman. 'Can't say why, just never have.' 'Then you've obviously never tried a Very Old Money Lager,' he heard himself say, still astonished. The Barrier was pierced and he was conversing, he was perceptible. He'd be able to conduct interrogations, be able to search out clues. Meanwhile he heard Margaret saying 'Don't demean your signature with a second-rate writing implement. Once you've tried the Eiger fountain pen you'll never want to go back to those hen-like scratchings and scrawlings,' and the woman seemed interested and so Margaret went on 'Our Empyrean Sterling Silver Collection features one-of-a-kind hand-etched casings –' In fact the man seemed captivated too he turned ignoring the beer pitch and gave Margaret his attention. 'Our brewers hand-pick the hops and malt,' he was unable to stop though he'd obviously lost his mark, 'and every single batch of fire-brewed Very Old Money Lager is individually tasted –' Following the couple through the corridor they bumped into another Advertising woman who'd been on the hovercraft, and she began singing, 'Vis-it the *moon*, it's nev-er too *soon*,' dancing sinuously and batting her eyes, distracting them all from fountain pens and beer for the moment and then the five of them swept into the larger space of the Undermall and suddenly there were dozens of people who needed to be told about the beer, 'Thirsty? Hello, hi there, thirsty? Excuse me, thirsty? Yes? Craving satisfaction, sparkle, bite? No? Yes? Have you tried Very Old Money? What makes it different, you ask – oh, hello, thirsty?' and also dozens of people working as Advertising, a gabble of pitches – stern, admonitory: 'Have you considered the perils of being without success insurance?' flippant, arbitrary: 'You never know you're out with the Black Underwear Crowd, not until you get one of them home!' jingly, singsong: 'We've got children, we've all got children, you can have children too –' and as they scattered and darted along the endless marble floors of the Undermall he was afraid he'd lose her, but there was Margaret, earnestly discussing pens with a thoughtful older couple and he struggled over towards her, hawking beer – 'Thirsty? Oof, sorry, uh, thirsty?' The crowd thinned as customers ducked into shops and stole away down corridors back to their apartments, bullied by the slew of Advertising except for the few like this older couple who seemed gratified by the attention, he actually had to wait as they listened and took down some information from her about the Eiger fountain pen while he stood far enough away to keep from barking at them about the beer. Then once the older couple wandered off he took Margaret's hand this time, why not, she'd done it, and drew her down a corridor away from the crowds, hoping to keep from engaging with any more customers, and also in the right direction if he had his bearings. He thought he did. He led her into the shadow of a doorway, a shop called FINGERTOES that wasn't doing much business. 'Listen, I've got to tell you something, I haven't been completely truthful, I mean, I haven't lied, but there's something –' She looked at him, hopeful, confused, but generous in her interpretation, he could tell, what a pure and sweet disposition, maybe her dad wasn't such a bad guy after all if he'd raised a plum like this. 'I'm a detective, I mean, what does that mean, really, but the thing is there's been a murder and I'm trying to look into it –' and then he plunged in and told all, the Apartment On Tape, pulling it out of his satchel to show her, the shadow, the strangling, his conversation with the dealer and then his brainstorm to slip inside the citadel, slip past the One-Way Permeable Barrier that would of course have kept his questions or accusations from even being audible to those on this side, and so he'd manipulated her generosity to get abroad the hovercraft. 'Forgive me,' he said. Her eyes widened, her voice grew hushed, reverent. 'Of course, but what do you want to do? Find the police?' 'You're not angry at me?' 'No, no. It's a brave thing you're doing.' 'Thank you.' They drew closer. He could almost kiss her, just in happiness, solidarity, no further meaning or if there was it was just on top of the powerful solidarity feeling, just an extra, a windfall. 'But what do you think is best, the police?' she whispered. 'No, I have in mind a visit to the apartment, we're only a couple of blocks away, in this direction I believe, but do you think we can get upstairs?' They fell silent then because a man swerved out of FINGERTOES with a little paper tray of greasy fried things, looked like fingers or toes in fact and smelled terrific, he couldn't believe how hungry he was. 'Thirsty?' he said hopelessly and the man popping one into his mouth said, 'You called it brother, I'm dying for a beer.' 'Why just any beer when you could enjoy a Very Old Money –' and he had to go on about it, being driven nuts by the smell, while Margaret waited. The moment the grease-eater realized they were Advertising and broke free, towards the open spaces of the Undermall, he and Margaret broke in the other direction, down the corridor. 'This way,' said Margaret, turning them towards the elevator, 'the next level down you can go for blocks, it's the way out eventually too.' 'Yes, but can we get back upstairs?' 'The elevators work for us until the patches run out, I think,' and so they went down below the Undermall to the underground corridors, long echoey halls of tile, not so glamorous as upstairs, not nice at all really,

the lengths apartment people went to never to have to step
out onto the street and see car people being really appalling
sometimes. The tunnels were marked with street signs, names
of other Undermalls, here and there an exit. They had to Advertise
only once before reaching East One Thousand, Two Hundred
and Fifteenth Street, to a group of teenage boys smoking a joint
in the corridor who laughed and asked Margaret questions she
couldn't answer like are they mightier or less mighty than the
sword and do they work for pigs. They ran into another person
Advertising, a man moving furtively who when he recognized
Margaret was plainly relieved. 'He's got a girlfriend,' she explained, somewhat enigmatically. So those Advertising could, did
– what? Interact. But caught up in the chase now, he didn't ask
more, just counted the blocks, feeling the thrill of approaching
his Apartment On Tape's real address. They went up in the
elevator, which was lavish again, wood panelled and perfumed
and mirrored and musical. An expensive building. Apartment
16D so he pressed the button for the sixteenth floor, holding his
breath, hardly believing it when they rose above the public floors.
But they did. He gripped her hand. The elevator stopped on the
sixth floor and a robot got on. Another of the creepily efficient
braincase-showing kind. At first the robot ignored them but then
on the fifteenth floor a woman got on and Margaret said, 'The
most personal thing about you is your signature, don't you think?'
and he said, 'Thirsty?' and the robot turned and stared up at
them. The doors closed and they rode up to the sixteenth floor,
and the three of them got out, he and Margaret and the robot,
leaving the woman behind. The hallway was splendid with plush
carpeting and brass light fixtures, empty apart from the three of
them. 'What are you doing up here?' said the robot. 'And what's

in that bag?' Clutching his satchel he said, 'Nothing, just my stuff.' 'Why is it any of your business?' said Margaret, surprisingly defiant. 'We've been asked to give an extended presentation at a customer's private home,' he said, wanting quickly to cover Margaret's outburst, give the robot something else to focus on. 'Then I'll escort you,' said the robot. 'You really don't have to do that,' he said, and Margaret said, bizarrely, 'Don't come along and screw up our pitch, we'll sue you.' Learning of the investigation had an odd effect on her, always a risk working with amateurs he supposed. But also it was these robots, the way they were designed with rotten personalities or no personalities they really aroused revulsion in people, it was an instinctual thing and not just him, he noted with satisfaction. He squeezed her hand and said, 'Our sponsors would be displeased, it's true.' 'This matter requires clearance,' said the robot, trying to get in front of them as they walked, and they had to skip to stay ahead of it. 'Please stand to one side and wait for clearance,' but they kept going down the carpeted hallway, his fingers crossed that it was the right direction for 16D. 'Halt,' said the robot, a flashing red light on its forehead beginning to blink neurotically and then they were at the door, and he rapped with his knuckles, thinking, hardly going incognito here, but better learn what we can. 'Stand to one side,' said the robot again. 'Shut up,' said Margaret. As the robot clamped a steely hand on each of their arms, jerking them back away from the door, its treads grinding on the carpet for traction, probably leaving ugly marks too, the door swung open. 'Hello?' The man in the doorway was unshaven and slack-haired wearing a robe and blinking at them as though he'd only turned on his light to answer the door. 'They claim to have an appointment with you sir,' said the robot. The man only stood and stared. 'It's very important, we have to talk to you urgently,' he said, trying to pull free of the robot's chilly grip, then added, regretfully, 'about beer.' He felt a swoon at looking through the doorway, realizing he was seeing into his Apartment On Tape, the rooms etched into his dreamy brain now before him. He tried to see more but the light was gloomy. ' – and fountain pens,' said Margaret, obviously trying to hold herself back but compelled to chip something. 'I apologize sir I tried to detain them to obtain clearance –' said the robot. *Detain, obtain*, what rotten syntax, he thought, the people who program these robots certainly aren't poets. The man just stood and blinked and looked them over, the three of them struggling subtly, he and Margaret trying to pull free of the robot, which was still blinking red and grinding at the carpet. 'Cooperate,' squawked the robot. The man in the robe squinted at them, finally smiled. 'Please,' said Margaret. 'Fountain pens, eh?' the man in the robe said at last. 'Yes,' said Margaret desperately, and he heard himself add 'And beer –' 'Yes, of course,' mumbled the man in the robe. 'How silly of me. Come in.' 'Sir, for your safety –' 'They're fine,' said the man to the robot. 'I'm expecting them. Let them in.' The robot released its grip. The man in the robe turned and shuffled inside. They followed him, all three of them, into poorly-lit rooms disastrously heaped with newspapers, clothes, soiled dishes, empty and half-empty take-out packages, but still unmistakably the rooms from his tape, every turn of his head recalling some camera movement and there sure enough was the wall that had held the shadow, the momentary stain of murder. The man in the robe turned and said to the robot, 'Please wait outside.' 'But surely I should chaperone, sir –' 'No, that's fine, just outside the door, I'll call you in if I need you. Close it on your way out, thanks.' Watching the robot slink back out he couldn't help but feel a little thrill of vindication. The man in the robe continued into the kitchen, and gesturing at the table said, 'Please, sit, sorry for the mess. Did you say you'd like a beer?' 'Well, uh, no, that wasn't exactly – if you drink beer you ought to make it a Very Old Money Lager for full satisfaction – but I've got something else to discuss while you enjoy your delicious, oh, damn it –' 'Relax, have a seat. Can I get you something else?' 'Food,' he blurted. 'Which always goes best with a Very Old Money,' and meanwhile Margaret released his hand and took a seat and started in talking about pens. The man opened his refrigerator, which was as overloaded as the apartment, another image from the tape now corrupted by squalor. 'You poor people, stuck with those awful patches and yet I suppose I wouldn't have the benefit of your company today without them! Ah, well. Here, I wasn't expecting visitors but would you like some cheese? Can I fix you a glass of water?' The man set out a crumbled hunk of cheddar with a butterknife, crumbs on the dish and so long uncovered the edges were dried a deep, translucent orange. 'So, you were just Advertising and you thought you'd pay a house call? How am I so lucky?' 'Well, that's not it exactly –' Margaret took the knife and began paring away the edges of the cheese, carving out a chunk that looked more or less edible and when she handed it to him he couldn't resist, but tried talking through the mouthful anyway, desperately trying to negotiate the three priorities of hunger, Advertising, and his investigation: 'Would you consider, mmmpphh, excuse me, consider opening a nice tall bottle of Very Old Money and settling in to watch this videotape I brought with me because there's something I'd like you to see, a question I've got about it –' The man in the robe nodded absently, half-listening, staring oddly at Margaret and then said, 'By all means let me see your tape – is it about beer? I'd be delighted but no hurry, please relax and enjoy yourselves, I'll be right out,' and stepped into the living room, began rummaging among his possessions of which there certainly were plenty. It was a little depressing how full the once glorious apartment had gotten. He envisioned himself living in it and cleaning it out, restoring it to the condition on the realtor's tape. Margaret cut him another piece of cheese and whispered, 'Do you think he knows something?' 'I can't know he seems so nice, well if not nice then harmless, hapless, but I'll judge his reaction to the video, watch him closely when the time comes –' grabbing more cheese quickly while he could and then the man in the robe was back. 'Hello, friends, enjoying yourselves?' His robe had fallen open and they both stared but maybe it was just an example of his sloppiness. Certainly there was no polite way to mention it. There was something confusing about this man, who now went to the table and took the knife out of Margaret's hands and held her hand there for a moment and then snapped something, was it a bracelet? around her wrist. Not a bracelet. Handcuffs. 'Hey, wait a minute, that's no way to enjoy a nice glass of lager!' he heard himself say idiotically cheese falling out of his mouth jumping up as the man clicked Margaret's other wrist into the cuffs and he had her linked to the back of her chair. He stood to intervene and the man in the robe swept his feet out from under him with a kick and pushed him in the chest and he fell, feet sliding on papers, hand skidding in lumps of cheese, to the floor. 'Thirsty!' he shouted, the more excited the more fervent the Advertising, apparently. 'No! Beer!' as he struggled to get up. And Margaret was saying something desperate about Eiger

Fountain Pens '– *self-refilling cartridge* –' The man in the robe moved quickly, not lazy and sloppy at all now and kicked away his satchel with the tape inside and bent over him and reached behind his ear to tear the patch away, another momentary sting. He could only shout 'Beer!' once more before the twilight world of the One-Way Permeable Barrier surrounded him, it was every-where here, even Margaret was on the other side as long as she wore the patch, and he felt his voice sucked away to a scream audible inside the space of his own head but not elsewhere, he knew, not until he was back outside, on the street where he belonged and why couldn't he have stayed there? What was he thinking? Anyway it wouldn't be long now because through the gauze he saw the man in the robe who you'd have to call the man half out of his robe now open the door to let the robot in, then as the naked man grinned at him steel pinchers clamped onto his arm and he was dragged out of the room, screaming inaudibly, thrashing to no purpose, leaving Margaret behind. And his tape besides.

The Wrong Arm
★ ★ ★ ★ ★ Sam Lipsyte

★ ★ ★ ★ ★ There were marks in it, divots in it, a feathering of weals and burns. These were all the scars from all the times something tried to kill her in that arm. The stove tried to kill her. The cleaver tried to kill her. The brillo nearly did it, too.

Winter, she hid the wrong arm in her home sweater. Summer was bees and bad nails in the porch door. We were worried about summer, until it was summer and we forgot to be worried anymore. We packed all the food we needed in the plaid bag, sandwiches and sandwich stuff and twist-off cups of lemon pop, packed it up and drove away. She sat up front, packed in her proper place, beside our father, wrong arm pressed against the window glass.

We were going to see the boats. The boats of the world were sailing up some river.

I wondered what the wrong arm looked like to the drivers driving by. I wondered if they saw its wrongness spread there on the window, the burnt part, the brillo'd part, the cleaver'd.

All we knew about the wrong arm was that it was wrong to touch it, to pinch it, to rub it. Any other part of her was there for us to hold. The wrong arm was not for us to take her by and lead her. The wrong arm was not for us to tap it for her to turn.

The wrong arm would never heal right. That's why everything knew to try and kill her there. If harmed, our father told us, the wrong arm could be the end of her. He said end of her as though he meant no harm.

Our father told us about that man who died from how his mother dipped him in a river.

He had a wrong heel.

I figured I'd take the heel over the arm any day. This was given my pick. This was given if they let me pick, not just given being given what you got. Our father said sometimes you had to deal with the cards life dealt you, but I knew games where you got new ones. Lantern men granted wishes, too. I wanted to be the kind of boy who would wish the wrong arm wasn't wrong anymore. I was worried I was the kind of boy who wouldn't waste a wish.

My brother, my sister, we did not behave on the way to the boats. Some of us had to piss. The car needed gas. The pipe in the gas-place bathroom almost killed her. Maybe it was filled with boiling piss. We got back on the road to the boats.

There would be bees out where the boats of the world were sailing, but our father said you couldn't be scared of everything, or you might as well be dead.

'It's nothing to worry about,' she said to us. 'I've had worse than bees.' She lifted the wrong arm a little where it stuck to the window.

What could be worse than bees?

Maybe wasps were worse. Maybe porch-door nails that could stick you with sickness even if your arm was right. Maybe porch-screen teeth where it was ripped and curled and our father never fixed it. Why didn't he fix it? Wasn't he summer worried, at least in winter? The bees were asleep then. There had been time. Who was I to say it, though? Me, who wouldn't waste a wish.

My brother, my sister, they had their parts of the seat, to eat sandwiches on, to sing. Each of them was nothing to me. Everything that was everything was in front of me. My father was in front of me on the other side of the car. She was in front of me with just the seat between us. The wrong arm pressed through the secret slot between the seat and the door. It was our slot. I could see the blister from the hot-piss pipe. The arm would flutter whenever the road went hard.

We stopped to sit at a picnic bench, to take a picture of us, with trees.

The bench was bad with splinters.

I walked the clear and hunted for hornets. I hunted for ticks. I counted all the things that could kill her here. A piece of bottle, a broken comb. A thorn, even. No lantern man would ever let you wish it all away at once. You could only do it one at a time, and you'd never get it all. You'd just waste your wishes that way.

'What about here?' she said to my father.

'Not yet, not here,' my father said.

Now we were on the river road. We spotted mast tips over the river hills. The plaid bag was on the floor. I was the keeper of it now. I put my hand in to feel the sandwich wax. I heard my father talking to her under the brother-and-sister songs.

He said, 'One fucking opinion.'

He said, 'Don't think that way.'

He said, 'A specialist in New Paltz.'

He said, 'Don't think you're getting away from me yet.'

He said, 'We have to tell them. That's the whole point. Who cares about the boats?'

I was beginning to care about the boats.

I was beginning to be someone who wanted to see what kind of boats the world had sent to sail here. I wanted that to be the point.

I started to ask a lot of questions about the boats. I didn't think it was wrong to ask.

Our father said the boats would be big and from every sea-going land. He said sea-going as though he meant some harm. He said the boats were one thing, and there was also another thing we would all have to talk about when we got to the boats.

I said I had some things I wanted to talk about, too. I said I wanted to know why they boiled piss at the gas station, what purpose did it serve. I said I wanted to know why he didn't just fix the porch screen while the bees were sleeping. I said I wanted to know if there was an Old Paltz, too.

'You shouldn't eavesdrop,' she said. 'We'll tell you everything.'

I asked why the wrong arm was so wrong, whether what we were going to talk about was an even wronger wrongness.

'Look,' she said, 'the boats.'

My father pulled the car onto a high plain, a meadow. The plaid bag slid when we braked.

We got out of the car and stood in the grass. We stood in our places from the car. People sat on blankets and bedsheets, pointed at the boats.

'Look,' said my father, and we were looking.

'Does this answer any of your questions?' he said to me.

'Some,' I said.

The wrong arm was backways in front of me like it was still

in our secret slot. There were scars, blisters, sun peels, stains. There were birthmarks and marks from after being born. It could be anybody's arm, I thought. We were making it wrong by saying it was wrong. We should be holding it and rubbing it and taking her by it to lead her somewhere. To lead her by it to the boats. We didn't need a lantern man's one fucking opinion in New Paltz to make my mother's wrong arm right again. We didn't need all the bees to go to sleep to keep the wrongness in my mother from getting wronger. We just needed to waste all our wishes.

'Let's go closer,' I said.

And then I did the wrong thing.

Circulation

★ ★ ★ ★ ★ Rick Moody

1. Of Office Supplies

★ ★ ★ ★ ★ Bern Lewis, divorce lawyer, opened the file folder before him and removed the offending paper clip from a portion of the materials relating to Westman v. Westman. He pursed his lips thoughtfully as he dropped it, dropped the paper clip – it inappropriately bound together pages of two separate documents – carelessly onto the surface of his rolltop desk. The Westmans' divorce was Mexican – this was back in the era of Mexican divorces – and his client, Mrs Westman, would soon be leaving for that debt-ridden, oil-producing, microbially infected nation. He was rushing to get the last details in order.

This story however does not concern Bern whose successful practice is its own reward. It does not concern his convertible Alfa Romeo nor his house in East Hampton nor his daughter (at the Spence School) nor his wife – the first Jewish person to be admitted to the Junior League of Westport. Nor, in fact, does this story concern the Westmans themselves and their divorce or recent unscientific theories (no control group in the landmark study) of developmental problems in young adults who have suffered through the agonies of a broken home. No, this story is about something else entirely. It's about the paper clip.

At seven-thirty that evening Bern Lewis buzzed his assistant Kathy Gennaro, who sat in a somewhat remote cubicle in the corridors of Gerbasi, Wellman & Crabtree. Kathy was a young, attractive woman from Bay Ridge, Brooklyn, who Bern felt, managed with her heavily made up look to affect a genuine radiance. When she smiled at Bern he had this feeling that some marriages never unraveled. While Kathy took no pleasure in her job she was good enough at it – she'd been a secretary for eight years – to give the illusion of loyalty and affection. Bern's voice over the intercom that evening – p's popping, s's susurring – gave her a few last minute instructions about appointments in the coming week. Then he asked sheepishly if Kathy would mind cleaning up his desk.

– Of course not, she told him. But this wasn't entirely true. Actually she did mind. She felt it was something he should have been able to do himself.

– Oh, and have a great weekend, Bern said. Hey, are you going to make it out to the beach?

– No, um, just a quiet weekend, Kathy answered. Bern wasn't really listening.

When she made her way to his office, the paper clip wasn't the first beneficiary of her crusade for desktop order. First Kathy organized a large stack of pending files – a whole host of divorce cases, a whole town's worth of sorrow – into one substantial pile that she balanced in Lewis's In box. She then lined up pens and pencils in a compartment in the right hand top desk drawer. Rubber bands she retired into a small duck decoy container. It was only just before taking leave of her boss's desk for the weekend that Kathy swept all the paper clips on the desk into her palm and crammed them into a magnetized plastic cup which conveniently offered, in a *space age* design, several for easy access.

Since her boss was gone now – eight minutes before, having waved on the way to the elevator – she could safely make her escape. Wait. The appointment book.

It was while Kathy was exasperatedly trying to figure out what to do about the double-booked lunch for Monday that she plucked what had once been the Westman paper clip from the magnetized dish and stuck it in her mouth. She intended to attach it immediately to this problem day in Bern's calendar. However, she forgot about the clip entirely and carried it – in her mouth – and the appointment book back to her own desk. She set the leather bound appointment book on top of her own In box. First thing Monday morning she'd deal with the darned lunch. Then she crossed the hall to the coat rack in the supply closet and found her second-hand fur.

– Night, Kath! shouted one lonely assistant as Kathy Gennaro passed through the expanses of shuttered desks by the elevator. Most of the associates occupied this large teamwork-oriented space.

– Mmmnn, Kathy replied.

She laughed. Because she suspected the nervous things lawyers did with paper clips. Who knew for sure? They used them for anything but holding documents together. Who knew how many people had sucked on this very paper clip? Was there any way it was still sanitary?

Delicately, she removed the paper clip from her mouth before burying it deep in the pocket of her fur coat, beneath a spare lipstick, a subway token holder, three pennies, and a note to herself reminding her to reschedule the dental hygienist.

– Night! she called. Have a wild weekend!

Among the problems that Kathy Gennaro faced – her parents' constant and depressing arguments, her brother's service in the Armed Forces, the terminal condition of her AMC Gremlin – there was one that really made its mark on her. It was her boyfriend Al. Two months ago he had suffered a bad accident at the foundry where he worked. A very serious burn on one hand. He'd had skin grafts to replace what was lost, but later the grafts had become infected. Bronze had gotten into the wound, or something. In the end Al lost two fingers. They'd been amputated: the middle and ring fingers of his left hand.

Kathy and Al had quarreled a little bit even before the accident. Theirs was a star-crossed romance. This Kathy knew in part from voluminous reading of soft reference books and women's magazines. She had also spoken with a priest at her parish, who recommended that she give Al as much room as he needed during this difficult portion of his recovery. A quiz in one of the women's magazines agreed. She should keep her mouth shut if she wanted that engagement ring, if she wanted peace of mind. She didn't comment on his relentless television watching at both his apartment and hers, she didn't bring up her own problems – such as her toothache, or the unusual lump in one of her breasts – and she helped him fill out his OSHA and medical insurance forms.

In this way, one Saturday, the Westman paper clip became attached to the claim forms of Alfred F. Shaughnessy (emergency service, including skin graft, X-ray, consultation, two nights semi-priv. on burn ward, observation, anesthetic, amputation, physical therapy, psychiatric counseling, follow-up and aftercare), and mailed across county lines to the offices of the Atra Insurance Corp. of White Plains, New York.

Three months Shaughnessy's paperwork languished in the Atra headquarters. Three months. The middle management at Atra was trying to evolve a computer-based claim processing system that would hasten refunds, but it had a lower priority than some income-generating management gambits. Thus, Al's form got a lot of relaxed personal contact over the months. First the claim was entered by hand onto an enormous main-frame computer of the sort they had back then – with gigantic spools of information going through some telecommunication spin cycle – from which it was downloaded and distributed to the filing department, where, again by hand, it was broken up into component documents and filed in perpetuity. Just before this last step, just before Al's claim was filed, an employee of this massive insurance bureaucracy finally rubber-stamped the documents. Funds were disbursed without a hitch.

However, in the midst of a misfiling spree several months later, a fellow who only worked at Atra through nepotism (and to keep him out of trouble until Manhattanville College was back in session), a guy named Randall Evans, actually trashed the Alfred Shaughnessy forms, threw them out, and while he was doing it he bent the paper clip, yes, the Westman paper clip, out of shape – out of the shape of the most profitable patent in the history of intellectual property, as he, Randall, had once heard a science teacher remark – into a straighter, sturdier projectile that could easily have *put someone's eye out.* He did this in order to clean beneath his nails, which were not particularly dirty. It was 4:15 on a Friday afternoon and his feet were propped up on a stack of human tragedies. The radio at his back blasted a fledgling, free form, album-oriented FM rock and roll station. He leaned back in his chair.

And then Randall did it. Leaned too far. He hit his head on the filing cabinet behind him as he fell backwards – as always in these situations, *it almost seemed to happen in slow motion* – and the paper clip was driven far into the sensitive skin underneath the nail of his index finger. It hurt like hell. It was only in there a quarter inch or so, but it hurt like hell, especially when he yanked it out and the blood began to flow. His finger was throbbing. Randall Evans shut off the radio when he collected himself. He was rubbing his head with the good hand. Shit. He kicked an empty desk drawer. Dented it. And then he deposited the rogue paper clip in the wastebasket underneath his desk. From which it was carted to a dumpster, from which it was hauled to a landfill, in which it was buried, never again in all of the centuries of elemental existence to be touched by human hands.

2. Of Blood Cells

Of lineage and biology we now have cause to speak! Of the movement of genetic destiny and the spheres writ smaller in veins and arteries!

Okay, the circulatory system, as you know, carries oxygen from the lungs to cells and organs throughout the body. These red corpuscles nourish tissue that needs oxygen to thrive and they likewise carry away a byproduct, carbon dioxide. That's their job. Feast and waste are their cargo. By means of this circulation, by means of its damming and flowing it's possible to read all the geographies and histories of an organism. That's circulation.

Likewise, in the modern age, blood cells from donors are shipped and frozen and reused in transfusion. Transfusion allows for a whole new circular pattern in which strangers are attached by gossamer coincidences. We can therefore follow a history of Randall Evans's blood along a trail of generous low-level philanthropists.

Like many of his generation, Randall had run afoul of the D.W.I. traffic regulations enacted by his home state. This was a year or so after his stint at the insurance company. It started with staying out late. He liked to drink, take speed, smoke pot, bird-dog chicks, stay out all night. He liked to take his parents' car and enact revenge fantasies with it. His dad was tough on him and he resented this toughness. One Thursday night he was racing his girlfriend – he was *dragging her* – on the back roads of Harrison, New York. It was maybe 2:30 in the morning. Perfect time for dangerous automotive games. Realizing that she was about to be victorious, though, that his imported sub-compact was slower – unbelievable! – than an American luxury sedan, Randall's eyes strayed momentarily, sheepishly, up toward the heavens.

He hit a mailbox. That was first. This initial lapse of concentration resulted in his striking a mailbox, and the wheels seemed to lock on something, the mailbox post (anchored in a cement base), and there was a sudden shower – in the headlights – of uprooted and shredded daffodils, and then he was swerving across a lawn uncontrollably – holy shit! he was heading for a house! and he *couldn't stop the vehicle!* The car came to rest finally when he collided with an above ground pool, a Doughboy. He was unconscious when the pool-owners, awakened by the sound of impact, pulled him from the wreckage. Water rushed through a jagged crack in the pool housing.

Because he hadn't been wearing his seatbelt he had innumerable lacerations and contusions, pre-eminent among them a large head wound. It was *gushing* (to use the language of the witnesses) in the minutes after impact, and, as a result, he received his first transfusion, in the Emergency Room at White Plains General.

Into Randall's body pulsed the AB positive blood of Arne Bennett, bank teller. Responding to a well-publicized plea by local medical authorities – he'd heard it on the all-news radio station one morning while stuck in traffic on the Cross County Expressway – Arne donated his blood precisely forty days before it hit Randall's veins. It reached this needy party just two days shy of its expiration date.

After the donation, Arne, who had never stopped to consider that his initials were the same as his blood type, tried – and the effort was characteristic of his good-naturedness – to rise immediately from the gurney at the makeshift Red Cross donor station. It was a masculine thing. He was in the branch conference room of a competing bank, Marine Midland. He wanted to get back to work. Immediately upon giving up the pint of blood in question he swung his massive, tree trunk legs to the edge of the cot. Perhaps he intended in part to impress a matronly and friendly nurse. Perhaps he was worrying a little about his toupee – the color of scorched straw – about whether or not it was going to stay on as he lay prone there. In any case, as soon as feasible he worked his legs down to the carpeted floor and stood.

Then he collapsed. Through sheer teamwork, the nurse (by the name of Eleanor) and several impromptu volunteers hefted Arne back up onto the folding cot. His toupee stayed rooted to his scalp. In all the commotion, though, he missed the chance to ask Eleanor if they might somehow meet. He was so embarrassed by his fainting spell he wouldn't have found the courage for it anyway. He disliked his timidity with women. He worried that he would never marry. In spite of everything, Arne was back at work in forty-five minutes.

Randall Evans, on the other hand, was hospitalized for several

days of observation. Concussion accompanied his more super-
ficial wounds. Meanwhile, Evans's girlfriend, Mary Cassell,
escaped without a scratch. She had pulled over twenty yards
ahead of him that fateful night and watched the whole thing
in her rearview mirror, a hand clamped worriedly across her
mouth. She visited him in the hospital – against his wishes,
because his face with all its stitches looked like a *railroad map* –
and at that moment something began to sour in their relationship.
Where crises might have brought other couples closer, it pried
this one apart. Randall couldn't accept her indulgence anymore;
he wouldn't let her straighten him out. He was uncomfortable.
He wanted out of the hospital. He wanted to be left alone.

Soon Evans *was* released. The injuries weren't terribly compli-
cated, it turned out. He had scars, but they were the scars of a
tough guy. And he prospered in his second life, in his life of good
fortune. Despite his family's wishes, Randall became a large
crane operator. It was a union job. It paid very well. At union
headquarters he too frequently donated blood. In early 1974, for
example, he donated in the large, undecorated union hall that
served his local. Sinatra was playing on the radio. The donation
went smoothly. Randall's story thereafter – with its placid,
middle-aged heavy drinking and its relatively amicable divorce –
diverges from this one and is lost.

Not long after Evans's donation, Debby Fahnstock, a wealthy
woman who had always favored corporal punishment in the
instruction of children, took Randall's blood (also AB+) into her
own depleted physique. The transfusion occurred during her 1974
triple bypass operation. She was a patron of the city opera and a
collector of various types of miniatures. In her fifties she became
remorseful about her past, about her life, about the prospects for

earthly love, for *agape*, for simple human kindness. She began to refuse visits from her family and friends.

Debby survived the operation. She grew stronger. But four years later, in 1978, when her son Ansel was thirty-four years old, he came down with a rare kidney disorder. It was likely, actually, that he'd had it all along. The disorder – Osborne's Syndrome – ran in the remote tributaries of the Fahnstock family. Transplant was the only successful treatment but it was risky. Nevertheless, Mrs Fahnstock ventured forth from her self-imposed exile and, at great personal risk, donated blood for Ansel's kidney transplant. The hospital was Lenox Hill, New York City; the presiding physician, Debby and Ansel's general practitioner, was John D. Westman, M.D.

Though perhaps Arne Bennett's very blood cells did not flow between the generations that night in 1978 – that night when the differences between the Fahnstocks were forgotten for a moment, when a mother and son who had never much liked one another were of like mind and like flesh – some remnant of these red cells did persist, some atavistic genetic material, some trace of Bennett's ardent faith (in the Baptist church), for example, or perhaps some watered-down approximation of Randall Evans's simple love of life. Something must have been in that blood. Something must account for the change of heart that passed that night through that transparent plastic tubing, unless it was just the sheer enthusiasm of survival.

3. *Of Ideas*

Chain letters circulate. Coinage. Wealth through inheritance. Moisture circulates, through the ecosystem. Disease circulates, venereally, virally, et cetera. The planets circulate. Books circulate (*Go little quair! Fly!*) and stories circulate and through them ideas and opinions and doubts and hopes. Gossip circulates. Philosophy trickles down. Jokes spread like wildfire, beginning at the Wall Street trading desk of Kidder, Peabody.

Ansel Fahnstock, unemployable heir to the heavily diversified Fahnstock portfolio, recoiled from violence of any kind. He never in his life, even as a child, initiated any instance of fisticuffs. When as a young man he was struck by his mother he took the blow and prepared for another, usually sneering with a really arresting vehemence. She then beat him harder. However, these pugilistic altercations were short. As he grew into manhood, Ansel married, and his marriage – like his parents' marriage – was typified by sullen disagreements that never escalated to the pitch of a real fight. He never struck his wife, but he didn't attend to her either. He was no ally. Likewise, he never struck his daughter, Joy, although there were occasions when the thought crossed his mind. He followed her up the stairs one day, his palm open on the backswing. Her diapered ass swayed above him on the step. He felt deeply ashamed of this. Any kind of laying on of hands disgusted him.

Meanwhile, Ansel gave himself over to two consuming avocations – philately and numismatics. Gleaming freshly minted coins and cellophaned, untouched stamps – never to be circulated, never to know the decay that always starts with human contact

– were the subjects of much of his thinking. To occupy himself, he substituted as a teacher of high school mathematics. As an instructor he was neither loved by his students – too passive, too impersonal – nor hated.

And then in 1978 his kidney problems flared. The transplant was accompanied by transfusion, as they always are, and steroids (to avoid tissue rejection). In the days after the procedure his family gathered often at his bedside – his sisters, his wife, his daughter, and even his mother. *If only his father were here*, they each said. *If only his father would come.* If only his father would cover over the wound of his paternal abdication; if only, after all this time, that one terrible fact could be undone; if only the marriage had not failed.

Among the Fahnstocks, then, persisted *the notion of the American family* with its respectful marriages, its rivalrous but loving siblings, its dogs and cats, its vacations, its meals, its tennis matches, its boating trips. This idea of theirs was like some perennial weed that grabs every square inch of topsoil, choking off all other vegetation, until the countryside of American notions featured this weed alone and no others; it reproduced limitlessly from coast to coast; no energy or water or sun or cash was needed for it; it wasn't even subject to the laws of thermodynamics.

Ansel's private room was piled high with borrowed vases. These hospital flowers were more beautiful for being ephemeral. To and from consciousness he drifted fighting off infection. His remote and cranky moods were forgiven. His wife forgave his silence, his daughter forgave him, even his mother forgave him. Forgiveness was in the room like a dignified perfume and it wasn't even contingent upon his recovery. Forgiveness became its own reward.

Because of his death. Because Ansel passed away. He came to some celestial dead stop. His mother's blood cells went with him, as did any cells belonging to Arne Bennett or Randall Evans, as did the transplanted kidney in him, the one that had formerly belonged to Kapoor S. Nigam, also deceased, a kidney which, before it was Nigam's, had belonged only to the awesome pool of things yet to happen.

Ansel's daughter was married eight years later to Howard Gates and again, I'm afraid, the marriage was not happy. Though a gentle and thoughtful son was issued by this union – it was me, in fact, the narrator of this story – a young man she had occasion to discipline only rarely, Joy Gates soon sought the representation of a divorce lawyer, Bern Lewis, and the results of these proceedings are a matter of public record, filed both in the offices of Gerbasi, Wellman & Crabtree (in triplicate, velo-bound and paper-clipped) and with the Manhattan District Court on Park Row. To maintain liquidity, and because the legal fees in the case were not insignificant, Joy Gates found one day that she was removing her father's coin and stamp collections from the safety deposit box at Marine Midland so that she might take them to dealers to be appraised. And in this way the history of her family and its notions, *thought to be retired from the harsh light of scrutiny*, were once again adrift in the universe of brief attachments.

Thereafter Joy Gates conducted herself quietly, peaceably, never again to reappear in this or any other public account.

A Primer for the Punctuation of Heart Disease

★ ★ ★ ★ ★ Jonathan Safran Foer

★★★★★ ☐ The 'silence mark' signifies an absence of language, and there is at least one on every page of the story of my family life. Most often used in the conversations I have with my grandmother about her life in Europe during the war, and in conversations with my father about our family's history of heart disease – we have forty-one heart attacks between us, and counting – the silence mark is a staple of familial punctuation. Note the use of silence in the following brief exchange, when my father called me at college, the morning of his most recent angioplasty:

'Listen,' he said, and then surrendered to a long pause, as if the pause were what I was supposed to listen to. 'I'm sure everything's gonna be fine, but I just wanted to let you know –'

'I already know,' I said.

'☐'

'☐'

'☐'

'☐'

'OK,' he said.

'I'll talk to you tonight,' I said, and I could hear, in the receiver, my own heartbeat.

He said, 'Yup.'

■ The 'willed silence mark' signifies an intentional silence, the conversational equivalent of building a wall over which you can't climb, through which you can't see, against which you break the bones of your hands and wrists. I often inflict willed silences upon my mother when she asks about my relationships with girls. Perhaps this is because I never have *relationships* with girls – only *relations*. It depresses me to think that I've never had sex with anyone who really loved me. Sometimes I wonder if having sex with a girl who doesn't love me is like felling a tree, alone, in a forest: no one hears about it; it didn't happen.

?? The 'insistent question mark' denotes one family member's refusal to yield to a willed silence, as in this conversation with my mother:

> 'Are you dating at all?'
> '☐'
> 'But you're seeing people, I'm sure. Right?'
> '☐'
> 'I don't get it. Are you ashamed of the girl? Are you ashamed of me?'
> '■'
> '??'

¡ As it visually suggests, the 'unxclamation point' is the opposite of an exclamation point; it indicates a whisper.

The best example of this usage occurred when I was a boy. My grandmother was driving me to a piano lesson, and the Volvo's wipers only moved the rain around. She turned down the volume of the second side of the seventh tape of an audio version of 'Shoah,' put her hand on my cheek, and said, 'I hope that you never love anyone as much as I love you¡'

Why was she whispering? We were the only ones who could hear.

¡¡ Theoretically, the 'extraunxclamation points' would be used to denote twice an unxclamation point, but in practice any whisper that quiet would not be heard. I take comfort in believing that at least some of the silences in my life were really extraunxclamations.

!! The 'extraexclamation points' are simply twice an exclamation point. I've never had a heated argument with any member of my family. We've never yelled at each other, or disagreed with any passion. In fact, I can't even remember a difference of opinion. There are those who would say that this is unhealthy. But, since it is the case, there exists only one instance of extraexclamation points in our family history, and they were uttered by a stranger who was vying with my father for a parking space in front of the National Zoo.

'Give it up, fucker!!' he hollered at my father, in front of my mother, my brothers, and me.

'Well, I'm sorry,' my father said, pushing the bridge of his glasses up his nose, 'but I think it's rather obvious that we arrived at this space first. You see, we were approaching from –'

'Give . . . it . . . up . . . fucker!!'

'Well, it's just that I think I'm in the right on this particu–'

'GIVE IT UP, FUCKER!!'

'Give it up, Dad¡' I said, suffering a minor coronary event as my fingers clenched his seat's headrest.

'Je-sus!' the man yelled, pounding his fist against the outside of his car door. 'Giveitupfucker!!'

Ultimately, my father gave it up, and we found a spot several blocks away. Before we got out, he pushed in the cigarette lighter, and we waited, in silence, as it got hot. When it popped out, he pushed it back in. 'It's never, ever worth it,' he said, turning back to us, his hand against his heart.

~ Placed at the end of a sentence, the 'pedal point' signifies a thought that dissolves into a suggestive silence. The pedal point is distinguished from the ellipsis and the dash in that the thought it follows is neither incomplete nor interrupted but an outstretched hand. My younger brother uses these a lot with me, probably because he, of all the members of my family, is the one most capable of telling me what he needs to tell me without having to say it. Or, rather, he's the one whose words I'm most convinced I don't need to hear. Very often he will say, 'Jonathan~' and I will say, 'I know.'

A few weeks ago, he was having problems with his heart. A visit to his university's health center to check out some chest pains became a trip to the emergency room became a week in the intensive-care unit. As it turns out, he's been having one long heart attack for the last six years. 'It's nowhere near as bad as it sounds,' the doctor told my parents, 'but it's definitely something we want to take care of.'

I called my brother that night and told him that he shouldn't worry. He said, 'I know. But that doesn't mean there's nothing to worry about~'

'I know~' I said.

'I know~' he said.

'I~'

'I~'

'☐'

Does my little brother have relationships with girls? I don't know.

↓ Another commonly employed familial punctuation mark, the 'low point,' is used either in place – or for accentuation at the end – of such phrases as 'This is terrible,' 'This is irremediable,' 'It couldn't possibly be worse.'

'It's good to have somebody, Jonathan. It's necessary.'

'☐'

'It pains me to think of you alone.'

'■ ↓'

'?? ↓'

Interestingly, low points always come in pairs in my family. That is, the acknowledgment of whatever is terrible and irremediable becomes itself something terrible and irremediable – and often worse than the original referent. For example, my sadness makes my mother sadder than the cause of my sadness does. Of course, her sadness then makes me sad. Thus is created a 'low-point chain': ↓↓↓↓ . . . ∞.

❋ The 'snowflake' is used at the end of a unique familial phrase – that is, any sequence of words that has never, in the history of our family life, been assembled as such. For example, 'I didn't die in the Holocaust, but all of my siblings did, so where does that leave me?❋' Or, 'My heart is no good, and I'm afraid of dying, and I'm also afraid of saying I love you.❋'

☺ The 'corroboration mark' is more or less what it looks like. But it would be a mistake to think that it simply stands in place of 'I agree,' or even 'Yes.' Witness the subtle usage in this dialogue between my mother and my father:

'Could you add orange juice to the grocery list, but remember to get the kind with reduced acid. Also some cottage cheese. And that bacon-substitute stuff. And a few Yahrzeit candles.'
  '☺'
'The car needs gas. I need tampons.'
  '☺'
'Is Jonathan dating anyone? I'm not prying, but I'm very interested.'
  '☺'

My father has suffered twenty-two heart attacks – more than the rest of us combined. Once, in a moment of frankness after his nineteenth, he told me that his marriage to my mother had been successful because he had become a yes-man early on.

'We've only had one fight,' he said. 'It was in our first week of marriage. I realized that it's never, ever worth it.'

My father and I were pulling weeds one afternoon a few weeks ago. He was disobeying his cardiologist's order not to pull weeds. The problem, the doctor says, is not the physical exertion but the emotional stress that weeding inflicts on my father. He has dreams of weeds sprouting from his body, of having to pull them, at the roots, from his chest. He has also been told not to watch Orioles games and not to think about the current Administration.

As we weeded, my father made a joke about how my older brother, who, barring a fatal heart attack, was to get married in a few weeks, had already become a yes-man. Hearing this felt like having an elephant sit on my chest – my brother, whom I loved more than I loved myself, was surrendering.

'Your grandfather was a yes-man,' my father added, on his knees, his fingers pushing into the earth, 'and your children will be yes-men.'

I've been thinking about that conversation ever since, and I've come to understand – with a straining heart – that I, too, am becoming a yes-man, and that, like my father's and my brother's, my surrender has little to do with the people I say yes to, or with the existence of questions at all. It has to do with a fear of dying, with rehearsal and preparation.

✂🕸 The 'severed web' is a Barely Tolerable Substitute, whose meaning approximates 'I love you,' and which can be used in place of 'I love you.' Other Barely Tolerable Substitutes include, but are not limited to:

→|←, which approximates 'I love you.'
🦟 ☐, which approximates 'I love you.'
🔒, which approximates 'I love you.'
✕✈, which approximates 'I love you.'

I don't know how many Barely Tolerable Substitutes there are, but often it feels as if they were everywhere, as if everything that is spoken and done – every 'Yup,' 'O.K.,' and 'I already know,' every weed pulled from the lawn, every sexual act – were just Barely Tolerable.

: : Unlike the colon, which is used to mark a major division in a sentence, and to indicate that what follows is an elaboration, summation, implication, etc., of what precedes, the 'reversible colon' is used when what appears on either side elaborates, summates, implicates, etc., what's on the other side. In other words, the two halves of the sentence explain each other, as in the cases of 'Mother::Me,' and 'Father::Death.' Here are some examples of reversible sentences:

My eyes water when I speak about my family::I don't like to speak about my family.

I've never felt loved by anyone outside of my family::my persistent depression.

1938 to 1945:: ☐ .

Sex::yes.

My grandmother's sadness::my mother's sadness::my sadness::the sadness that will come after me.

To be Jewish::to be Jewish.

Heart disease::yes.

← Familial communication always has to do with failures to communicate. It is common that in the course of a conversation one of the participants will not hear something that the other has said. It is also quite common that one of the participants will not understand what the other has said. Somewhat less common is one participant's saying something whose words the other understands completely but whose meaning is not understood at all. This can happen with very simple sentences, like 'I hope that you never love anyone as much as I love you¡'

But, in our best, least depressing moments, we *try* to understand what we have failed to understand. A 'backup' is used: we start again at the beginning, we replay what was missed and make an effort to hear what was meant instead of what was said:

'It pains me to think of you alone.'
'← It pains me to think of me without any grandchildren to love.'

{} A related set of marks, the 'should-have brackets,' signify words that were not spoken but should have been, as in this dialogue with my father:

'Are you hearing static?'
'{I'm crying into the phone.}'
'Jonathan?'
'☐'
'Jonathan~'
'■'
'??'
'I::not myself~'
'{A child's sadness is a parent's sadness.}'
'{A parent's sadness is a child's sadness.}'
'←'
'I'm probably just tired¡'
'{I never told you this, because I thought it might hurt you, but in my dreams it was *you*. Not me. *You* were pulling the weeds from my chest.}'
'{I want to love and be loved.}'

'☺'

'☺'

'↓'

'↓'

'⚲'

'☺'

'□↔□↔□'

'↓'

'↓'

'⏭○⏮'

'▨ + ▨ → ■'

'☺'

'🜊 □'

'⊠ ⌫' ''

'◎□❖◆○○□◆⊙●'

'■'

'{I love you.}'

'{I love you, too. So much.}'

Of course, my sense of the should-have is unlikely to be the same as my brothers', or my mother's, or my father's. Sometimes – when I'm in the car, or having sex, or talking to one of them on the phone – I imagine their should-have versions. I sew them together into a new life, leaving out everything that actually happened and was said.

Biographical Notes

★★★★★ **George Saunders** has published two collections of short stories, *CivilWarLand in Bad Decline* and *Pastoralia*, and a children's book, *The Very Persistent Gappers of Frip*. His stories have appeared in the *New Yorker* and *Harper's*. He teaches at Syracuse University.

★★★★★ **Matthew Klam** published his first collection of short stories, *Sam the Cat and Other Stories*, in 2000. He has contributed non-fiction pieces to the *New York Times Magazine* and *Esquire*. He lives in Washington DC.

★★★★★ **Judy Budnitz**'s first collection of short stories, *Flying Leap*, was published in 1998. Her novel *If I Told You Once* was published in 1999 and was shortlisted for the Orange Prize. She lives in New York City.

★★★★★ **Myla Goldberg**'s first novel, *Bee Season*, was published in 2000. The short story 'Comprehension Test' won a competition organized by *Salon* in 1998. Myla Goldberg lives in Brooklyn.

★★★★★ **Jeffrey Eugenides** lives in Berlin. In 1993 he published *The Virgin Suicides*, a cult-book which was made into a film directed by Sofia Coppola in 2000. In 2002 he published his second novel, *Middlesex*.

★★★★★ **David Foster Wallace** is the author of two novels, *The Broom of the System* and *Infinite Jest*, two collections of short stories, *Girl with Curious Hair* and *Brief Interviews with Hideous Men*, and a collection of essays, *A Supposedly Fun Thing I'll Never Do Again*. He teaches at Pomona College in California.

★ ★ ★ ★ ★ **Amanda Davis** lives in New York City. In 1999 she published the short story collection *Circling the Drain*. The main character of 'Faith', the story published here, also appears in her first novel, *Wonder When You'll Miss Me* (2003). Amanda Davis died in March 2003.

★ ★ ★ ★ ★ **Dave Eggers** founded the independent publishing company McSweeney's Books and is the editor of *McSweeney's Quarterly Journal*. His memoir, *A Heartbreaking Work of Staggering Genius*, was published in 2000, and his novel, *You Shall Know Our Velocity*, in 2002. He lives in San Francisco, where he helps to run a non-profit-making tutoring centre called 826 Valencia (www.826valencia.com).

★ ★ ★ ★ ★ **Julia Slavin**'s collection of short stories, *The Woman Who Cut Off Her Leg at the Maidstone Club and Other Stories*, was published in 1999. The recipient of a Pushcart Prize, she lives in Washington DC.

★ ★ ★ ★ ★ **A. M. Homes** has written four novels – *Jack*, *In a Country of Mothers*, *The End of Alice*, *Music for Torching* – and two collections of short stories, *The Safety of Objects* and *Things You Should Know*. She lives in New York and teaches at Columbia University.

★ ★ ★ ★ ★ **Shelley Jackson** is the author of many hypertexts, including the highly acclaimed *Patchwork Girl*, and a short story collection, *The Melancholy of Anatomy*, which was published in 2002. She lives in Brooklyn.

★ ★ ★ ★ ★ **Stacey Richter** has won the Pushcart Prize three times, and her fiction has been published in *GQ* and *Granta*. Her first collection of short stories, *My Date with Satan*, was published in 1999. She lives in Arizona.

★ ★ ★ ★ ★ **Aimee Bender**'s stories have been published in *Granta* and the *Paris Review*. She has published a collection of short stories, *The Girl in the Flammable Skirt*, and a novel, *An Invisible Sign of My Own*. She lives in Los Angeles.

★ ★ ★ ★ ★ **Ken Kalfus** has published two collections of short stories, *Thirst* and *Pu-239 and Other Russian Fantasies*, and a novel, *The Commissariat of Enlightenment*. He divides his time between the United States and Russia.

★ ★ ★ ★ ★ **Arthur Bradford**'s stories have appeared in *Esquire*, *The Face* and *McSweeney's* and were collected in a book, *Dogwalker*, in 2001. He has also directed a documentary, *How's Your News?*

★ ★ ★ ★ ★ **Jonathan Lethem** lives in Brooklyn. He is the author of five novels: *Gun, with Occasional Music*, *Amnesia Moon*, *As She Climbed Across the Table*, *Girl in Landscape* and *Motherless Brooklyn*. He has also edited *The Vintage Book of Amnesia*.

★ ★ ★ ★ ★ **Sam Lipsyte** published the collection *Venus Drive* in 2000. His first novel, *The Subject Steve*, was published in 2001. He lives in Queens, New York.

★ ★ ★ ★ ★ **Rick Moody**'s most recent book is *The Black Veil: A Memoir with Digressions*. He has also written three novels, *Garden State*, *The Ice Storm* and *Purple America*, and two collections of short stories, *The Ring of Brightest Angels Around Heaven* and *Demonology*.

★ ★ ★ ★ ★ **Jonathan Safran Foer**'s novel *Everything is Illuminated* was published in 2002, and won the *Guardian* First Book Prize. He is the editor of the anthology *A Convergence of Birds*, and his stories have been published in the *Paris Review* and the *New Yorker*.

Marco Cassini (1970) is the co-founder and editor-in-chief of minimum fax, an independent publishing house in Rome.

Martina Testa (1975) works as an editor for minimum fax. She has also translated books by Thom Jones, J. T. Leroy, Jonathan Lethem and David Foster Wallace.

Acknowledgements

'I CAN SPEAK!™' © George Saunders, 1999, first appeared in the *New Yorker* (June 1999).

'There Should Be a Name for It' © Matthew Klam, 2000, first appeared in the collection *Sam the Cat and Other Stories*.

'Flush' © Judy Budnitz, 2000, first appeared in *McSweeney's* (Issue 3).

'Comprehension Test' © Myla Goldberg, 1998, first appeared in the anthology *Virgin Fiction*.

'Timeshare' © Jeffrey Eugenides, 1997, first appeared in *Conjunctions* (Issue 28).

'Incarnations of Burned Children' © David Foster Wallace, 2000, first appeared in *Esquire* (November 2000).

'Faith *or* Tips for the Successful Young Lady' © Amanda Davis, 1999, first appeared in the collection *Circling the Drain*.

'Letters from Steven' © Dave Eggers, 2001, first appeared in *McSweeney's* (Issue 5).

'Dentaphilia' © Julia Slavin, 1999, first appeared in the collection *The Woman Who Cut Off Her Leg at the Maidstone Club*.

'A Real Doll' © A. M. Homes, 1990, first appeared in the collection *The Safety of Objects*.

'Sleep' © Shelley Jackson, 2001, first appeared in the collection *The Melancholy of Anatomy*.

'The First Men' © Stacey Richter, 1999, first appeared in the collection *My Date with Satan*.

'The Leading Man' © Aimee Bender, 2000, first appeared in the *Paris Review* (Fall 2000).

'Invisible Malls' © Ken Kalfus, 1986, first appeared in the *North American Review*.

'The Snow Frog' © Arthur Bradford, 2002, appeared in *Zoetrope All-Story* (August 2002).

'Access Fantasy' © Jonathan Lethem, 1998, first appeared in the anthology *Starlight 2*.

'The Wrong Arm' © Sam Lipsyte, 2000, first appeared in the collection *Venus Drive*.

'Circulation' © Rick Moody, 1995, first appeared in the magazine *Columbia*.

'A Primer for the Punctuation of Heart Disease' © Jonathan Safran Foer, 2002, first appeared in the *New Yorker* (June 2002).